WHEN IT BURNS

A SPRINGSIDE NOVEL

HOLLIE LUCKIE

AUTHOR'S NOTE

Thank you so much for reading *When It Burns*. I hope that you fall in love with the town of Springside the same way I have. This book is full of banter, spice, and all the found family you could want. However, Theo is also a man struggling with his past, so please be aware that some heavier topics are discussed as well.

When It Burns contains mature content that may not be suitable for all audiences. For a list of content warnings, flip to the content list at the back of the book. Please note that some of these content warnings may contain spoilers.

DEDICATION

To anyone who has ever needed the reminder that there's always brighter days ahead.

PLAYLIST

High Hopes by Panic! At The Disco
The Good I'll Do by Zach Bryan
Dancin' In The Country by Tyler Hubbard
Different 'Round Here by Riley Green
Depending on the Night by Muscadine Bloodline
Cowboy Hat by Jon Pardi
Would Have Loved Her by Chris Bandi
Ride by Chase Rice
Save Me (From Myself) by NURKO and Kyle Hume
hole in the bottle by Kelsey Ballerini
When She Comes Home Tonight by Riley Green
Strawberry Wine by Deana Carter
You Found Yours by Luke Combs
Don't Give Up on Me by Zach Bryan
Wide Open Spaces by The Chicks
I Want Us by The Roads Below
Love You Again by Chase Matthew
I'LL QUIT LOVIN' YOU by HARDY
Lady May by Tyler Childers

Banks by NEEDTOBREATHE
What My World Spins Around by Jordan Davis
Alabama by Cross Canadian Ragweed

CHAPTER ONE
CAROLINE

Was it even really a Monday at Springside High without a little bit of chaos?

My internal question is answered promptly by the repeated screech of the fire alarm and the announcement over the loudspeaker that this is a school-approved fire drill. It isn't even 8 AM, but here I stand, classroom roll in hand and attempting to shuffle all thirty-two of my high school juniors outside in less than ninety seconds. It is too early for this, and I am not even caffeinated yet. I was just in the middle of making my morning cup of coffee when the fire alarm started going off. Our principal mentioned the fire department would be dropping by when they had a spare moment today to do a state-required drill, but I didn't think it would be this early.

"Okay everyone, leave your stuff. Hopefully, it will only be a moment. Let's move quickly," I tell my class. A series of groans erupt from the room, and one of the boys points at the window. "Miss Caroline, you do realize it's raining right?"

I look out the window and sure enough, a steady drizzle has just started. Great. Getting teenagers to do anything at 7:47 in the morning requires an act of Congress, never mind making them walk outside in the rain. "You're right, Wesley. Let's go."

I quickly turn off the light before leading my class down the hall. We make our way outside and stand in the misting rain. I hurry to read the roll, hoping to make my way down it before it becomes too smudged to read. "Olivia, Jack, Michael, Ty." I continue down to make sure everyone is accounted for, before turning around to face the building. It's a warm and humid late August morning—pretty much the norm for South Alabama. Typically by the time I call roll, we've been cleared to go back inside. Of course, that wasn't in the cards for me this morning.

My students huddle under umbrellas and the hoods of their rain jackets for a few minutes before I see other teachers beginning to take their classes inside. "Come on guys," I yell to my class before leading them back into the side entrance and down the hallway to my room.

When I turn the corner, I see one of the firefighters standing in front of my door. I don't recognize him, which is weird considering I thought I knew all the firefighters in Springside. Clearly, this guy is new to town. A man like this would have been the talk of the town, and now I'm trying to figure out how I know nothing about him.

As we make our way closer, I look at him—all six feet of him—along with his chiseled biceps and tousled brown hair. I catch myself momentarily drooling over how sexy he is until I realize he seems to be deep in thought. He glowers at my door as he bites the corner of his lip, and I can't help but wonder what it would feel like to have his lips on mine.

"Are you Miss Tyler?" the man asks as I near my classroom. He stares at me with the biggest scowl I have ever seen and looks as though he is more frustrated with the events of this morning than I am.

"Yeah, but you can call me Caroline," I say politely, trying to diffuse whatever tension was floating in the air around us.

"Miss Tyler, I just need to know, are you incompetent or just plain irresponsible?" he asks, glaring at me with such contempt you would think I had kicked his puppy.

"Mr. —" I stop, reminding him that he hasn't even introduced himself. I have no idea what I have done to earn the wrath of this man. My kids stand behind me unsure of how to handle this situation. I make eye contact with a few of them trying to show them that I'm fine and this is nothing to get upset over.

"It's Chief Johnson," he barks at me gruffly. "I am the new fire chief in town."

"Mr. Johnson, it's lovely to meet you also," I say, deliberately ignoring his title. "What happens to be the problem this morning?"

"I said it's CHIEF Johnson, Miss Tyler! The problem is that you left a damn candle burning in your classroom. FEMA just released the latest statistics that said over 23,600 fires were started last year thanks to candles just like the one in your room. There were 165 fatalities last year alone. So I will ask you again, are you incompetent or just irresponsible?" the angry man in front of me asks as I can feel my students shift at my back.

"Well Mr Johnson," I say as I watch his face contort in frustration that I have once again ignored his proper title. "Around here, we earn our titles so the rank on your badge doesn't mean a whole lot to me. Secondly, I would like to remind you that you are in a school. Your language isn't appropriate," I scold him, and to his credit, he does look a bit embarrassed.

"IT'S CHIEF JOHNSON!" he yells, ignoring my other point. "And you also left your door wide open during the fire drill. A closed door can make the difference between life and death in a fire."

"Listen, Chief Johnny, I truly apologize for my candle. I usually light it in my room in the morning while I get everything set up for the day before students come in. Something has to combat the Axe body spray and Victoria's Secret lotion, right? And I swear I pulled the door closed. I put in a maintenance request last week for that handle. I don't think it's catching right," I say while maintaining eye contact.

He continues to scowl at me and is clearly trying to intimidate me.

My students behind me laugh awkwardly at my comment about their body spray and one or two try to come to my rescue. The mysterious new fireman straightens and looks down at them, silencing their retorts. *Wow, tough crowd*, I think to myself.

"Miss Tyler, get your damn candles off school property. If I come back and find any wax in that room we are going to have problems. I would expect a teacher to have the common sense to understand with all the paper on your desk that a candle can get out of control fast. So as for my original question, I'm inclined to believe you are more on the irresponsible side. It is a miracle this place hasn't burned to the ground after all the crap the old chief allowed. He clearly lost his mind and was willing to put everyone at risk. And get your door fixed. Do you know how reckless it is to have a door that doesn't lock properly in a school?" Once again the man continues his tirade oblivious to the fact that his previous statement was fighting words.

Our old fire chief, Huey, retired last month and was absolutely beloved by everyone in Springside. He volunteered with the youth basketball and baseball leagues, oversaw the town softball tournament, and created a program to partner local fire and police employees with teenagers interested in careers in public service. Out of the thirty-two sixteen-year-olds I have standing behind me, I'm willing to bet Huey had a part in coaching or mentoring at least half of them.

Sure enough, when I glance behind me, I see several enraged faces and a group of kids beginning to whisper about this new hotshot fire chief. I know I need to get the situation under control quickly to prevent any of my students feeling the need to defend ol' Huey's honor.

Have I mentioned I still haven't had my coffee yet? Sighing, I decide to swallow my pride in the effort to diffuse the situation.

"Chief Johnson, I sincerely apologize for my candle this morning. I understand that it's against policy and it won't happen again. As for my door, I will call the maintenance department again this morning. I promise you won't have any other issues from me."

I look him in the eye, trying to convey to him that we are done here. But he continues to sneer at me in disgust before walking off and throwing a disgruntled "I better not," over his shoulder.

I turn around to my students who are glaring after the new chief in anger and simultaneously trying to shake the water off themselves. I remember at that moment that I probably resemble a drowned rat. Sure enough, I wipe under my eyes and see my mascara has run down my face. Great. Happy Monday to me I guess.

WE ARE HALFWAY through second period when I feel my Apple Watch ping with a notification. I look down to see a text from my best friend, Hannah. She teaches science on the other side of the school, and I have a pretty good idea of what I'm about to find. I grab my phone and scroll down to see her message.

Hannah: WHAT THE HECK CAROLINE?! A bunch of your kids came to my room and said the new fire chief was a total asshole to you. What the hell happened?!

> Me: Yeah, it's definitely been a morning. Monday night margs at Maracas tonight? We can discuss then.

> Hannah: You're on.

I throw my phone in the drawer of my desk, trying to turn my focus back on the lesson I created on *The Great Gatsby*. As we are still early into the school year, I'm trying to hook my students' attention while also building relationships with them. So far today, all I have managed to accomplish is becoming the talk of the school.

When we returned to the room after the incident with Chief Johnson, I spent the remainder of class trying to distract the students from my humiliation. I launched into a monologue about Jay Gatsby and the ideals represented in the novel of the American Dream. Despite my efforts, all my students wanted to discuss was the new chief.

It was clear that Chief Johnson did not make a favorable impression on the students of Springside. While part of me is exceptionally angry at the way he talked to me, I certainly don't envy the position he is in now. Springside is a tight community, and it's hard enough for outsiders to find their place here. I'm not going to go out of my way to tell anyone about the encounter, but I have no doubt that the community gossip is already running rampant about the new fire chief. Plus, something tells me that his outburst probably has very little to do with me at all. I wasn't sure what happened to make him upset, but I was almost positive I'd been a convenient scapegoat. After a few years in education, I've gotten used to diffusing situations between my students, and occasionally some of my coworkers, so I wasn't as upset as I probably should have been.

I try to hold on to my anger, but I know I hadn't been innocent in our encounter this morning. I generally try to see the best in people, and I know that the new chief will be facing the town firing squad after his inadvertent insult to Huey.

"Okay everyone, don't forget we will be reading Chapter One tomorrow in *The Great Gatsby*. Make sure you bring your books to class and be ready for a pop quiz on the Roaring 20s and F. Scott Fitzgerald," I declare loudly to my students right before the bell rings. "Have a good day! I will see you tomorrow!" I yell at each of them as they walk out the door.

I start the slideshow over and go to stand outside my door to welcome my next class of juniors into my room. As soon as I enter the hallway I notice Coach Will Thompson coming my way. Will is the Springside equivalent of John B from Outer Banks, and I often find my female students writing his name with hearts in their notes. He graduated a year before me, but we have always been friends.

Will stayed in Springside and has risen through the ranks of football coaching quicker than anyone in town has ever seen. Really anyone could have predicted this since he was the captain of the team all four years of high school. Plus, his charisma, his ability to bond with his players, and his love for Springside combine to make him incredibly popular.

Throughout the years, there have been plenty of meddling women in town who hoped we would end up together, but it was just never in the cards for us. He's more like a brother to me than any type of love interest.

I always secretly thought he and Hannah would be perfect together, but since the school board frowned on workplace dating, I have never voiced those thoughts to either of them.

"Caroline, what's this I keep hearing about an asshole fire chief yelling at you this morning?" he asks when he gets close enough to talk to me without the students in the hall overhearing.

"Oh, well yeah, he wasn't happy with me. He accused me of trying to burn the school down because I had my Volcano candle burning during the fire drill. I meant to blow it out before we went outside but I was uncaffeinated and totally forgot," I explain sheepishly.

"I heard the fucker started shit-talking Huey in front of everyone," Will says with a look of horror on his face. Will and Chief Huey have been close ever since Will's sophomore year of high school. Will had caught his dad in a compromising position with one of his rival teammate´s mom from the next town over, and his parents went through a nasty divorce and custody battle when we were in high school. When his dad lost, he ran off on Will and his four younger siblings. He hasn't seen him since.

Huey caught Will drinking on the football field late one night and instead of busting him, he sat down and started talking to him. They talked for hours, which led to Will revealing a lot of the anger and hurt that he'd been repressing from his father's absence. That night on the football field changed Will's life, and Huey became a stand-in father ever since. Huey sat in the first row when Will graduated high school, found him scholarships for college, helped him get his first job as a coach, and hasn't missed a Springside game since.

"I think he was just voicing his frustration at the way some of the rules hadn't been as strictly enforced as he prefers" I reply, trying to reign in his anger.

"What a dick. Are you okay?" he asks, his concern evident on his face.

"Yeah, I'm great. Really." I add when he hesitates.

"Okay well, I better go. I have a meeting with the mayor and superintendent on our new season in ten minutes, but if you have any problems let me know. I plan to let them know that I don't appreciate the way the new fire chief handled today," he says.

"Oh, please don't. There is no need in getting your panties in a wad. Everything is fine." I smile at him to prove I'm truly okay, but I could tell it was futile. When Will got something on his mind, there was nothing we could do to change it.

"I'll see you later," he calls out over his shoulder, and it doesn't escape my notice that he completely ignored my plea.

CHAPTER TWO
THEO

To say I was having a shit day would be the understatement of the century.

My first day at work started with a frantic call from the principal at the high school begging us to come before the state department came. After my altercation with the beautiful teacher in the hallway I had the distinct impression I had majorly put my foot in my mouth. I hadn't meant to come on as strong as I did, but people needed to take fire safety more seriously. If my life wasn't proof of that I don't know what is.

We made the rounds to the other schools in town conducting their state-mandated drills, and thankfully, they went more smoothly than the high school this morning. However, it hadn't escaped my notice that there were still a ton of issues. It seemed to me that Huey and his older crew turned a blind eye to some of the problems and now it was going to be my job to fix them—great. I took a minute to be grateful that several of his most faithful crew members had retired when I'd entered. They had trained their replacements, but as a result, the small station was mostly younger guys.

The sinking feeling only grows stronger as I pull up to the

fire station, now later in the afternoon. As I put the truck into park, I notice the mayor's silver Ford pickup in the lot, and I know my day is about to get a lot worse.

I enter the station and make my way to my office. Sure enough, as I turn the corner, I see Mayor Brian Jones sitting in my office typing away on his cell phone. Great. Might as well get this shit show over with.

I walk into my office feigning confidence. At thirty, I know he took a chance hiring me last month as the youngest fire chief in Springside's history, so I feel like I owe him. Mayor Jones was my older brother, Jake's, college roommate. They both attended the University of Alabama on a full ride for football, and by Jake's sophomore year, it had felt as though Brian was a part of our family. But all of that changed the night our world was turned upside down, and I fell out of touch with Brian until a few weeks ago when he called me about the job.

I can feel my heart rate picking up and my skin growing clammy as it always does when I think about that night, but I know I can't think about that right now. Attempting to shift my attention back to Brian, I give him an apologetic grimace. Damn, I really need a beer and some fresh air.

We shake hands and I sit down at my desk. Considering all of my things are in boxes I'm grateful that I have somewhere to sit. I add unpacking to my growing list of things to do ASAP.

I can tell by the way Brian is waiting for me to get comfortable that he has something to say. I have a feeling I won't like whatever it is either.

"Theo, you know I hired you because I believe in you right?" Brian starts. Damn, I do not like the way this is starting, but I nod at him to continue. "But can I just say I don't think you could have gotten off to a more rocky start if you tried? You have been here less than twenty-four hours, and I've gotten at least forty calls today asking me about the outsider I hired who yelled at a teacher and committed blasphemy in the eyes of the town. Dude, do you realize you insulted the most beloved man in a hundred-mile radius on your first day?"

"Well I didn't, but I'm well aware now," I say more to myself than him.

He nods at me looking a little more sympathetic than he did when I walked in. "Listen, Theo, I know you take fire safety seriously, and God knows I understand why. It's part of what makes you so great at this job. It's why I brought you here. But we have a major problem now. Springside is a small town. And they're going to take your insult to Huey personally. We need to get ahead of this before they're trying to run both of us out of town."

"I'm assuming you have an idea of how we can do that?" I ask him skeptically.

"I do but I don't think you're going to like it," Brian warns. "It's the beginning of fall and you know how big football is to a town like us. I thought about it during my meeting with the coach this morning. I know you know the game better than anyone, thanks to Jake. So you're going to volunteer as a coach. I talked to the head coach this morning, and he wasn't happy but I got him to agree to let you help out. One of his assistants decided to move to Mobile last month so there is an opening and he needs help."

I feel like I can't breathe. I haven't touched a football since the night my world fell apart. My chest tightens, and my vision blurs. I know what I'm feeling is the start of a panic attack, but I try to calm down enough to focus on what Brian is saying.

Football? The mayor can't be serious. But the more he talks the more I realize he is. I zone out as he starts talking about practice schedules and ways to make it fit into my job at the station, then mentions team dinners hosted by the local church and community pep rallies at the high school followed by bus rides and pregame warm-ups.

Brian looks at me and must realize I am lost to the demons

of my past because he gives me an apologetic grimace. "Listen, I'll email you all of the details. But you need this Theo. I need you to do this. And it's what Jake would have done."

"Brian, you can't ask me to do that!" I say, feeling the panic rising in my chest. "Plus none of us have a God damn clue what Jake would want! He's gone and he's not coming back!"

"Theo, I know this—Jake cared about you more than just about anything. He was so excited about the idea of getting to play at Bryant Denny with you. And he couldn't wait to start coaching. Right now, you've got two options: stay in Springside and make an effort with the community and the team, or live out of boxes for the next two weeks while the town does everything they can to make you quit," Brian says, and I see the sincerity in his eyes. "And just in case you need a reminder, you aren't the only one who lost their best friend that night. We're both just trying to make him proud."

Any rebuttal I have to this idea dies at those words. Usually, comments like that do nothing but piss me off, but Brian was almost as close to Jake as I was. And I know he's right. Jake loved anything to do with football and had planned to give up his chance at the NFL to coach younger players.

Knowing that there's nothing else I can say, I nod at Brian and tell him, "You're right. So when do I start?"

"I'm glad you asked. Coach Thompson is expecting you at practice in an hour. I am gonna warn you. He's really protective of Miss Caroline, the woman you yelled at today. So don't be surprised if he doesn't give you the warmest welcome. That being said, you won't find a guy that cares more about his team and his players. It took a little bit of convincing to get him to agree to this, so please don't screw it up. Otherwise, your time in Springside will be a lot shorter than planned."

Great, I think to myself, as all hopes of a quiet evening unpacking with a beer in my hand quickly vanish from my mind. "Well, I'd better get ready for practice then," I say to Brian. He stands from his chair and goes to shake my hand.

"Listen, man, I know you got off to a rockier start than you hoped, but it's gonna be alright. You're damn good at your job, and I know once the town gets a chance to know you this will be something we laugh about later. We just have to get them there first."

"Yeah, you're right. Thanks," I tell him, standing to shake his hand as he rises from his chair.

"Don't sweat it. Gotta love the small-town politics, am I right? You head on to practice and maybe one night next week we can grab a beer once you get settled in," Brian says as he walks out of my office.

"Sounds good," I call out down the hall.

Crap. I guess I have a practice to get to. And after fourteen years of running from my past it looks like today might be the day that I have to face it.

I PULL up to the high school stadium and take a breath. I haven't stepped foot on a field since the accident. I gave up the game I loved more than anything at sixteen and haven't looked back, but it looks like my time of avoidance has come to an end.

Knowing I have no other option if I want to keep my job, I sigh and get out of my truck. I try to ignore the sinking feeling in my stomach as I make my way down to the field. I attempt to pretend the late August Alabama heat is the cause of the sudden sweat I can feel breaking out over my body, but the reality is, I know better.

I can see the team on the field as I make my way down, and suddenly each member stops and looks up at me. I can feel the distrust and general dislike for me coming off them in waves. Once I make it to the field, a dark-headed man, who looks to be in his mid-twenties, looks me over, and yells to the team. "Alright guys, as you know Coach G had to move for his wife's job down to Mobile last month, so we had an opening on our staff. After speaking with several of the stakeholders of our team, Chief Johnson will be our new Wide Receivers coach. He's gonna observe practice today and will get started working with y'all tomorrow."

I should have known better than to expect a warm welcome after Brian's warning, but I wasn't expecting these high schoolers to absolutely hate me. The look on their faces says they would rather bear crawl over rocks every day for the season than have to listen to anything I have to say. The tone of the man, who I'm assuming is Coach Thompson, didn't give me much hope that he's happy I'm here. I would have liked to meet him without all the players' eyes on us, but considering the fact that I came straight from my meeting with Brian, there hadn't been time.

A boy steps forward that I recognize from my encounter with Miss Caroline this morning. "Hey Coach, you know he insulted Huey this morning and he was a total jackass to Miss Caroline in front of everyone. You really think he's what's best for our team?"

I look over to see several of the boys nodding along in agreement with him. Coach Thompson's face grows grim as he looks at his team. "Well Wesley, as much as I appreciate your desire to take up for Miss Caroline, I don't recall asking for your opinion. And since the rest of you seem to agree with him, why don't y'all start at the end of the field down there and roll until you don't doubt my coaching abilities anymore."

The boys let out a loud groan of frustration but immediately run to the end of the field and start rolling on their stomachs. It occurs to me that this gives the players another reason to hate me. Great. I may be frustrated, but I can't ignore the fact that this team and these players are my ticket to staying in

Springside, and this isn't winning me any fans. I remember having to do this as a player a few times and it sucked. Between the grass, the dizziness, and the sore body it brought, I know these kids won't be questioning Coach Thompson again anytime soon.

I walk over to the coach and stick my hand out. "Good afternoon, I'm Chief Johnson, but you can call me Theo," I say.

The man looks at my hand for a moment before deciding to shake it begrudgingly. "Coach Thompson. I guess you can call me Will. And before we get started I want to get one thing out of the way. The mayor is one of our biggest supporters here at Springside, and I couldn't turn him down. But Caroline and I have been friends for years, and I don't appreciate the way you spoke to her this morning. I said yes to giving you a shot, but you're gonna have to prove to me and everyone else that you're not the asshole everyone thinks you are."

I nod at him. "I understand."

He looks at me and continues, "So, the mayor told me you're Jake Johnson's little brother huh? That man was a legend. My dad took me to my first game at Bryant Denny in 2009 against Arkansas, and I still remember that eighty-yard catch your brother made."

I shake my head in a sign of affirmation. "Yeah, that's me," I reply, trying to keep the tightness out of my voice. Just like any other time that I think about my brother, I can feel my chest constricting and my pulse quickening.

Will seems to notice that I would rather do anything else than continue this line of conversation and takes pity on me. He changes the subject by saying, "As for the team, I think we're showing signs of promise. Last year was a bit of a rebuilding year. But we've got a young team with some real potential. If you've got half the talent your brother had, I think you can help us out. But to be clear, I still don't like you very much."

Realizing that this is as close to a proverbial olive branch as

I am going to get from him, I nod quickly. "Thanks, man. I understand, and I apologize."

He looks at me sharply and says, "I am not the one you need to be apologizing to. You find a way to make it up to Caroline, and I'll think about easing up on you."

"Got it," I respond as he jogs out to join the team. I sit on the bleacher set up on the field and settle in to watch practice. I wait for the panic of missing my brother to set in, but the longer I sit here the more at ease I feel. I realize I've been putting off this moment for far too long. I had expected to feel like I was suffocating sitting on the field. But the reality is I feel much closer to Jake than I have in years. Brian was right when he said that this is what Jake would have wanted.

Clinging to that thought, I focus on practice and try to figure out how to fix the mess I made today.

CHAPTER THREE
CAROLINE

The only thing I can think as I walk into Maracas is that I have never needed a Margarita Monday more than I do tonight. I walk into the familiar Mexican restaurant feeling like I can finally take a deep breath. This day has sucked. I've been coming here for dinner on Mondays with Hannah since we moved back to Springside. Maracas is small, but it's within walking distance to the old, downtown building the city made into apartments where I live, and their food is incredible. The restaurant was once a gas station, but when the original owner decided to retire, the building was purchased and transformed into a local hang-out. The antique gas pumps still sit outside, adding to the restaurant's charm.

I smile at the trademark "Save water, drink tequila" neon sign that takes up the entire back wall, and let out a little laugh. *Don't have to tell me twice,* I think to myself.

After the fire fiasco, I struggled all day getting my students to focus in class. After the second period it had only got worse, since the news had spread through all of the kid's group chats. Those things spread gossip faster than anything else I have ever seen before. If they weren't so annoying I would almost admire their power.

By the time lunch rolled around I'd gotten texts from two cheer parents, some friends in town, and my Aunt Sue asking if I was okay. The preacher from church also reached out to see if he could pray for me. Sometimes living in Springside really is like a cliché Hallmark movie, but after living here all my life I tend not to notice.

Even my parents, who had moved to Brazil years ago and only messaged on my birthday, heard the news from one of their old friends and sent an email to check on me. I don't necessarily have a bad relationship with my parents, but we've never had much in common. I drifted apart from them pretty quickly after high school, and I was okay with where our relationship stood.

After all that, cheer practice rolled around. I took over the Springside Varsity squad three years ago, and it is one of my favorite parts of my job. After convincing Hannah to come on as a tumbling coach the following year, we've become unstoppable. I am incredibly proud of the program we've built. Pushing the girls to try new stunts or tumbling passes and helping them develop the confidence to carry themselves through life never fails to excite me.

But today the girls only wanted to talk about the hot new fire chief and how much of a jerk he'd been. By the time four o'clock rolled around, I banned the topic of conversation and the girls had run too many laps to count.

As usual, I arrive to Maracas before Hannah so I grab us a table and order my first peach margarita of the night and some queso. Hannah is my best friend, but she's notorious for running late.

Some people think it is because she's flighty or rude, but I know it's due to her efforts to take care of her grandfather's farm. His health has been declining slowly for years, but he refuses to sell any of the animals. Hannah's parents moved away when she was in middle school and left her with her grandparents, which meant she now bore the responsibility of taking care of the farm.

Hannah and I both attended Springside High, and while we've always been best friends, our decision to room together at Alabama freshman year cemented her place as the closest thing I have to a sister. Our shared love of teaching, nineties country music, and smutty romance novels, combined with the fact that both of our parents wanted a life far away from us, makes our bond pretty much unbreakable now.

Hannah used to be the most carefree person I knew, but lately the farm has added a ton of stress to her life. She tried hiring a couple of caretakers to sit with her grandfather around the clock to keep him company, but as his health problems grew more serious, she'd been forced to put him in a nursing home. Most of her teaching salary goes to his medical expenses and farm equipment. That being said, she can't afford to pay someone for the farm work as well. Members of the community help out on occasion, but Hannah is too proud to ask for help unless she is desperate. There is no telling what she'd gotten into between practice and dinner.

I sip my drink and snack away on chips while I wait for her to arrive. Picking up the Kindle that I always keep stashed in my purse, I start to read my latest cowboy romance.

I've had a fascination with cowboys for as long as I can remember, but the only cowboys I know in Springside are pushing seventy. Just last month Mr. Wilkerson passed away leaving the most beautiful farm in the county up for sale. I'd heard last week someone purchased it, but I haven't met them yet. *Maybe it's a sexy cowboy in his early thirties looking for someone to take a ride on his bronco*, I think to myself knowing that was like hoping to find a needle in a haystack.

I get lost in my book and before I realize it, I've finished the first small bowl of chips and the margarita. I am a bit of a light-weight, so I know I need to slow down, but after the day I've had, I can't find it in myself to care.

I order another drink as Mrs. Sally, the town gossip, stops by my table. I swear that woman is in her seventies, but she still gossips worse than any of my students at school. She tries to look nonchalant but I know she's dying for all the details of what happened at the school today. I skirt around her questions with a bit of success, attempting to tune her out and wanting nothing more than to get back to the sexy cowboy railing his love interest underneath the stars after a long day on the farm.

However, my interest skyrockets when she says, "Can you believe the school agreed to let him volunteer as a coach on the football team? Such a damn shame. I don't know if someone with a temper like that should even be allowed around children."

While it's news to me that he was helping with the football team, I try not to let it show on my face. I may not be the mystery fire chief's biggest fan, but after living in Springside my entire life I knew how it felt to be dragged through the town's gossip mill. It makes me crazy when people like Mrs. Sally start sticking their nose in other people's business just to cause problems. Especially when they start making accusations that have absolutely no basis. I have grown accustomed to the meddling, but after the day I had and the tequila making its way through my system, I'm at my limit.

"Well Mrs. Sally, you and I both know that Coach Thompson wouldn't let anyone near those boys that he thought could be dangerous. That's a pretty big accusation to be making out here in front of God and everybody. Plus, I was in the wrong this morning anyway. It was all just a big misunderstanding. So let's just leave it there," I say with the biggest smile I can manage on my face.

Thankfully the waiter chooses that moment to make his appearance with my second margarita, and Mrs. Sally walks off looking somewhat scorned. I have no doubt she'd be starting a rumor that I'm a raging alcoholic in no time, but the woman needs to stop talking. The difference between me and the new fire chief is I have plenty of people to stick up for me in town. And while I'm frustrated with the way he treated me today, I know rumors like Mrs. Sally was starting for an outsider could be career-ending.

I turn back to my book and read a few chapters with only a few interruptions. It is impossible to go anywhere in Springside without running into someone you know. As a town of less than six thousand, everyone knows everyone which makes me even more curious about the town's newest resident.

I just finished speaking to two of my cheerleaders who stopped by on their way out of the restaurant when Hannah blows in the door, running as fast as her legs can carry her. That's Hannah though. She never does anything slowly or timidly. She is a complete whirlwind, and I love her even more for it.

"Oh my gosh, I am so sorry I am late. Leroy got out and started running wild through the pasture. To be such a fat lil booger he can move."

Leroy is the nine-year-old American Yorkshire pig that Hannah's grandfather bought her as a teenager. I am obsessed with the six-hundred-pound pig and know from experience that when he is feeling playful, he can run a whole lot faster than most people believe.

Laughing at the mental image, I respond, "It's no problem. I almost finished my book."

We immediately launch into a discussion on what we've read over the last week as Hannah orders a drink. Hannah's go to is sports romance while mine is cowboys, but we are both avid romance readers and love to debate the merit of sex positions and meet-cutes.

Just as we are discussing the hot, sexy cattle rancher in my current read, Hannah stops to take a sip of her margarita and exclaims, "Oh my gosh, I love smut and tequila."

She says it loud enough to gain the attention of a few of the nearby tables, but she sips her drink in content oblivion. If she and I hadn't been friends for so long, I might have been embarrassed by her outburst, but after being friends for over fifteen years I'm used to it.

I see a girl sitting alone at the bar beside us, and we make eye contact. It's unusual for there to be anyone in town on a Monday that I don't recognize. I smile and she timidly walks over to our table.

"Hey, y'all. My name is Margaret. I know this is super random, but I'm new to town. I heard you talking about romance novels, and I'm completely obsessed as well. Just wanted to come over and say hi," the visitor says with a shy smile.

"WHAT?" Hannah exclaims loudly, once again drawing the attention of everyone in our vicinity. "We never get new young people. Sit with us! Where are you from?! What are you doing in Springside? Are you single? Where are you living? Tell me everything."

I look over to Margaret who looks like she's regretting the decision to come over and say hi with each passing moment. "Woah, Hannah. Let the poor girl breathe."

Margaret smiles thankfully over at me and turns back towards Hannah. "I moved from Birmingham. I am twenty-four and newly single. I arrived today, so I'm still getting the lay of the land, but I bought the empty building downtown. I want to make it into a coffee shop and bakery eventually, but it needs a lot of work."

"Shut up," Hannah yells. "Springside is gonna have a coffee shop?!"

"We've been dying for one for years! Driving forty minutes for Starbucks gets really old after a while," I add excitedly.

Margaret's smile grows. "Oh, it makes me excited to hear that. This is a big step for me, but I have wanted this for so long. I can't believe it's really happening."

Hannah scoots over in the booth. "You have to join us. It feels like Caroline and I have been the only single twenty-somethings in town for as long as I can remember."

Margaret looks to me as if she's waiting for me to give her permission so I smile and nod at her. She sits down, and Hannah immediately launches back into conversation as if we've been friends for years. She jumps from books to boys to work while we all sip on our peach margaritas and even my head is spinning slightly before she exclaims, "Caroline, I don't know how I forgot. What the hell happened this morning? All I've heard from my kids was that the new fire chief is a major asshole!"

A look of genuine concern covers Margaret's face as she asks, "Oh my goodness what happened?"

Hannah jumps in before I can get a word out. "We had a fire drill this morning, and the new fire chief completely screamed at her in front of everyone. He also insulted the most beloved man within one hundred miles and was a total ass."

"Oh, really?" Margaret says with interest, picking up her phone and typing away.

"Well, I don't think he meant it. My door has been broken to my room, and he's just doing his job," I say, unsure of why I am trying to defend the new fire chief from my best friend's wrath.

"Did he ask you any questions before he started screaming at you?" Margaret asks.

"Well, no," I say and before I can get a word in, Hannah is

off on a tangent again. I notice Margaret texting furiously on her phone, and when she looks up I ask, "Is everything okay?"

She laughs at me and sits her phone down on the table as she takes a big gulp of her margarita, "Oh yes, I'm good. I guess I didn't tell you my last name. I'm Margaret Johnson, and the new asshole fire chief is my brother. I was just reiterating to him that he truly is an asshole."

Hannah and I stare at each other, my face blushing from embarrassment and hers breaking into ferocious laughter.

"Oh my God, we're totally gonna be best friends," Hannah yells with a laugh.

CHAPTER FOUR
THEO

It's almost 7 o'clock by the time I get out of practice, drive the twenty minutes to my new house, and grab a quick shower. I am just stepping out of the room-sized walk-in shower when I see my phone lighting up with a text.

Margaret: WHY do you have to be such an asshole???

Margaret: We've barely been here twenty-four hours. You've shown your tail, AND screamed at the closest thing I have to a friend here in town.

Margaret: When I get home you better be ready to figure out a way to make this right.

Sighing I throw my phone on the bed and glance at my chocolate Labrador, Bear, as he stretches across my pillow. "Well bud, what a crappy day. You aren't mad at me are you?" It was supposed to be a joke but it feels like a slap in the face when he stands up and lays back down, this time with his back to me.

Great. Even my dog thinks I'm an ass.

Grabbing a pair of boxers and old gym shorts out of the top of the box closest to me, I throw them on and start to take inventory of what I have in my room. I planned to tackle a good bit of the unpacking tonight when I got home from work but that was before I'd been assigned to football duty. I enjoyed the practice more than I thought I would. Watching the team work together to complete passes and learn plays made me feel closer to my brother than I have in years.

Leaving Bear stretched across my pillow, I make my way back down the hall and look into the mostly bare refrigerator. Right. In my haste to get away, I also hadn't gone to the grocery store. Damn it, today really did not go how I planned. I run back to my room and pick up my phone to text my sister.

Me: Yeah, yeah I know I'm the worst.

Me: Where are you?

Me: If you're coming home from town, would you please bring me something to eat?

I wait for a second and see the dots that signify she's typing.

Margaret: Are you for real?

Me: Please. I'm hungry and I've had a shit day.

Margaret: I don't have any sympathy for you. All everyone is talking about is how much they hate the new fire chief.

Me: Yeah, yeah. I get it. I'm an asshole. You know, we can't be liked by everyone.

> Margaret: Fine, I hope Bear is willing to share his kibble with you because that sounds like it's as close as you're gonna get to supper.

Sighing, I take a breath and try not to lose my temper. The worst part is I know she's right. I never should've lost my cool the way I did this morning.

> Me: Okay you're right. I'm sorry. I want to figure out a way to make this right, and I'll talk to you whenever you get here. But there really isn't anything to eat at home. Would you please consider bringing me something to keep me from starving?

> Margaret: I know there's nothing at home. Why do you think I came into town? And I'll bring you something. But you better hope that I don't put laxatives in it. It's what you deserve after making us the talk of the town.

Blowing out a breath, I decide to sit on the only piece of furniture and search through the listings of farm animals for sale that Brian acquired for me when I took the job. When I saw the farm property for sale, I couldn't pass up the opportunity. Since I'd started with a fire station when I was eighteen, I'd managed to save enough for the down payment on the fifty-acre property.

When Brian offered me the job and the property fell into place, I started feeling like my life might be starting to take a turn for the better. I should have known that it wouldn't take long for me to screw it up. Lo and behold, after barely twenty-four hours in Springside, at least five thousand of the six thousand residents currently hate me.

Sighing, I wait for Margaret to make her appearance. I should have known in a town as small as this one that she would make friends with the woman I yelled at earlier today.

As I wait, I scroll through Instagram trying to decide how to apologize for my behavior. Coming into this job with my age and new status in town, I'd thought coming on strong was my best option for proving I was serious, but I can see now where that was a major mistake.

Finally, I see headlights coming up our long driveway. After a minute, Margaret makes her way into the house. "Have I mentioned you are a major ass?"

Sighing and running my hand through my hair, I reply, "You think I don't already know that? Are you gonna help me fix it?"

Margaret looks at me with a sneer before softening her facial expression. "I really should leave you to clean up the mess you made but since I know how seriously you take your job, and the fact I'm sort of tied to the town dickface at the moment, I guess I will help you figure something out."

She takes out her phone and starts typing away. Getting frustrated I snap at her, "I thought you were helping me. What the hell are you doing?"

"I'm inviting my new friends over for dinner tomorrow night. You better figure out how to grovel between now and then."

CHAPTER FIVE
THEO

My first thought when I wake up is that it's much hotter than it should be. In my groggy state, I think that the air conditioner must have broken, but I quickly realize that this heat is way different from a normal Alabama night.

It's dark when I open my eyes, but I can feel the heat on my face. I look around and notice the gap under the door shows a bright light and smoke is billowing in through the space. Coming to terms with what's going on, I scramble out of bed and start screaming for my siblings. Calling out for my parents. Looking for a way out of my bedroom. I grab for the door, but the knob burns my hand, warning me not to open it. I cough and sputter still trying to yell for anyone that could help me. But help isn't coming. My heart races out of my chest and I continue screaming "MOM, DAD. HELP ME! JAKE!!!! MARGARET!!!"

I'm jerked awake by my screams, and Margaret pounding on my door. It takes me a minute to realize where I am before realizing I'm in the farmhouse in Springside. Trying to force air back into my lungs, I grab for the water on my bedside table. I'm covered in sweat and my throat is raw from calling out in my sleep.

"Theo, you gotta wake up!" Margaret screams, still pounding on the door. I stand from the bed and walk over to the door trying to dodge all the shit I still need to unpack on the floor. Opening it, I see the clear signs of worry on her face. "Another nightmare?" she asks.

"Yeah, you know the usual," I tell her.

"I'm worried about you, Theo. You can't keep living like this." My sister tries, clearly worried about me becoming upset with this line of conversation.

"I'm fine," I snap. "Yesterday was fucking hell. I made a fool out of myself, and now I have to figure out how to make good with this damn town along with the teacher I was a complete ass to." I don't bother to mention that the nightmares have been a constant for the last several years. Margaret and I have talked every day since the night our lives fell apart, but this is the first time we've lived together since I moved out.

Margaret was living with her asshole boyfriend until she walked in on him last month with his cock down another girl's throat. He's a high-powered attorney in Birmingham, and she'd thought he'd been the one. They'd looked at wedding rings this summer, but it turned out he'd been sneaking around with one of his clients' wives for over six months. They'd met as he was defending her husband's company for fraud. I knew my sister was still healing from his betrayal and that it had been a major factor in her deciding to move to Springside with me.

"Okay, well Caroline and Hannah confirmed they are coming over tonight. I'll take care of the sides and dessert, but I need you to be in charge of the grill. I figured you could grill some steaks and I'll make a pasta salad and baked potatoes. I've been itching to make some fresh bread and I have a new cookie recipe that I am thinking about making as a signature item for the bakery."

Margaret and I had stayed up through the early hours of the morning to make the living room and kitchen somewhat welcoming for visitors. We'd unpacked the lamps and some of the other girly shit Margaret insisted we needed from throw pillows and area rugs to lemon verbena candles. She'd refused to let me touch anything in the kitchen since she's obsessive about knowing where everything is while she bakes. I was dog-tired by the time we finished, but I had to admit that it felt good to finally feel like I had a home.

After the fire, I decided to go straight into fire training. I eventually went back and got my degree online from a community college while I was working my way up to Captain, but I always knew city life wasn't for me. While I worked in the suburbs outside of Birmingham, I still felt suffocated by the lack of fresh air. I'd worked my way through the ranks and rented a small apartment close to the station, but it had never felt like home. I hadn't even bothered to buy much furniture other than a bed and sofa in the twelve years I'd lived there, much to Margaret's frustration.

I was grateful for the opportunities at the old station, but I never felt like I'd found a place to belong. Add on the fact that I had beaten a few older members of my old squad out for Captain, easy to say I hadn't been sad to leave the tension in the station. I'd been worried that would be a problem in Springside but everyone I met yesterday seemed fine—until I insulted Huey.

"Well I have to get going to work, but get whatever you need for tonight. I'll leave some cash on the bar for groceries before I leave, and just so you know, I'll be taking care of our expenses until you get the coffee shop opened. I don't want you to be stressed about money. I have to jump in the shower before I head to the station," I tell Margaret as I grab a clean pair of boxers and shorts and start to walk out of my room and toward the bathroom down the hall. I'd given her the master bedroom, considering that she has about four times the shit that I do.

As I started to walk past my sister she put out her arm to

stop me and threw herself into my arms. "Theo, you know I give you a whole lot of shit, but you know you can always talk to me," she says as she looks up at me with tears in her eyes.

Swallowing an unexpected lump in my throat, I hug her back. "I know Marg, I'm good. I promise," I tell her, trying to make sure my voice is as convincing as possible.

I may be a broken man, but I'll be damned if anyone else knows that.

CHAPTER SIX
CAROLINE

"Run it full out this time, ladies," I shout Tuesday afternoon as my squad marks the last count of their first routine of the season. "Y'all know that Meet the Saints sets the tone for the whole season, and I'm expecting perfection."

"Yes ma'am," the squad choruses at me as I turn to run the music again.

Once I make sure the girls are set, I hit play on my phone and hear the Bruno Mars mix start to play. Hannah and I worked this summer to choreograph all the material we would need for the season, and we were spending today running several of our upcoming performances. As "That's What I Like" blasts through the gym, the girls dance and flip through the routine for Meet the Saints. The single base extension stunts fly through the air and they cradle to the beat of the music. Finally, the girls move to the ending formation and yell, "Go Saints!" with huge smiles on their faces.

"Okay, good job girls. Now that you're warmed up, let's run our competition routine we're using for later in the season." I instruct the girls, and they all move to their formations.

We've worked on this routine for months, and I am so anxious for us to finally hit it. I press play again, and this time the remix of "High Hopes" by Panic! at the Disco fills the speakers. I watch to make sure everyone is hitting the choreography perfectly before all three stunt groups execute flawlessly synchronized basket tosses.

Smiling to myself, I hold my breath a little, as I always do, while they move to their final pyramid. We spent all summer sweating our asses off and trying to perfect this stunt sequence.

I look over at Hannah to see her completely zoned in on the routine. It took a bit of convincing to get her to agree to come on as a coach for my squad, but I eventually wore her down and she's fallen in love with the sport the same way I have.

We both stand extremely still as Maggie, our team captain, sets for her back handspring tuck into the stunt. We've spent days of practice discussing grips and hand placement to make sure that she lands the tuck and is immediately ready to go up and pull her heel stretch so that the other groups can link up for the final sequence. We came close last week, but the stunt still wasn't hitting exactly where we wanted it to. Hannah and I spent the weekend texting about ways to correct the timing, and I am so nervous to see if it's going to work.

When I took over three years ago, the program was in chaos. They'd been through six coaches in the last five years before I accepted the position. No one knew anything about tumbling or stunting, and the squad had a reputation for drama since there wasn't any oversight. Since I came in, I've managed to turn it around with Hannah's help. I take a lot of pride in what I've built and I know that this year could be the year that we're ready to take on regionals.

By the time Maggie perfectly hits the tumbling pass, both Hannah and I are close to screaming. When she pulls the heel stretch I can feel my excitement mounting, and by the time the flyer on the side grabs her foot and helps her flip over the top, we are barely containing our excitement. Finally, all three groups finish in libs as the music ends with a yell of "Go Saints," and Hannah and I explode into cheers.

The girls dismount cleanly and all of a sudden they rush Hannah and me with hugs and yells of "We did it!" We both laugh as we try to get them to settle down.

"Okay, okay girls. Calm down. Let's get it together," I call, unable to contain my smile. "That was awesome and I am so proud of y'all! We still have a lot of work to do this season, but I couldn't be more proud of the progress y'all have made so far. Grab some water and we're gonna run it again."

The girls run off to the bleachers across the gym, but Maggie doesn't move. "Oh my gosh that was crazy!" she exclaims with a big smile on her face. Maggie is seventeen, but she carries herself with the maturity of someone who's been forced to grow up faster than she should've. Her mother died her first year on the squad due to breast cancer. She fought for two years and went through several major surgeries, but every time the doctors thought they helped her beat the disease, more would show up. She'd been at practice when her dad showed up to tell her that her mother had lost her battle. She'd taken one look at his broken expression, and ran to me and fell in my arms in tears. Ever since that day, she's come to me for advice, and I try to be the best mentor I can be for her. She is incredibly sweet and talented, and I am holding out hope that I can help her get a cheerleading scholarship to Crestview University.

"I am so proud of you," I tell her, my smile matching hers. "You've worked so hard, and I can't believe how far you've come!"

"Thank you, Miss Caroline. I couldn't do any of it without you and Miss Hannah. Do you think we have a real chance for regionals this year?" she asks with so much hope and excitement that I can't help but feel the same way.

"I think this could be our year," I tell her and she nods.

"Okay well then I think we have some work to get back to," she states, returning to her competitive mindset. As she walks back over to the rest of the squad, I hear my phone ping and look down to check it. I see a text from Will and roll my eyes at his insane protective nature.

> Will: Theo is at practice and when I asked him what he was going to do to make up for yesterday, he said you're having dinner at his house tonight. What the hell Caroline?

> Me: What? I met his sister at Maracas last night. Hannah and I are going to their house for dinner.

> Will: I don't like it. He's new to town, and no one knows anything about him. I don't like the idea of you being alone with him.

> Me: I'm not gonna be alone. Hannah is coming.

> Will: Really? You and I both know that she will be at least thirty minutes late. I'd feel better if I was there just in case.

> Me: You can't just invite yourself over to the new fire chief's house because you think he'll hurt my feelings.

> Will: Watch me.

Blowing out a frustrated sigh, I put my phone down. Hannah gives me a look and immediately asks, "What's wrong?"

"Will is being a total drama queen and thinks that he needs

to be at dinner tonight. He doesn't trust the new guy," I say with annoyance.

Hannah rolls her eyes at me. "Great. He does have a tendency to be a bit dramatic, but usually only when it's related to you. And honestly, it's probably not the worst idea in the world. I just wish he wasn't such a dick to me," she says, blinking innocently.

"He's not a dick. You just intentionally push all his buttons. And both of you are used to being the loudest person in the room," I say with a laugh.

"Whatever," she says indignantly. "Are we gonna get back to practice or what?"

"Okay girls, let's run it again," I shout. If nothing else, tonight should be interesting.

CHAPTER SEVEN
THEO

"Did you remember sour cream for the potatoes?" I ask Margaret while opening the fridge.

"Yes! It's behind the bottle of wine," she replies.

"Got it." I move the bottle of Moscato and grab the container I'd been searching for.

"We have ten minutes until they're supposed to be here. Caroline said she and Will are on the way, and Hannah is finishing up with something for her grandfather. Have you started the grill?" Margaret yells at me from her bedroom where she's getting ready. I know this night is about me attempting to make up for some of my behavior, but I know she also needs to feel like she has a place here in this new town. I came home to the kitchen overflowing with fresh bread, three different types of cookies, a charcuterie board, along with pasta salad, and a garden salad.

"Yep, it's ready to go when they get here!" When Margaret suggested this get-together, I had thought it was just an excuse for her to cook a ton of food. But after Will told me at practice that he didn't trust me yet to be alone with Caroline and Hannah, I knew tonight was going to be more than I'd bargained for. And while I wanted to hate Will for not trusting me, I didn't. I was new to town and had come on as an aggressive asshole yesterday. I know he still doesn't care for me, but he's trying because the mayor had played the politics card with him.

I pace the house as Bear pads out of Margaret's room and throws himself in the middle of the floor with a yawn. Rolling my eyes at his antics, I grab one of his toys and throw it. He makes no move to get it and blows out a sigh at me. I've had Bear for two years, and I don't know if I've seen him excited about anything. He's a low-energy dog, but I love him anyway.

"They're here," Margaret yells back at me. "Get the door, please. I am finishing my makeup now."

"Got it," I mutter as I hear a knock on the door.

I walk to the alcove by the front door and pull it open to see Caroline and Will standing on the porch. Caroline is carrying a small wrapped box with a smile on her face, while Will scowls at me immediately.

"Hey! Glad y'all made it. Y'all come on in," I say amicably, as I motion for them to come inside. As Caroline enters the house, I'm suddenly struck by how beautiful she is. Of course yesterday, I'd thought she was pretty, but without my anger clouding my vision I see that she is one of the most gorgeous women I have ever seen. She's wearing denim shorts that show off her perfect ass and legs with a black short sleeve shirt. Her long, dark brown hair is pulled away from her face, and she's wearing just enough eye makeup to bring out the green in her hazel eyes. How the hell did I miss this yesterday? Not only am I an asshole, but I must be blind as well.

Trying to refocus myself on the current moment, I walk to the kitchen and ask, "Would y'all like something to drink? We have sweet tea, water, wine, and beer."

Will looks at me for a minute like he's sizing me up and finally replies with, "Sweet tea is fine for me. I have to drive this girl home." He says it casually, but I can't help but wonder if there is something between the two of them.

Caroline must pick up on the questions I want to ask because she replies, "Will and I both live in the same apartment building along with our friend Seth. Since Will insisted on coming along, I let him drive my car in exchange for serving as my DD. Anyway, we live above the post office. A few years ago the city converted some old retail spaces into apartments, since single-person housing options are pretty much nonexistent in Springside.

"Have you met Seth yet? He teaches the construction classes at Springside and coaches the Varsity baseball team."

I'm spared from having to come up with a response to that when Margaret walks into the room. Caroline's face brightens as she stands and makes her way over to my sister and gives her a hug. They start talking immediately as if they've been friends for years instead of less than twenty-four hours.

I set to work fixing Will a glass of tea and waiting for the girls to take a breath so I can ask them what they want to drink. As I'm waiting, Margaret walks over to the fridge, grabs the bottle of wine and the corkscrew out of the drawer, and pops the top without ever leaving a pause in their discussion. She pours them both a glass and looks over to me as if I'm a moron.

"Well, are you going to give our guest something to drink or not?" she asks.

I realize I've been standing here with Will's drink in my hand for the last several minutes. I hand it over to him as he glares at me. It's clear his amicable behavior isn't going to extend past practice.

"Hannah said she's on time for once and will be here in just a minute. Who knew all it would take for her to be on time is the new fire chief to act like an asshole and then be forced to grovel at my feet," Caroline announces with a laugh after hearing her phone ping. She looks at me and gives me a wink that has my dick starting to grow hard in my jeans.

"Why is she always late?" I ask, feeling like I've been left out of a joke and trying to calm myself down. What am I twelve?

Caroline opens her mouth to answer as Margaret and I listen, but Will cuts her off before she can start. "Because she has the shittiest parents on the planet. They moved away when she was in middle school because they wanted more freedom and said Hannah was 'too needy' because she needed dinner at night and clothes to wear to school." Will's face is overcome with contempt as he talks. "She became the caretaker for her aging grandfather and a shit ton of animals last year, and she's barely keeping her head above water with everything on her plate."

"She's managing just fine, Will. You just worry too much," Caroline responds with a laugh.

"Whatever," Will retorts. "She's just so damn stubborn. I've tried to help her, and she won't listen. Huey taught me everything he knows about farm animals, but she tells me she has it under control."

"These two are like oil and water," Caroline announces as Will stands to get the door for Hannah. "You'll get used to their constant bickering eventually but for now, buckle up because you're about to get your first show. I always say they're meant to end up together, but no one in town believes me."

"Oh I wish you'd drop that shit," the girl I'm assuming is Hannah says as she blows into the room with Will right behind her. The new girl and Caroline couldn't be more opposite physically if they tried. Where Caroline is brunette with hazel eyes, Hannah is blonde with blue eyes. Caroline has curves and can't be taller than five-four while Hannah is tall and slim. "It'll be a cold day in hell when I let him anywhere near my pussy."

"Hannah!" Caroline exclaims. "You don't have to be crass. We're guests here too!"

"Whatever," Hannah says, blowing off Caroline's concerns. She turns to me and her eyes narrow as she puts together who I am. "So you're the dickwad new fire chief, huh? You know everyone hates you right? If you'd asked me on Sunday I would have said it's impossible to make the whole town of Springside hate you in less than a day, but you my friend have talent. I think you may be less popular than Mrs. Sally and she once started a rumor that everyone that worked in the hospital had a drug addiction. The rumor made it all the way up to the Medical Board of Alabama. They came down and shut us down for almost a week while they investigated. Even after that, they all had to have drug tests done every day for a month. Apparently, she started the rumor because the hospital staff made her wait ten minutes past her appointment time for her colonoscopy. She's a royal bitch, but I'm pretty sure they hate you more now. That must really suck. Oh my God what a day, I need a drink," she announces as she walks to the fridge and helps herself to a bottle of water.

I swear this woman is a walking tornado. I have no idea how to respond to the monologue she just gave, so I decide to take the path of less resistance and simply settle for an introduction. "Hey, I'm the new asshole fire chief everyone's talking about. I appreciate the honesty, and I think this is a new record. I usually don't get the title of 'Biggest Asshole' until at least a month in. But anyway, you can call me Theo," I state, sticking out my hand to shake hers and smiling. I feel discomfort surging down my spine but I'm trying to be charming and polite.

Hannah just looks at my outstretched hand and frowns at me. "Caroline and I have been best friends since we were in elementary school. She forgives way too easily in my opinion, and even if she forgives you, I won't until I decide you've suffered enough. Do you know how toxic teaching has become? The last thing we need is someone coming and yelling at us in front of our students. Society already doesn't respect us, and you certainly didn't help that yesterday when you came in acting like you have never made a mistake in your life. So I'm sure once you apologize, Caroline is gonna tell you everything is rainbows and butterflies, but before you tear into anyone else, you need to remember that your actions have a consequence." With that Hannah walks over to Caroline who is deep in a conversation with Will on the sofa in the living room.

Damn. I hadn't thought about my actions that way. In my attempt to keep everyone safe and do my job well, I'd not only been a jerk, but I'd undermined Caroline's authority in front of her students. I knew from the last two days working with the football team that respect and authority were essential, and it hadn't been my intention to undermine hers. But, now that I think about it, I totally see where Hannah was coming from. Fuck.

Margaret just gives me a sad smile, letting me know that she overheard that exchange. "I'll be outside." I walk to the fridge and grab out the pan of steaks that had been marinating since lunch. I need some air and to figure out how to get the beautiful brunette out of my head. I couldn't ever deserve her anyway.

CHAPTER EIGHT
CAROLINE

I notice Theo looks frustrated as he walks outside to put the steaks on the grill. Margaret walks over and launches into a conversation with Hannah and Will about her new coffee shop and I decide there's no time like the present to make up with Theo. If nothing else, I at least should let him plead his case, if he wants to.

"Be right back," I tell the group as I go to follow Theo outside, "he forgot the tray to put the steaks on."

"Give him hell!" Hannah yells out at me as I close the door to the porch behind me.

Theo is standing mostly in the dark at the edge of the porch beside a large gas grill. The lid to the grill is up, and he seems focused on placing the steaks carefully on the metal grate. I think he is oblivious to my presence until he speaks without looking up, "What are you doing out here, Caro?"

I normally hate being called Caro, but the gruff way he just said my name has me blushing. I quickly imagine him growling it in my ear as he slides into me from behind, and I can feel the desire course through my veins. I remind myself that he asked me a question, and I try to refocus my attention on the question he asked me.

"I was bringing you the tray for the steaks. And I-I- I feel like we need to talk," I stammer, suddenly incredibly nervous. I force myself to take a few steps closer to him so that I can see his face, setting the platter on the table beside the grill. The light from inside the house casts shadows on his face, and another jolt of desire runs through me as I finally get close enough to stare at him for a moment.

"Yeah, we do. Listen, I'm an asshole. I don't mean to be. I totally deserve everyone hating me because I never should have talked to you the way I did. I was wrong. But I have a problem with fire safety. I have to feel like everything is exactly right at all times. It's been that way since the night—" Theo trails off for a minute like he's lost in thought before he picks back up. "Anyway, I am not good with people in situations like this. I snap and I say the wrong thing. I really don't deserve your forgiveness but if you could forgive me anyway I'd really appreciate it."

I fight the urge to touch him, rubbing my hand up and down my shoulder. "I get it. And while I don't condone being rude, I understand that you had, and still have, a lot on your plate. It would be hard for anyone to fill Huey's shoes, and with the added pressure now I don't envy you at all," I say with a smile. I don't mean to be as flirty as I feel, but it's clear my body is craving the new fire chief. I have never been very forward with men before, but I also haven't been super attracted to anyone in Springside. I dated casually when I was in college, but I never felt an instant attraction.

He gives me a shy smile, but I can tell he doesn't quite know how to respond to me. Part of me can't blame him considering how almost all of Springside indirectly hates him because of me. He turns back to the grill, flipping the steaks as we stand in a slightly uncomfortable silence.

"So, you coach cheerleading at the high school?" Theo asks

as he stares straight ahead. I am quickly realizing that Theo isn't uncomfortable around me; he's uncomfortable with how he treated me yesterday.

"Yeah, I do. I started cheering when I was six, and honestly, I never wanted to quit," I respond, standing next to him in the dark.

"That's cool," Theo says, "I don't know much about cheerleading, but Will mentioned that you and Hannah are really talented coaches."

"Thanks. Did you play a bunch of sports growing up?" I ask him, trying to ease the tension.

He winces a bit before saying, "For a bit." It's obvious that he doesn't want to continue the current line of conversation so I stand there awkwardly.

"So..." I start as he says, "Well..." We laugh and it seems to ease the tension momentarily.

"I am normally not quite this awkward," I say with a laugh as some of the hair I'd pulled to one side falls into my face. The Alabama humidity and I are not friends. Just as I raise my hand to brush it out of my face, Theo's large hand runs from the top of my head and brushes the stray hair out of my face. I feel a jolt of electricity run through my body, and I swear I've never felt so alive. It's an innocent touch, but it feels more sensual than some of the one-night stands I had in college. I have never thought of myself as a sexual person, but after less than five minutes in Theo's presence, I am beginning to wonder if I don't know myself as well as I thought I did.

Theo looks as if he is a bit taken aback by his own actions, and quickly grabs the tongs beside the grill. He busies himself with flipping the steaks again as I try to make myself stop fidgeting.

"So, what do you like to do Miss Tyler? You know other than cheerleading and witnessing me making a total ass out of myself?" he asks, and I let out a small giggle of laughter.

"Well, Chief Johnson, I read a whole lot of smutty romance novels and I drink a ton of wine. Other than that, I spend most of my time at school or helping Hannah with her farm," I respond before taking a sip of my wine.

"So you and Hannah are pretty close, huh? Does your family live in Springside?" he asks.

"Nope, they moved out of the country when I graduated high school. My parents are both just free spirits. So Han's pretty much all I have."

Theo nods and opens his mouth to say something, but he's interrupted by Margaret sticking her head out of the door.

"Caroline?" she yells, squinting her eyes into the darkness.

"Yes," I shout and step towards the door so she can see me.

"Sorry but Will and Hannah are arguing, and I am not sure what to do. Are they always like this?" she asks.

Laughing, I respond, "Welcome to my world. They've been like this since middle school. It can get brutal, but they're harmless. I am coming to save you though."

"Sounds good!" Margaret calls back and closes the door.

"Okay, well I am gonna go check on those hooligans inside," I say with a laugh.

As I go to make my way inside, Theo grabs my hand, catching me off guard. His eyes seem to hold a world of chaos, but I smile at him because I feel the same way. "I really am sorry Caroline; you didn't deserve to be talked to the way I yelled at you yesterday. I am truly mortified by the way I treated you in front of those kids."

I start to reply, "It's fi-," but Theo stops me.

"I swear to God, Caroline, it's not. But I promise I am going to make it up to you. Margaret already loves you, and the last thing I want is to mess that up for her. So I am hoping we can be friends," he says, and I can feel the sincerity in his voice.

"Okay Theo, I am not going to argue with you. And I am so excited to have Margaret here in town. People our age never move to Springside. As for us, I look forward to seeing how friendly you can be," I say with a wink as I make my way inside. I don't know what's going on between us or what just came over me, but I wasn't lying when I said I was looking forward to seeing where it goes.

CHAPTER NINE
THEO

As I watch Caroline walk away from me into the ranch house, I can't help but wonder what the fuck is wrong with me. As she stood out here keeping me company after the way I treated her yesterday, I got furious. Not at her, but at myself. I realize I am a broken man. I've come to terms with the fact that women like Caroline and men like me —actually, just me—are never going to be more than friends. Unfortunately, I can't even seem to make it into the friendship zone without wanting what I can't have.

In my line of work, having trauma isn't unusual, but we have to get good at hiding it. Some stations are more supportive of the mental health movement than others, but after my first captain screamed at me for having a panic attack one night after a particularly bad nightmare, I've done everything I could to hide my scars—both the physical ones and the ones that lived in my memories. Now that I am the Chief in Springside, I want to make sure that no one under me is ever treated the way I was, but it's a little late for me, personally.

One thing I was damn sure of was I needed to get my shit together. Something about Caroline makes me feel like I can have a chance at a normal life, but I continue to remind myself that no one wants to put up with my mood swings and nightmares. If yesterday didn't prove that fact, I don't know what would.

I grab the tongs and take the steaks off the grill, placing them on the platter that Caroline brought me while working to convince myself that the attraction I felt to the beautiful brunette inside will burn out as quickly as it started.

As I walk inside, I see Bear curled up on top of Caroline's lap as she sits on the couch. He is usually considered pretty unsocial for a Labrador and prefers to hide out from company in the comfort of my bedroom. It's no surprise to me though that the eighty-pound pup has fallen in love with Caroline. She scratches his head and his tail wags as she talks to Margaret.

I can hear Hannah and Will arguing, but I don't stop to listen closely enough to try to determine what the argument is about. Caroline was right about them being oil and water.

"Steaks are ready," I say loudly as I sit them on the granite countertops. I'd been surprised when we toured this house and found that it was full of relatively modern amenities to have been a farmhouse owned by an elderly man.

"I'm coming," Margaret hollers back as she rushes from the couch to pull all of the dishes she had prepared earlier today. She walks over to the oven, and I can smell the scent of fresh rolls she'd made from scratch permeating the air. She also pulls out a large dish with at least ten of the biggest potatoes I've ever seen from the warmer and grabs bowls of two different pasta salads out of the fridge. She notices me watching her and announces, "There was a produce truck set up beside the grocery store this morning selling the most beautiful vegetables I had ever seen. Said he grew 'em local. I stocked up."

"And you thought the five of us would eat ten of the world's biggest potatoes?" I ask her with a smile on my face.

"Well, I didn't want to run out," she says defensively. "I want to make a good impression, unlike some people."

"Wow, low blow," I say, becoming more serious. "But you're right. I just want you to be happy here."

"I know you do," she replies, smiling at me now. We work together grabbing toppings for the potatoes from the fridge and making sure that everything is set up to her standards.

"Let's eat," Margaret declares to our guests, and after watching her smile and laugh with the girls, I decide no matter how rocky the start may have been, moving to Springside was the right decision for both of us.

DINNER IS A SUCCESS, and we are sitting at the table talking when Will brings the evening to a grinding halt. "So Theo, we haven't had an opportunity to talk much. You said you're Jake Johnson's brother. If you have half the talent he did, I am sure you had every college scout in the country after you. Did you play college ball anywhere?"

I tense and I can feel the three women looking at me. "Nope," I reply lightly, hoping that will be enough to change the subject. This isn't the first time this has happened, and I know Will isn't asking to make me upset. "I wanted to be close to my sister so I went straight to the fire academy and went back later for online classes at the community college."

Reading the confusion on the women's faces, Margaret smiles at them. "Yep. It didn't matter what our foster parents said, and Lord knows I tried, he wouldn't leave. I guess he does love me somewhere way, way, way deep down," she says with a wink.

I don't miss the look that Caroline and Hannah exchange when Margaret says the words, foster parents. There's no judgment in it, but it's clear they didn't know about the accident. I feel my chest growing tight as it does every time I think of that night. I manage to keep my voice level as I say quickly, "I trusted Bobby and Heather but after the accident, Margaret was the only family I had left. I still don't think there is anything wrong with that."

"Of course, there isn't," Caroline says with a sad smile. "I am so sorry to hear that happened."

"Thanks," Margaret and I say at the same time, used to this awkward silence whenever the topic of the accident comes up. I can tell from the way Caroline is looking at Hannah that she is willing her to not ask any other questions. Thankfully, she seems to understand since I can still feel my chest tightening and throat closing with each moment that this conversation continues. Will looks sheepish that he walked himself into such a touchy subject.

Ever the hostess, Margaret quickly perks up, diffusing the tension, and asks, "So who wants dessert? I tried a new cookie recipe today. I want to have a signature cookie when I open the bakery, but I haven't found the perfect one yet. Maybe you all can help me."

After a chorus of agreement, we make quick work of cleaning the table and Margaret returns quickly with a silver platter full of cookies. These aren't normal cookies though— they are at least five inches wide and look incredible.

"I want y'all's honest opinion," Margaret says sheepishly. "I've tried at least eight other recipes so it's okay if you don't love them. These are brown butter snickerdoodles with milk, dark, and white chocolate chips tucked in."

"Oh my God!" Hannah screams in what I am learning is her usual fashion after taking a bite. "I think I just had an orgasm."

"Damn, you must be really desperate then. Don't those porn books you and Caroline love teach you that's not how it works," Will says with a laugh. "If you weren't such a brat, I'd take pity on you and offer to help you out."

"Right, like you and your sad little micro penis know anything about how to make a woman orgasm," Hannah fires back.

I am a little afraid to see how this argument is going to progress until Caroline interjects, "I wish y'all would just screw and get it over with." I laugh at her, surprised by her outburst. Hannah and Will object, but Caroline ignores them. She doesn't seem embarrassed, and continues breaking apart the humongous cookie in front of her and popping it in her mouth. It's been a long time since a girl made me laugh out loud, and Margaret looks at me quickly letting me know that fact didn't go unnoticed by my nosy sister.

"Anyway," Hannah continues as if the argument with Will had never happened. "I know you two are new to town," she says pointing at Margaret and I, "but we are thinking about going down to the beach for the day on Saturday. You know it's less than an hour from here and the crowds should have died down with school being back in. If you boys can promise to keep your micropenises and asshole behaviors to yourselves, you can come with us. Margaret, you're invited no matter what."

Margaret squeals, and I can see the first bit of genuine excitement on her face since that dickface ex-boyfriend of hers broke her heart. "We're in!" I don't miss the fact that Will is still glaring at me like he isn't particularly happy that I am being welcomed into the group as easily as I am after what happened at the school yesterday. I don't blame him, but I am tired of letting life pass me by because of the shitty hand that my sister and I have been dealt. I nod in affirmation along with Margaret. Besides, I may have decided that I don't deserve Caroline Tyler, but I would damn sure enjoy spending the day with her in a bikini. My time in Springside may have gotten off to a shitty start, but even I have to admit, things are looking up.

CHAPTER TEN
THEO

Around eight the next morning, I make my way into my office at the station. Given Springside's size, it isn't particularly surprising that we are a smaller station with eight firefighters in addition to me. At first, I had wondered why none of them had applied for the Chief position, but after working with them for a couple of days, it seems that everyone is simply comfortable in their position. They definitely are a lot closer than I'd expected, but I don't mind the family vibe the station gives off, even though I am definitely still seen as the outsider.

As I sit down at my desk to check emails, a young, dark-headed firefighter knocks on my door. I met him on Monday, and I am pretty sure his name was Zach. "Hey, Chief," he asks from the doorway. "Is it okay if I come in?"

"Sure, come on," I reply, typing a response to Mayor Jones asking to meet him for drinks next week before swiveling my chair around to face the young firefighter. I know I would still be considered young for the position I am currently in, but Zach can't be more than twenty years old. "What can I help you with?"

I try to smile at him, but it feels awkward on my face so I just continue looking at him while I wait. "Well, I am sorry to bother you Chief, but I just wanted to let you know that I am the sole caretaker for my younger sister, Bethany. I am not asking for any special treatment, but I wanted to make you aware. If she's ever sick or anything like that, I am all she has. The guys here have always covered for me or let me pick up an extra shift when she has extra expenses, but if you aren't okay with that arrangement I will make something else work."

The kid looks like he is ready to ramble for several more minutes, but I cut him off, "Zach, I appreciate the professional courtesy of coming to me, but that won't be a problem. If you ever need anything else, don't hesitate to come to me, okay?"

A visible relief overtakes Zach's entire face. It makes me feel a little sick to my stomach that he was this nervous to come to me. I take my job seriously and I refuse to turn a blind eye to obvious infractions, but it was never my intention to have the men working under me walking on eggshells. I don't really know how to walk the line between being firm and being a dick, but I hope I haven't screwed it up so thoroughly that no one wants to work for me. "Thank you so much, Chief. Really, you don't know how much I appreciate this."

"Of course," I say, fidgeting uncomfortably with his obvious relief. "How old is your sister?" I ask, trying to fill the silence and prove that I am not the completely self-absorbed asshole everyone thinks I am.

"She's fifteen. Our parents died in a car accident the week after I turned eighteen. It's just the two of us. But she was in the car with them, and she sustained some pretty serious injuries. She lost her left leg, and while she's worked hard over the last year to gain some independence, I still worry about her. She has lots of doctor's appointments, and honestly, some days are just better than others for her. But I need this job. Working for the fire station is the best thing that's ever happened to me. It has given Bethany and me the income and the assurance we needed to get back on our feet. I promise you won't have any problems out of me."

"I don't doubt that," I reply. "I have a little sister I would do anything in the world for, even though she can be an annoying little shit at times. I would never ask one of my men to choose the station over their family's health as long as I can help it. If you need anything, just come talk to me, and I will do what I can."

Zach nods at me so fiercely, I worry he is going to injure himself. "Of course Chief Johnson. Thank you so much. You have a great day." He turns to leave, continuing to thank me as he makes his way out the door and around the hall.

Shaking my head, I turn my attention back to my computer. After sifting through several emails, I see one from City Hall providing me with some of the procedures I hadn't had time to review yet. I decide to spend the remainder of the day memorizing them and writing out a list of questions to ask when I see Brian.

Around eleven, my phone buzzes with a text. I flip it over to see it's from my foster mom, Heather.

> Heather: Hey! I am dying to know how the move went. Are you settled in? Do you need anything? How's the new job? Bobby and I are so proud of you. Love you big.

Blowing out a breath, I rub my hand over my face and sit my phone down. Heather and Bobby Jenkins had been close friends of my parents from church, and it had been a huge blessing that they took us in. Clairville, where we'd grown up, was the only home we'd ever known and thanks to the Jenkins' generosity in taking us both in, we didn't have to move schools in the middle of the most difficult season of our lives. But I still felt a bit guilty because I'd always held them at arm's length.

Add that to the list of wrongs I needed to make right. I pick my phone back up and reply.

> Me: Good morning. We are good. Thanks for checking. I'll call when things settle.

> Heather: Sounds great. I just talked to Margaret— we miss you both! Give your sister a hug for me!

Checking that off my list of things to do, I throw myself back into the protocols. By the time I look up, I realize that it's two o'clock which means I worked through lunch and it's almost time for practice today. While my position with the football team isn't something I ever really thought I would do after the night everything changed, I have to admit that I am having fun working with the boys. I am jealous of their passion for the sport. I remember feeling the same way when I was sixteen and carefree. It makes me sad to realize all that the accident took from me, but I am proud of my attempts to make it right, even if it is a bit later than I'd have liked.

I begin to gather my things as my mind wanders to Caroline once again. I have to admit I am thinking about her more and more. Last night as I showered, I briefly imagined her dark brown hair wrapped around my fist after stripping her bare as I bent her over the counter and pounded into her wet pussy. This morning as I got ready for work, I imagined her in my bed, sleepy and satisfied as I woke her up by running my tongue from her tight hole up to her clit and back again. As I worked at my desk today, I imagined her hiding in the cove under my desk, sitting on her knees waiting to take my cock down her tight throat while I worked, struggling to stay quiet as I made calls and reviewed protocol.

I have always had an overactive imagination and an incredibly high sex drive, but I'd spent most of my junior year in a deep depression and had worked overtime senior year to graduate on time with my class. After I graduated, I'd had a few one-night stands, but I didn't want anyone to have to put up with my trauma bullshit for more than a few hours.

Even still, Caroline has gotten in my head and I am not sure how to get her out. Hopefully a few hours at the football field will clear my brain from anything to do with her. Otherwise, it looks like I will be taking a lot of cold showers in my future because I will never be worthy of touching Caroline Tyler.

CHAPTER ELEVEN
CAROLINE

Thursday morning I make my way to my classroom and go through my usual routine of checking my email and writing my learning objectives on the board. I am not sure how writing a sentence on what I am teaching along with the strategies I am using will improve student learning, but the State requires it so I try to keep it updated. After that's done, I bump the air conditioner down and project my slides onto the board with the morning bell-ringer on it. We've been in school for almost a month now, and I am happy with the way my students have settled into the routine.

I take a big sip of my favorite homemade caramel cold brew before my students rush in; I grab my phone and text the group chat with Margaret and Hannah.

Me: Just checked the forecast for Crestview this weekend. Sunny and eighty five. Can't wait to have my toes in the sand.

Hannah: Oh my God me either. One of my freshmen just asked me if Shakespeare is the guy that plays in Criminal Minds. I know we've only been in school for a month but I need to get the hell out of here.

Margaret: Bless you both. I am so excited. I am working on making us some snacks and treats that we can take on the beach. Any requests?

Hannah: THE COOKIES

Me: OH MY GOD THE COOKIES

Margaret: Haha they are in the oven now. I played around with the ratio of chips. I will need your opinion so get ready.

Me: Done. I can't wait.

Tucking my phone into my desk, I open the door for my students to enter the room for the day. I make my way into the hall for morning duty to ensure students all make it into first period safely. After standing there for a few minutes and speaking to the teachers next door, the bell signaling the beginning of first period rings so I enter the room and close the door.

As class begins, my students reach for the composition notebook and work quietly on the bell ringer question. Since we are currently reading the beginning of *The Great Gatsby*, I'd asked them to explain their idea of the American Dream. I monitor the room and notice that Michael Adams is the only student not working. He has his phone out and headphones in to listen to the show he's watching on HBO. Springside High School has a no-phone policy during instruction, and while I generally try to pick my battles with cell phones in class, Michael is blatantly disrespecting the policy and me.

I take a breath and walk over to his desk. I tap on his desk and motion for him to remove the headphones so I can speak with him. He looks up at me and rolls his eyes before going back to his movie. Really? I do not make enough money to deal with this crap.

I blow out a breath before tapping on his desk again. He pulls out an AirPod and looks up at me, "What?" he asks as if he hasn't blatantly disrespected me twice before eight in the morning.

"I need you to put up the phone and headphones and answer the bell ringer. This one could be a grade," I say, trying to force a bit of a smile.

"No thanks," he responds as he goes to put the earbud back in his ear.

"Michael, you can't have those out in class. I've asked you nicely twice. If I see them again I will have to confiscate them and turn them into the office. After that, your parents will have to come get them. Plus I don't want you to get a zero on your bell ringer," I say calmly. I learned early on to do my best not to let my frustration show even when I was ready to snap. It isn't foolproof, but voicing my frustration just puts me at a higher risk for the student to escalate.

"You know what Miss Caroline? Fuck you, fuck your bell-ringer, and fuck your policy. If you want the AirPods and the phone you're gonna have to come take them, and since I am assuming you're not gonna do that, I am gonna sit right here and watch my movie while you drone on about whatever stupid, useless shit you have planned to talk about today," Michael explodes at me.

It isn't very often that I am stunned speechless while teaching, but this moment is definitely one of them. I look around at the rest of the class who are staring at me with expressions that I am assuming mirror mine. I have dealt with all sorts of behavior issues over the last few years, but I have never been cussed at so blatantly by a student during class. A few of the boys shift in their seats like they are ready to jump to my rescue if Michael becomes violent, but I know I need to do everything in my power to prevent that from happening. I rack my brain trying to figure out why Michael is behaving this way, but I come up empty. He hasn't been overly friendly, but I am pretty sure if I check his grades it will show that he is normally an all-A student.

I calmly walk over to the school phone that sits on my desk and pick it up. I enter the extension for the office, and after a few rings our school secretary, Mrs. Bess, picks up. Mrs. Bess is in her mid-forties and is adored by most of the kids at Springside High.

"Springside High School, how can I help you?" she asks politely.

"Good morning Mrs. Bess, this is Miss Tyler. Are any of the administrative team in the office? I am having an issue in first period, and I need someone down here."

"Let me check Miss Tyler. These kids just keep getting crazier I swear, honey. Give me just a second," Mrs. Bess says as she places me on hold. The whole room has given up any semblance of pretending to work on their assignment, and everyone is staring at me to see how this will go down. Meanwhile, Michael sits at his desk continuing to watch his movie while throwing sneers at me every few minutes.

"I'm sorry Miss Tyler, but they're not in their offices right now."

"What about the resource officer?" I ask, and she must hear the desperation in my voice.

"Oh dear. He's here somewhere. Let me find him, and I will get him over there to you," Mrs. Bess says apologetically.

"Thanks so much," I respond to her quickly before hanging up. In the time that I have been on the phone, Michael has removed his AirPods and is continuing to watch his show without the headphones. The students around him look uncomfortable and, as I look closer, I realize he is watching the latest episode of *Euphoria* which is certainly not school-friendly. As cursing and moans fill the room, everyone begins fidgeting awkwardly.

"Michael Adams, turn that off right this instant," I say, once again shocked at how openly he is defying me.

"What's the matter, Miss Tyler? You're just mad you're too much of a prude to have someone warm your bed at night. You should go smoke a blunt and calm your tits," he taunts.

Truly at a loss for words, I can do nothing but blink at him. I notice two or three of the boys looking at him like they are ready to handle it themselves, but I make eye contact and shake my head at them. After a few minutes of an intense stare-off, I hear the resource officer putting the key in the door to come inside. Officer Stewart comes in and immediately waits for me to explain what's wrong. Over the last three years, I've never had to call for him so he knows it must be something big.

"Well, Mr. Adams has caused a major disruption and needs to be removed. He had his phone and AirPods out, and when I asked him to put them away, he cussed at me several times. Then as I was waiting on the office to find you, he started playing an inappropriate video out loud and made some derogatory comments at me. He is refusing to leave," I explain in a rush.

Officer Stewart looks at me like I have spoken to him in a foreign language. Springside High is definitely not perfect, but I doubt he has ever been called in for anything like this before. I would empathize with him if I wasn't so tense and desperate for this incident to be over.

"Well, uh Mr. Adams, you're gonna have to come with me," Officer Stewart states. I have to admit that he doesn't sound convincing to my ears so I doubt Michael is concerned. When

Michael refuses to leave, Officer Stewart picks up the walkie-talkie he keeps with him to connect to the office.

"Hey Mrs. Bess, we're gonna need backup," he says.

Great. I blow out a breath and sit down at my desk and resist the urge to put my head down. Looks like today isn't my day either.

CHAPTER TWELVE
THEO

I walk up to the locker room before practice on Thursday, and I immediately notice that there is a different feel to the atmosphere at the school. I tell myself I am making a big deal out of nothing and try to get myself ready for practice. As I walk back to the little makeshift office Will made for me on Monday where I leave my notes, I hear the murmur of boys talking about some incident that happened earlier today.

I ignore it as I continue making my way through the rows of lockers until I hear one of them say Caroline's name. I turn and look for Will so that I can ask what the hell is going on, but I don't see him. I grab my papers and make my way outside where I see Will and one of the other coaches, Marcus, talking.

"Good afternoon," I yell to them as I walk over. They stop talking and both of them glare at me. "What's going on?"

Will sighs and looks pissed and defeated. "There was an incident in Caroline's room today. She's fine but one of the kids that saw you yell at her went off on her. She was able to keep it from escalating, but it was bad. He cussed her out and refused to do anything she asked. Then he played a sex scene from *Euphoria* and refused to put his phone up. He threatened physical violence if anyone tried to do anything, and still didn't comply with the resource officer. He sat there through all of first period and the office finally sent the rest of her classes to the library. It took the threat of handcuffs to get him out of his desk."

As I listened to Will, I feel the blood draining from my face. The logical part of my brain knows that I didn't tell this kid to disrespect Caroline, but I did model that behavior in a way when I yelled at her on Monday. I blow out a frustrated break as one of the other coaches asks what the school is going to do.

Will lets out a laugh that has no trace of humor in it. "Well our principal is big on second chances, and as much as I appreciate what he's done for me, he's on my shit list today. No one could get up with any of the student's emergency contacts because all the numbers were disconnected. So he sat in the office all day, and he'll have four days of out-of-school suspension. He'll be back in her room by Thursday of next week."

Shit. I want to punch something. Will must see the anger in my face because he amends. "Listen, man, it's not your fault. I can tell by the look on your face that you're feeling guilty and ready to explode. I am feeling both of those things as well, but it's not gonna do us any good. At the very least, I can appreciate that you seem to care about Caroline. From a coaching standpoint, some of the boys are really fired up about it, and it's our job to try to calm them down today. Let them run drills and get some aggression out and then remind them that as frustrated as we might feel, any actions made in response to the events today will be severely punished. Caroline texted me that she had to talk a few of them down earlier today. We can't have our whole team suspended for fighting before our first game."

I nod, knowing he is right, but at the same time wanting nothing more than to fix this mess. I can't help but think that this is the perfect example of why I need to stay away from Caroline. The logical part of my brain knows that this doesn't have anything to do with me. I try repeating that thought to myself over and over, but it doesn't do much good. Instead, it serves as a reminder that my brokenness is contagious, and I'll be damned if I break anything as perfect as Caroline Tyler.

AFTER RUNNING drills for two hours in the sweltering Alabama heat, Will finally calls practice to an end. As the boys huddle up, they listen quietly.

"Remember that we have Meet the Saints tomorrow night in the gym. You will all be recognized and you need to wear your blue jersey and some jeans. Some of your parents have volunteered to help with decorating, and some of them will be selling shirts and programs to help us raise some money. If we make enough, we could possibly spend the night in a hotel for the away game in Huntsville at the end of the season," Will announces to the team.

That announcement is met with a chorus of cheers and appreciative whoops. Wesley, the player who came to Caroline's defense earlier in the week, speaks up, "Hey Coach Thompson, if we spend the night, will the cheerleaders stay too?" The team around him nods making it clear they were all thinking the same thing.

I can tell Will is trying not to laugh, but he manages to keep a straight face. "Well boys, y'all should already know the answer to that. I believe the cheerleaders are just as much a part of this team as any of us. They don't miss a game, and they practice just as much as we do. With that being said, you knuckleheads don't need to worry about that because you won't be anywhere close to the girls. Y'all stay in enough trouble as it is. And speaking of trouble, I am going to say this once and only once. Please stay out of trouble. I know we all have tempers, and we don't like watching people we care about being mistreated. That makes you good men, and I am proud to have you on my team. But South Springs School Board has a strict policy concerning physical altercations. In addition to out-of-school suspension, I am required to suspend you for at least one game if you are involved for any reason. We have a real chance at a state championship this year, and I need you all eligible to play. Do you understand?" he questions the team.

"Yes sir," the boys chorus back.

"Okay, six-thirty tomorrow night, and come dressed. We will see you then," Coach Thompson says as he dismisses practice.

The boys walk off muttering under their breath about a kid named Michael needing to get what is coming for him. I couldn't help but agree with them, but since I feel like it was my fault Caroline was in this position, I decide to try to make it up to her instead.

CHAPTER THIRTEEN
CAROLINE

"Miss Caroline, are you okay?"

"Miss Tyler, what happened?"

"Oh my gosh, I cannot believe what a jerk Michael was to you this morning."

I am bombarded with questions as I step into the gym for today's cheer practice. I lace up my tennis shoes, having decided to condition with the squad in an attempt to let off some of the aggression that's built up since the showdown this morning. I am normally not a runner, but since going home and curling up in bed wasn't an option today, I decided this was the next best thing.

"I am good," I assure them, trying to force a smile. "We're gonna condition for a bit today. Lace-up your shoes, and let's go."

We start off by stretching and then we go outside to do a few laps around the school. I've never been much of a runner, but I have to admit that it feels good to turn my brain off and focus on the sound of my feet hitting the pavement.

We run almost two miles in amicable silence until I call everyone back into the gym. Hannah despises conditioning, so she offered to work on arranging transportation to the games later this season while we were outside. I walk up to her, grabbing the water bottle I'd left on the bleachers while the girls all collapse in a heap on the mats we'd rolled out before our run.

"Hey, everything ready to go for the season?" I ask, sitting down on the bleachers beside her.

"Yes, I talked to the transportation department and they have us set up with Mark as the driver for the season. But enough about that. Are you okay? What the hell happened today? I wanted to come check on you, but I couldn't get away. My kids came in talking about it, but I didn't believe them." Hannah's mouth doesn't seem to be able to keep up with the speed that questions are entering her brain.

"Ok, perfect. Thanks for taking care of that for us. I'm okay. It's crazy though. That behavior seems really out of character for Michael. I really don't know what to do. Mr. Hale suspended him for a week for defiance and inappropriate use of technology, but you know we can only do so much. I tried to call his parents after everything went down, but the number was disconnected," I reply with an eye roll.

Hannah rolls her eyes and says, "Imagine that." It has become a recurrent issue, especially in high school, that parents like to ignore calls from the school or give us faulty numbers. If I had to bet, at least half the phone numbers in the system were wrong or disconnected.

"Yeah, I just hope that I can figure out a way to handle it better next time. Maybe his behavior will correct itself, but if it doesn't I'm not really sure what to do," I say trying not to show how defeated I feel. After a few years in education, I've learned to try to only focus on the problems I have control over, but damn it's tough. The longer I teach, the more I am reminded of the fact that I am not superwoman and I can't save everyone as much as I wish I could.

Hannah gives me a sad smile because I know she understands. My best friend might be loud and over the top at times, but I have never seen anyone care more than she does. She is fiercely protective over the people she loves, and she's also the biggest advocate for her students. I know she can tell by the look on my face that today hit me hard. "Brighter days ahead right?"

I smile at our saying and repeat "Brighter days ahead," feeling a real smile touch my face for the first time all day. When Hannah's parents left, she'd tried to act like she was unphased until one morning I found her on my doorstep crying. I'd let her in and sat with her while she cried, and we'd talked for hours. Finally, she finished crying and said, "But hey, brighter days ahead, right?" She told me that she needed the reminder that hard times don't last forever, and she'd asked me to repeat it back to her when she needed perspective. Ever since, it had become a bit of a motto in our friendship and it always makes us smile.

"You ready to get this started?" I ask her, and she smiles at me with a nod.

"Let's do it," she says.

"Okay ladies, let's hop on up and get ready to run our routine for the first game next week," I instruct the squad that's still recovering from the run. They slowly rise to their feet and walk over to the bleachers to place their water bottles out of the way and grab their pom poms before taking their place on the mats to prepare for the routine.

"Music's on!" I yell, pressing play on the "High Hopes" mix.

The girls lift their heads and are synchronized as they complete a triple toe touch sequence, and they execute the dance portion perfectly before moving to their tumbling formation. Maggie executes a flawless back handspring full combination she spent all summer working on and I resist the urge to squeal in excitement. The girls keep going, walking to their stunt formation with big smiles on their faces. There is an energy in the gym that feels magnetic, like everything we've worked for all summer is finally at our fingertips. They hit the rippled heel stretches perfectly, and I look over to share an excited look with Hannah. Finally, Maggie flies through the air and flips over from the pyramid to land safely in her bases' arms before shooting back up to the ending liberty. The squad calls out "Go Saints" and the music cuts out. I jump up screaming alongside Hannah. They've hit the routine before, but the girls are starting to hit their stride, and it's mesmerizing to watch.

I know it's most likely due to the day I've had today, but I feel tears start to sting my eyes. I blink them back quickly, not wanting the girls to tease me about being emotional. This program has come so far since I took over, and I am just so proud that I can finally see the work and planning I've put in come together.

"Oh my gosh girls! That was incredible! I am so proud of every single one of you," I scream as they jump around, unable to stand still due to their excitement. "We're gonna run it a few more times because I want to make sure it's perfect. Make sure y'all hit that triple toe touch hard and point your toes during the entire jump sequence. Great job! Once this is perfect, we will run the Bruno Mars routine again for tomorrow night. This routine is pretty close to perfect already, but I want to save it for the field."

As the girls take their places and get ready to run the routine again, Hannah leans over and whispers, "See I told you, better days." In that moment, I realize she's right because, despite the shitty day I've had, I can't keep the smile off my face.

AFTER RUNNING both routines a few more times, we call the girls in to end practice. They are sweaty and look exhausted, but they are smiling so big it hurts my cheeks to look at them. "Great job today girls! You have all worked so incredibly hard, and I cannot wait for everyone to see what I saw tonight."

The girls cheer, and I turn it over to Maggie to close out practice, "Okay, y'all I've talked to Miss Caroline and we are going to wear our white uniform with the vintage lettering. Make sure your hair is up with the blue bow. Meet the Saints starts at seven, so we can warm up around six-thirty. If y'all have any questions send them in the group text. I am so proud of how far we've come this season. See y'all tomorrow!" There are a few hoots of approval from the other girls, and then everyone is gathering their things to leave.

As most of the other girls make their way to the door, I notice Maggie fidgeting nervously a few feet away like she doesn't know what to say. Hannah and I make eye contact, and she nods at me whispering, "Go see what's going on. I'll hang right here."

I give her a grateful smile and make my way up to Maggie. "Hey, what's up?"

She'd been so deep in her thoughts I think I've scared her, but she grins and says, "It's been three years today since I lost my mom, and I just wanted to say thank you. This day always makes me sad, but right now all I can think is, she would be so damn proud of me.

"I miss her so much, but today she doesn't feel so far away. When she died, I didn't think I would ever cheer again, but you didn't let that happen. And it's making me realize that I don't want to stop feeling the way I do right now after I graduate. I know I told you no when you asked me if I was interested in pursuing cheerleading in college, but I've changed my mind. Do you think you and Miss Hannah can help me?"

My eyes are full of tears but I attempt to blink them back.

"Oh my goodness, of course I will help you. I didn't know your momma well, but I know she would be so incredibly proud of the woman you've become. There's been no better joy than getting to coach you and the rest of this squad and watch y'all make a name for yourself. Let me talk to Hannah and see who all we need to contact."

She rushes me with a hug before backing up and replying, "Thank you so much! I'd better go. Dad and I are going to Maracas, and I don't want to be late. But really Miss Caroline, thank you for believing in me when I didn't believe in myself."

I don't really have words to say but manage to choke out "Of course" before turning back and walking over to where Hannah is waiting for me. I collapse onto the seat beside her and after ensuring the gym is empty except for the two of us, I burst into tears.

I've always been a bit on the emotional side, but these are the parts of teaching that I wish everyone saw. The extreme highs and lows. Feeling like nothing I do will ever be enough. Feeling like I have to hold the whole world together. Knowing I can't fix all my kids' problems, but still feeling guilty when they're struggling. The way it feels when I think I've made a difference coupled with the shame I feel when all my attempts at help are met with negativity. Between the events of this morning, practice, and Maggie's speech, I feel like I've been on an emotional roller coaster today. I'll be ready to face tomorrow head-on in a second, but first I need a minute with my best friend to process all of these emotions.

Hannah rubs my shoulder comfortingly and says, "They tell us all the time we can't save them all, and they're right. But I'll be damned if you didn't save that one." I let out a small laugh because she's right. I might not be able to fix whatever Michael is struggling with, and I may not have all the answers. But in this moment, I can cling to the fact that I've made a little bit of difference and right now that's enough.

❧

I'M COVERED in sweat as I swipe away on Instagram while leaving the gym almost two

hours later. After practice, I stayed behind and used the weight room to work out some of the remaining pent-up energy that felt as if it had been vibrating just under the surface of my skin since this morning. Between a few rounds of circuits and my run at practice, paired with a smutty audiobook, I feel more relaxed than I have all day.

I'm exhausted, and all I can think about is showering and curling up on the couch. I have big plans to watch *Love Island* wrapped up in my fuzzy pink blanket with a large glass of Moscato and my favorite snack–melted M&Ms. Hannah always laughs at the fact that I have to microwave my M&Ms, but I will forever stand by the fact that it's the only way to eat them.

As I walk outside, I notice that my SUV is the only car left in the parking lot, which isn't surprising since it's after seven. Making my way closer to my vehicle, I see a box sitting on the hood. I can make out my name written across the top in a messy scribble along with what looks to be a piece of copy paper sticking out of the top.

Grabbing the piece of paper first, I flip it open and read it.

Miss Tyler,

I heard about your day and thought you could use
a pick me up. Consider this my attempt at an olive
branch. I know I was a dick about your candle
on Monday, but here's a replacement.
See you Saturday,
Chief Johnson

Shaking my head at the note, I open the box and find a pink oil diffuser and a couple of scents in the box. I feel a smile take over my face as I repackage the oils and throw the box in the car with my bag. I have to admit, Chief Johnson is full of surprises.

Damn, what a day.

CHAPTER FOURTEEN
THEO

Friday afternoon, we don't have practice so I leave the station and run home to let Bear out and change clothes. I swear the Labrador rolls his eyes at me when I walk in the door, but I grab some treats out of the container for him anyway. He gives a single twitch of his tail, so I call it a win before I let him outside.

"Hey, Margaret!" I yell through the house as I throw my bag down and make my way to the bedroom to grab the coaches polo Will threw at me as I left practice yesterday. I have to admit that while this isn't how I ever imagined my life would go, I am having fun with the team. I still feel my throat close up every time I think of my brother and his love for the sport, but I know that Brian was right when he said this is what Jake would have done.

"Hey!" Margaret responds. After changing, I walk back her way and find her in the kitchen talking on the phone. "Yes, Heather. We are getting settled in. Y'all will have to visit soon. I am baking some snacks for us to take to the beach this week-end. Theo just walked in the door and is getting ready to go up to the high school. Did you know he is coaching football? I know I can't believe it either. Yeah, we have a lot to catch up on. Maybe y'all can come down in a few weeks? Okay sounds good. Love you too." She hangs up the call and looks at me. "Are you going to Meet the Saints?"

"Yeah, I am about to head that way," I tell her as I grab a bottle of water out of the fridge.

"Hannah and Caroline were texting me about it earlier today. Can I ride with you? I haven't met anyone else in town, and I want to start meeting people since we're the outsiders," my sister asks looking hopeful.

"Sure that's fine, but only if you let me have one of those cookies you just took out of the oven. But hurry your ass up, we don't have all night," I respond before taking a long swig of my drink.

"Deal. I am going to go change clothes. I'll be back in just a minute," she mutters over her shoulder, already making her way to her bedroom.

I take a seat on the barstool Margaret picked out for the counter and grab for one of the warm cookies. It melts in my mouth and I fight the urge to let out a groan. I usually don't like sweets but these things are like heaven.

While I wait, my mind drifts to how different this moment would be if my family hadn't fallen victim to death's grimy fingers. I have no doubt that Jake would be coaching at an incredible high school and our parents would be his biggest fans. Margaret would probably have gone off to a fancy culinary school like she'd dreamed of, but she couldn't bear to move too far away after everything'd happened. I have a hard time even picturing what my life would look like. The carefree, funny boy of my youth had died along with my family that night, and all that's left is the shell of what used to be. I shake my head and try to pull myself out of the pit of my thoughts. I know the 'what if' game is useless, but it's a trap I fall into more often than I care to admit.

Trying to focus on something else, I get up and fill up Bear's bowl. He scratches on the door, obviously ready to eat. I scratch his head and let my mind wander to Caroline. I don't know how the hell she's managed to get so far under my skin, but it's obvious she has captivated me more than I would like to admit. I imagine her in the kitchen grabbing a cookie off the pan before tearing off a piece and placing it in my mouth. I'd lick the melted chocolate off her finger and suck on it until she let out a whimper. I'd push her against the bar, wrapping her legs around my waist so she could feel how desperately I wanted her before pulling her shirt down to reveal her rosy-

"You ready to go?" Margaret asks, breaking up my fantasy. Fuck. What the hell is wrong with me? It seems like the more I tell myself that Caroline is so far out of my league, the more I crave her touch. I shake my head to clear my thoughts and take a breath, trying to get the image of the hottest girl I've ever seen out of my head.

"Yep, let's go."

WHEN WE PULL up to the gym at Springside High, I am once again reminded that football is life in this town. We are twenty minutes early, and there doesn't seem to be a parking spot anywhere. After making a few laps, I see some other trucks parking in the street so I follow suit and jump the curb. This is crazy; it's not even a real game tonight.

"Wow," Margaret says. "I feel like we've jumped into the set of *Friday Night Lights*."

"No kidding," I say, feeling overwhelmed by the crowd I'm about to walk into. "We'd better get going though." We open our doors and make our way to the gym's entrance. It's clear we are new to town, and we get a bunch of stares as we walk into the gym. Great. "This place has to be a goddamn fire hazard."

"Don't focus on that tonight. Pretty sure that's what got you in this position in the first place. I am going to sit with Hannah and Caroline. They texted and said they'd save me a seat with them in the front. You good?" my sister questions, concern evident on her face. She knows crowded and confined spaces are not my favorite thing, but I shake off her concern telling her I'm fine. I watch as she makes her way to the bleachers where I see Caroline and Hannah waving to her. They are both wearing jeans and shirts that say "Springside Varsity Cheerleading" across the front. For a moment I can't take my eyes off of Caroline. She's wearing those damn jeans again, and I know I can't think about it or I will have a whole other issue. I look around desperately for a distraction and finally spot Will with the rest of the team in the other corner of the gym.

I walk over and give the team and coaches a small head nod. Will speaks loudly enough that the huddle of boys can hear him, "Okay, Principal Hale will welcome everyone and then we're up first. When they call your name and number, just step forward and wave. They'll introduce y'all first and then the coaches. After that, Wesley will say a few words inviting everyone to come support us this season. We will have a seat, and we will watch the cheerleaders and the band perform and then they'll introduce the volleyball team. You already know that I expect you all to give them your undivided attention. Otherwise, we'll spend the entire practice on Monday running hills."

There's a chorus of "Yes sir," and "Okay, Coach," before the boys turn their attention back to the conversations they were having. I sit in silence for a few minutes before I notice an older lady making her way over. I look over to see Hannah and Caroline whispering to my sister with looks of concern on their faces. The woman can't be more than four-foot-nine and has to be at least seventy years old, so surely she can't be the reason the girls look like they've seen someone kick their puppy.

Their concern suddenly makes sense when the elderly lady walks right up to Will and pokes her finger in his chest. "Well, I never thought much of you as a coach, but even I didn't think you'd be stupid enough to put these boys in danger. Don't you know this coach you brought in is violent? It's bad enough that we're stuck with him as the fire chief, but to bring him into a space where kids are involved. It's despicable. You should be fired!" the woman spits at Will, raising her voice enough to gather the attention of most of the people in the packed gym.

I am stunned speechless. I open my mouth to defend myself, but no words come out. I know I am not close to winning any popularity contests around here, but for her to insinuate I would hurt any one of my players? She must be off her damn rocker.

Before I can restart my brain, Will steps in and says, "Now Mrs. Sally. We both know that's a big accusation to be throwing around and you don't have a bit of evidence to support it. And since you decided to spew your hate in front of my team, I'm gonna give you the courtesy of being as polite as I can possibly be. You're full of crap. I'll take you trashing my coaching ability all over town because nobody in Springside gives a dang what you say. But I will not have you undermining me and my staff in front of my team. Chief Johnson has cleared a background check, and I believe that he will be an asset to this team and this community. And I think that's more than you could say after that incident you caused last year don't you think?"

Mrs. Sally sputters at him, "Those pills were prescribed. It was all a misunderstanding."

"And that's why you showed up to the Safe Harbor luncheon high as a kite and it took three police officers to remove you?" Will asks in an innocent sounding whisper so that only she and I can hear him.

Mrs. Sally looks like she's ready to throttle Will, but he gives her his most charming All-American smile and says, "Thanks for your concern, Mrs. Sally, but next time you have a problem, don't address it in front of my players. Go Saints!"

He turns his back to her and she has no choice but to go find a seat. I look at Will, feeling like I should say something but coming up empty. He must read the expression on my face because he says, "Don't. You might not be my favorite person, but no one deserves the wrath of Mrs. Sally like that. Plus it looks like you're here to stay. Just don't be an asshole anymore."

I give him a tight nod and see the man I am presuming is Principal Hale making his way to the podium set up in the center of the floor. Will motions to the rest of the team, letting us know that it's time. We stand and line up after the introduction concludes. Will takes the microphone and runs down the row of all fifty-seven players before getting to the coaches. When he calls my name, I step forward and wave. For the most painfully awkward six seconds of my life, it's dead silent. No one claps. Everyone stares at me like they aren't sure what to think of me. I go to step back, effectively mortified, when Caroline, Hannah, and Margaret erupt into the most obnoxious cheering I've ever heard. The rest of the crowd finally jumps in, and Will gives me a shrug before moving on to Coach Marcus who's standing beside me. He makes it through to the end and Wesley walks up to the microphone.

"Hey everyone. Our season starts in two weeks here at home. We have a big game against the Saddle Ridge Wildcats, and we would love to have a packed house. We have been working hard all summer, and think it's time that Springside brings home a state championship. What do y'all think?" Wesley exclaims, and he's met with thunderous cheers so loud I swear I can feel the gym floor shake.

We make our way back to our corner bleacher and I see Hannah and Caroline make their way to the microphone. They quickly move the podium to the corner so that it isn't blocking the floor where her cheerleaders are setting up. Caroline picks up the microphone and says, "Hey everyone. My name is Caroline Tyler and this is Hannah Scott. We are the coaches for the Varsity cheer squad here at Springside, and we are so excited to give y'all a small preview of what we've been working on." She goes through the list of twelve names and each time she says one, a girl waves and flips in the air. "Your music is on girls!" she calls out as a song by Bruno Mars starts blaring through the speakers.

I don't know much about cheerleading but, in that moment, I feel like I can't look away. Caroline's squad jumps and flips in perfect synchronization and the next thing I know they are throwing several of the girls in the air as if they weigh nothing. The girls end their routine with a yell of "Go Saints!" and the gym becomes a mess of screams and cheers. I look over at Hannah and Caroline who are hugging and seem close to jumping up and down. I feel the first ghost of a smile touch my lips since I entered the gym.

AFTER THE BAND performs and the teams have been introduced, the crowd disperses. Will dismisses everyone after reminding them about practice on Monday, nodding at the coaches to let us know we were good to leave. I look over to see Caroline, Hannah, and Margaret standing beside the cheerleading mats, waiting for the gym to clear so they can roll them up and put them away. Walking closer, I overhear their plans for our beach day tomorrow.

After a few minutes, the gym is mostly empty. Hannah starts walking backwards, pulling up the tape from the mats the cheerleaders used earlier and rolling it neatly. Margaret watches her and starts on the same process on one of the other rows. Once they are halfway down the mat, Caroline bends over and begins folding one of the four carpeted mats into a tight roll.

"Want some help with that, Miss Tyler?" I ask, looking down at her crouched position and trying not to stare at her perfect ass.

"Sure, you can start that one right there," she says, tilting her head and pointing at the mat beside her. I give her a tight nod and start rolling behind her. This position gives me an opportunity to admire her curves, and damn if I'm not dying to touch her again. Just brushing the hair out of her face the other night had been enough to make me hard, and I can't remember the last time a woman had me this bent out of shape.

We spend the next fifteen minutes rolling the mats and binding them tightly with velcro straps and buckles. I fight a smile of amusement as Hannah and Caroline flip the hundred and fifty pound mats end over end to get them into a small supply closet in the corner of the gym.

"Hannah, did you bring that swimsuit top for me to try on?" Margaret asks as we walk toward the exit. "I know I have a black top somewhere, but I can't find anything thanks to the move."

"Yep, I sure did. It's in my car. Come grab it from me. I'm parked this way," Hannah says, pointing in the opposite direction from where I parked my truck.

"Coming. Theo, don't leave without me. I'll be right back," my sister throws over her shoulder already walking off with Hannah.

Caroline looks at the girls and laughs. "I'm this way," she tells them pointing towards where my truck is sitting. "I'll see y'all bright and early in the morning."

"Sounds good. See you then," the girls bellow over their shoulders as they continue walking through the dark night.

"I'll walk you. I'm parked this way too," I tell her and follow her as she walks to her small white SUV parked beside my truck.

"Your squad did a great job tonight," I say, desperate to get as much time with her as she was willing to give me.

It's dark in the street where we're parked but I don't miss the way her face lights up as she smiles at me. "Thanks. I am so damn proud of them. They've worked so hard and I love getting to see them finally getting the appreciation they deserve," she explains as she leans against her front door. "I'm looking forward to our first game next week. Will says we have a real chance at state this year."

I nod before agreeing, "Yeah, I know I haven't been here long, but we've got some real talent. Will is a great coach."

Caroline smirks, nodding her head in agreement. We both go still as her eyes meet mine. A moment passes between us, neither of us daring to speak. I think we both know that breaking eye contact will push us back into reality. I feel an incredible pull to her—one I know she feels too, if the look in her eyes is any indication. We stand for another minute, neither of us ready to make the first move.

But, when she softly bites her lower lip, I can't help myself anymore. I reach up to rub my thumb across her lip, and she inhales sharply. She leans into my touch, and I am seconds away from taking her mouth the way I want to, when a car pulls up and shines its headlights directly at us.

We jump apart immediately as Margaret hops out of Hannah's car and saunters over to us.

"Ready, Theo? I have so much baking to do when we get home," she says, completely oblivious to what she just interrupted.

Caroline gives me a small wink and turns to get in her car, "See you tomorrow, Chief Johnson. Bye, Margaret!"

As she pulls away, all I can think about is how desperately I've always wanted what I can't have– a normal life, a chance to change the events of that night, and my family back. But damn if Caroline Tyler isn't finding herself on the list too.

CHAPTER FIFTEEN
CAROLINE

After the girls' performance last night, I struggled to wind down, so seven o'clock on Saturday morning comes a lot sooner than I want. I'm sluggish when I first open my eyes until I remember that I am up at the ass crack of dawn to go to the beach with my friends. I am a big believer that there's no problem a beach can't fix. No matter what I am feeling, the sound of the waves crashing and the sight of the endless sea always reminds me how minuscule I am in the big scheme of things.

I get up and make the bed before I pad into the kitchen to get a cup of coffee. I fiddle with the machine until I hear it making my double shot of espresso, then I go to the bathroom and wash my face while I wait. On the way back to the kitchen, I grab my new bikini out of my closet and hold it up. Hannah convinced me I needed it when we were out shopping last week, but it is so out of my comfort zone I'm not sure I can pull it off. It is red and has hot pink straps on the shoulders and the hips, but it's much more risqué than the high-waisted bottoms and tops I usually gravitate towards. I throw it on my bed with a pair of denim cutoffs and a cropped black tee shirt. As I walk back into the kitchen, I hear my phone chirp with a text message.

> Hannah: It's Beach Day Bitches!

> Margaret: Oh my goodness I am so excited. I've packed a bunch of snacks and I told Theo to make sure he picks up some drinks. He offered to drive us.

> Hannah: Helllll yes! Theo the DD? I think he's growing on me. I'll spend the night at Caroline's after we get home tonight so y'all can just grab us from her apartment if that works? Will and Seth are coming a little later, so they can get themselves there.

> Margaret: Sounds good to me.

> Me: That's so sweet of Theo! Tell him thank you! What are y'all wearing?

> Hannah: C, you'd better have on that bikini you showed me last week.

> Me: I'm afraid it's too much.

> Hannah: I'm not dealing with your shit today. Put it on now. If not I'll make you when I get there.

> Me: *eye roll*

> Margaret: Y'all are a mess. See you soon.

> Me: I'm apartment 2A whenever you get here. Just come on up.

Knowing that Hannah isn't joking about finding a way to

make me wear the swimsuit, I begrudgingly throw it on and look at my reflection in the mirror. It doesn't look bad, but I am worried about the fish getting an eye full. Sighing, I throw the shorts on over the bottoms and decide to roll with it. I hear a knock at the door and walk to swing it open assuming it's Hannah.

Instead, I come face to face with Theo. I should have known Hannah wouldn't be early, but the coffee hasn't fully knocked out my brain fog. Theo looks at me and then glances down at the itty bitty swimsuit top I'm wearing, and I try not to blush as his eyes rake over my body. All of a sudden it seems like all of the air has been sucked out with a straw. Theo is all muscle, and his dark brown hair has gotten just long enough I can imagine grabbing it while sinking down onto his cock. Judging by his physical size, I am willing to bet he isn't small. I start to imagine leading him into my apartment and stripping him down before pushing him onto the couch and straddling him to let my dripping wet-

"You have everything you need?" he asks from the doorway, breaking me from my daydream. I jump a bit, mortified that I fell so deeply into the almost sex scene playing out in my head. Maybe Will is right and the smutty books have broken my brain. Oh well, my book boyfriends are worth it.

"Give me just a minute to grab my stuff. You're welcome to come in. Make yourself at home," I say over my shoulder, already making my way back to my bedroom. I throw the cropped tee on over my swimsuit and make quick work of grab-bing a beach bag. I throw in a change of clothes, a towel, sunglasses, some sunscreen, and run to grab my fully charged Kindle off my nightstand. Once I have all the essentials, I walk back to the kitchen grabbing my water bottle before turning back to Theo and saying, "Ready when you are."

"Okay cool, come on. We can wait on Hannah in the car," he says. I wonder if being alone with me in my apartment is making him uncomfortable, but considering the fact I was just imagining myself writhing on his dick, he may be warranted in that emotion. We silently walk down the hallway and make our way outside. Margaret is standing at the back of the truck checking on the cooler on the tailgate.

"Hey girl," I call out to her when we are close enough that I won't have to yell.

"Oh goodness, hey! I was just grabbing the muffins I baked for breakfast. Here you go, have one while we wait." She hands me a bag that must have at least four flavors of the biggest muffins I've ever seen. "I made a lemon blueberry, a banana chocolate chip, a cinnamon coffee cake, and an orange strawberry batch. Let me know what you think."

"Have I told you lately how glad I am that you decided to move to Springside?" I ask jokingly. As I grab out a banana chocolate muffin, Theo leans in to grab the bag from me. Even with the heavenly scent coming from the muffins, I can suddenly smell nothing but him. He smells of cedar and mint toothpaste, and I have to refrain from leaning closer to him. What the hell is wrong with me?

WE WAIT ROUGHLY ten more minutes, making small talk and snacking on the muffins before Hannah whips into the parking lot. She jumps out of the car after barely getting it in park and reaches for her bag in the backseat before she sprints over to us and jumps in the backseat of Theo's truck with me.

"So sorry everyone! Leroy was giving me absolute hell this morning, and he tried to charge the chicken coop to get some of their feed. I thought I was going to have to stay home and figure out how to replace the wall, but I got everything settled after I moved Cletus and Maryanna into a new field. Of course, after all that I smelled like shit so I had to take a shower," Hannah says, rolling her eyes as she throws herself into the truck. Sensing the confused look on Theo's face, I explain.

"Hannah takes care of the family farm for her grandfather. Leroy is her pet pig, but I am pretty sure he thinks he's a dog. If she would let him ride in the front seat with her I am pretty sure he would hang his head out the window," I say with a laugh. "And Cletus and Maryanna are the only two cows she likes. We went through a phase a while back that we thought all of them needed a name, but they have over one hundred. We couldn't even begin to keep up with what we'd called them, so we just had to say forget it. But Cletus and Maryanna stuck."

Margaret laughs out loud as Theo throws the truck in drive and turns onto the backroad that leads to the small coastal town about forty-five minutes away. Crestview is bigger than Springside, thanks to the college campus and beach property, but I love that it still has a small-town feel. I grab out my Kindle and we ride in polite silence listening to music and reading.

Around nine, Theo pulls into a parking spot at a secluded public beach. We make quick work of unloading the truck and start to make the trek towards the water. I grab my beach tote and one of the bags Margaret had filled with snacks. I haven't made it more than a few feet when Theo reaches out his hand and takes the bag from my shoulder. I immediately feel chill bumps run down my arm where he touched me, regardless of the ninety-eight-degree heat. "I'll take this."

"Thanks," I murmur, feeling incredibly shy all of a sudden. I am pretty sure I am blushing like a schoolgirl, but since there's nothing I can do to stop it I try not to worry about it. Hannah scouts out a great place on the beach for us, and we try to spread our stuff out enough to ensure that we have room when Will and Seth arrive. Hannah and Margaret run straight out to the water with some floats they'd brought with them, but I decide to lay out for a bit first. I expect Theo to keep to himself, but instead, he brings a chair and sits down beside me. I smile at him, wondering if he feels as magnetic with me as I do with him.

"I heard what happened at school this week with Michael. Are you okay?" Theo asks me after a few minutes.

"Yeah, I'm fine. I don't know what's going on with him. Obviously, my feelings are a little hurt, but I don't think any of his behavior was really about me. I'm just hoping that everything is okay," I reply, looking out at the vast blue ocean. It's moments like this that make me really glad to be alive. "How was your first week as Chief, Mr. Johnson?"

"Well, I'm damn glad it's ending better than it started. I know I've said it a million times before, but I really am sorry for the way I talked to you when we met," Theo says with a sheepish look on his face. I take pity on him and give him a smile.

"We all have our days. If I've learned anything as a teacher, it's to have a whole lot of grace. It's crazy what the people we see every day are going through, and we can be so clueless. I am sorry the town hasn't given you the warmest welcome. I think they'll grow to love you though. Except maybe Mrs. Sally but she hates everyone," I say with a laugh and Theo cracks a small smile.

I grab the sunscreen I packed in my bag and start applying it quickly, rubbing the lotion in on my legs and arms. I struggle to reach around and get my shoulders covered, and after a minute Theo says, "Do you want some help with that?"

I blush a little thinking about his big hands running across my body, but I quickly nod in agreement. "Sure, if you don't mind that'd be great."

He slowly reaches out his hand as if he is worried he's gonna run me off. He grabs the bottle from my hand and motions for me to turn around. I shift in my chair so that he can reach me and brace myself for the cold lotion to touch my exposed flesh. But as he makes contact with my shoulder, all I can feel is the heat from his fingers as he gently massages the sunscreen into my skin. He moves his hand down and I feel his hand brush the string of my bikini. The thought hits me that I would let him pull that string later tonight and stand there happily in front of him as it fell to the floor. I imagine him running his rough hands lower and teasing me gently until he runs a finger through my wet core until I'm screaming out his name. Blinking that thought away, I try not to let my lust-filled brain get the best of me. "Uh, thank you, Theo. Do you want me to do yours now?"

I cringe as soon as it registers what I just asked, and he gives me a small smirk that has wetness pooling between my thighs. "Darlin' let me let you in on a secret. I'll let you do me anytime," He lets out a small, uncharacteristic laugh before jerking his shirt off and throwing me the sunscreen.

I can feel the heat on my cheeks, and I am about to sink into another lust-induced haze when I look over to where Theo has turned around waiting on the sunscreen. There is a small patch of his back that looks as though it was singed off. It has healed well, but there is certainly still evidence of trauma. I grab the sunscreen and squeeze some into my hands before asking, "What happened to your back, Theo? Did something happen at work?"

As soon as the words are out of my mouth, I wish I could take them back. Theo visibly stiffens, and while I can't see his face, I know the grinning, grumpy man that was just before me is gone. In his place is a man lost to his demons, and I don't know how to get him back.

CHAPTER SIXTEEN
THEO

Goddamnit Theo. What the hell were you thinking? My brain continues to scream obscenities at me, and I try to put together a response to the beautiful woman sitting behind me.

I'd come to terms with my scars over the years, but no one had ever really questioned me about them. In my line of work, they weren't too out of place and the years of throwing myself into working at the station hadn't left much time for days at the beach. Never mind the fact that I'd lived like a recluse for the majority of my twenties.

"No, they're not from work" is the best response I can manage as I fight to stay in the present.

"Oh, okay. I'm sorry I asked," Caroline says softly as she slowly massages the sunscreen into the tense muscles of my back.

"It's fine," I say, looking out at the ocean as I try to pull myself together. Once I feel as though my mask is firmly in place again, I turn and settle back in my chair. I look out at the ocean and think of my Mom. She loved the beach, and we never went a summer without a trip south. She loved laying in the sun and sending Dad to chase us down when we were younger and wandered too far from her chair. As we got older, she'd sit in her chair reading a book and take as many pictures as she could. I know Margaret has a few saved on her computer, and I have the sudden urge to track them down.

Breaking out of my trance, I look over at Caroline who is watching me with a look of regret on her face and fidgeting with her swimsuit. Her question was innocent enough, and I'll do anything to get the carefree look back on her face. "So you help out around Hannah's farm?" I ask her, trying to steer the conversation back to a safe topic.

Her face breaks out into a wide smile as she asks, "I do. I really love the animals. Did you grow up around animals?"

"Not really," I reply simply.

Caroline laughs and says, "Not really? What does that mean?"

"My grandfather had a horse that we used to help take care of when we visited, but he died when I was in middle school and we didn't have room for a horse in town."

"I love animals," Caroline states. "I've been going out to Hannah's farm since we were in elementary school. Leroy is my favorite. He's mischievous, but he's so cute."

I look at her for a minute before asking, "That's the pet pig y'all were talking about?"

"Yep, he has a dedicated food bowl and everything. Her grandfather got him for her years ago, but I don't think he ever expected he would become so doglike. His little tail even wags when you pet him."

"You're shitting me," I say, trying not to let the smile I'm fighting show. The corners of my mouth lifting up feels foreign to me, but there's something about this girl that makes it impossible to contain.

"Nope, you'll have to come meet him sometime soon," she says with a smile.

"Okay," I respond simply, unsure of what else to say.

We sit in comfortable silence for a few minutes before she stands up and offers her hand. "Come on," she says, standing up and holding out her hand for me.

"Where are we going?" I ask looking up at her.

"Does it matter?" she asks with a quirk of her lips.

And at that moment, I decide I don't give a shit. I give her my hand and she pulls me up and tugs me along with her straight into the ocean. She laughs loudly as she tries to jump on me, forcing me underwater. We tussle and I fight to grab her to dunk her under the water. She screams and throws her body against my back as she wraps her legs around my front. I slowly reach around and turn her so that she is facing my front with her legs still wrapped around me. Her breaths are hard from the exertion of fighting with me and our lips are inches away from claiming each other. I have no doubt she can feel my hard length pressing into her center with the way she's pressed against me.

We stare at each other, both of us unwilling to break the spell we seem to be under.

She inches her face slightly closer to me, and all I can think is how badly I want to feel her hot mouth all over mine. I run my fingers under the string of her swimsuit, and she arches into me begging for my touch. I'm about to close the last bit of distance between us when a wave comes and knocks us both underwater.

We resurface, and Caroline's laugh is loud enough that I almost forget the way she felt wrapped around me. I grab her hand and lead her to the shore.

As Caroline and I emerge from the water, Hannah and Margaret return with Will and the man I am assuming is Seth. Seth is roughly the same height as Will, but he is leaner than me. His scruffy brown hair hangs down in his face and he has a wide smirk on his face. "This is Seth," Will explains to me.

I nod at him and say gruffly, "I figured," before shifting my attention to Seth. "Hey, man."

"Theo right?" he asks as he sticks out his hand, intending to shake mine. I nod and stand to shake his hand once before sitting down. "So you're the new asshole fire chief huh?"

Caroline makes a move to defend me, but I respond simply with, "Yep, that's me."

Seth lets out a loud laugh and shakes his head. "Nice to meet you. I gotta say, you made quite the entrance into Springside. I know everybody has their panties in a twist about your arrival. Will told me that you and your sister just moved down here from outside of Birmingham. I guess Springside has to be a pretty big adjustment."

"Yeah, a bit," I respond as everyone around us just stares. I know I'm being an asshole but I don't care. I am done apologizing to everyone in this stupid town.

The group titters awkwardly until Seth lets out a boisterous laugh and slaps me on the shoulder. "Listen, as long as you and Caroline are good, I don't give a damn what Mrs. Sally is spouting on about at the Dollar General. Everyone in Springside has gotten on her hit list at least once. It'll blow over. So let's grab a volleyball net and have some fun today.

The group lets out a loud echo of cheers in agreement, and Will reaches into the suitcase-sized beach bag Hannah brought to pull out a neon volleyball. As we run over the white sand to grab one of the empty nets, Will calls out, "Girls y'all head to the other side. We're about to kick your ass."

~

"WHAT THE FUCK WILL? Maybe if you weren't so worried about messing up your hair, you might be able to hit the ball in the boundary," Hannah taunts loudly as a ball flies past Will.

"I swear Hannah, since you're such a goddamn superstar

I'm about to let you play by yourself. I swear you never get tired of hearing your own voice do you?" Will snaps back, serving the ball back over the net.

We've been playing for well over an hour and while I should have guessed this crew would be competitive, I was totally unprepared for the trash-talking these two have done. I can't tell if they are ready to fuck or claw each other's eyes out. Margaret and Caroline let out loud laughs at the duo's antics as Caroline dives to set the ball up for Hannah. Her long legs were already covered with sand, but as Hannah expertly spikes the ball at Seth's feet, I notice Caroline's large breasts are now covered as well. She stands up trying to wipe the grains from her body, but it clings to her curves.

"Alright, guys. Play nice. I need a break. I am going to get in the water," Caroline yells across the beach with a laugh.

The group choruses their agreement, and everyone races to the ocean. Will grabs Hannah's waist and throws her over his shoulder as she kicks and screams. I fight a smile as he throws her into the water and she comes up sputtering.

"Will Thompson, I am going to murder you!" Hannah yells, gathering a few stares from the families lounging on the beach. I walk deeper into the water, getting some distance from what I am certain will be a knockdown drag out between the two.

Hannah and Will continue bickering, but all of a sudden I can't hear anything they're saying because I am completely captivated by the view of Caroline walking towards me. The sun makes her skin glow which is fitting with her bright personality. Saltwater glistens off every beautiful inch of her tanned skin, and her curves look as if they are begging me to reach out and touch them. It occurs to me that the thoughts I'm having about her are far from friendly, but I decide to give myself a pass since it's not like I am going to act on them. The almost kiss in the water today is as close as I'll ever get to knowing what Caroline Tyler tastes like. But damn what I wouldn't give to have her muscular thighs wrapped around my head while I licked her cunt. I have no doubt she would taste like the sweetest honey that's ever touched my lips. I am grateful for the water hiding what I am sure is my obvious arousal thanks to the fantasy playing in my head.

"We can't take them anywhere," Caroline says with a laugh as she nods her head to Hannah and Will who are now trying to tackle each other into the water.

"I'll say. Is she really trying to tackle a football coach? Will is at least three times her size," I point out incredulously.

"I think you'd be surprised. Hannah is little, but she's feisty. My money's on her. Wanna bet on it?" Caroline asks with a smirk.

"Sure, Sunshine. You're on. What are the stakes?" I ask. I hadn't meant to call her that out loud, but her smile tells me she doesn't mind.

"Sunshine huh?" she asks with a wink.

"Yeah. I've never met anyone that was so damn happy all the time. I think it fits. But don't change the subject now. What are the stakes?" I ask as Hannah and Will continue to flounder in the water.

"If Hannah takes down the football coach, you'll agree to drive us to the line dance next weekend. Will told us last time he was never coming back, and you know there aren't any Ubers in Springside. If Will somehow gets the best of Hannah, I'll help you around the farm."

I really don't give a damn about farm help right now, but this girl is impossible to turn down. I give her a small nod and reach out my hand to shake hers. "You're on," I tell her, trying to ignore the jolt of electricity I feel from touching her again. Once again she draws a bit closer, and my self-restraint to keep from pulling her into me is almost at zero when I hear a loud splash beside us. Caroline cheers loudly as Hannah dances in the water and Will tries to stand as a wave knocks him back down. I shake my head and try not to laugh as Will curses over and over again. "I'll be damned. Looks like you have yourself a driver."

We stay on the beach until the sun has slipped down toward the horizon, and the brightest sunset lights up the sky. The girls have had several White Claws throughout the day, and they are singing loudly as they sit in their chairs and sing about a cowboy taking them away. Caroline and Margaret giggle as Hannah stands and starts dancing to the music playing from the speaker. I may have gotten off to a rough start in Springside, but it's clear my sister has never felt more at home. It makes me more relaxed seeing her so happy.

Seth leans over as he watches the girls and asks, "So man, what brought y'all to Springside?"

"Well, the mayor is a family friend. When he called to ask if I was interested, I jumped at the opportunity to get out of the city. Plus, it worked out for Margaret to move with me. So here we are," I tell him.

"That's awesome that you're so close. I know you got off to a rough start, but I think Springside is lucky to have you. I don't remember the last time anyone under the age of fifty moved into town. The locals will come around," Seth says confidently.

I don't really give a damn about the town, but it feels good to have someone not believe I am a total asshole. "Thanks," I reply, unsure of what to say.

I look back over at the girls who are now holding hands and dancing to the latest Miranda Lambert song. I have always gravitated to country music, and the tune has come across my Spotify several times over the last week.

I can't take my eyes off of Caroline. It feels like she's awakened a part of me that I thought was dead, and I don't know the last time I felt so alive. She throws her head back and laughs freely at something that Margaret whispered to her, and I swear she glows once again with the way the sun glistens off her skin. The song ends and the girls throw themselves back into their chairs.

"Y'all ready boys?" Hannah asks us as she begins gathering the trash from around our chairs.

"Yeah, trying to load after dark sucks," Seth says standing to help.

With that, we begin packing our stuff to make the trek back to the truck. The group trickles in that direction as I stay behind to pick up any trash we might have missed. I think I am alone until I turn around from fiddling with the cooler to make sure it's firmly on the wagon we brought down to see Caroline standing there waiting on me.

"Come on Theo. Let's go home," she says with a smile as she wraps her hand around mine and leads me up the beach. Damn, if I don't love the way that sounds on her lips.

We work together to pull the heavy wagon to the board-walk, and I try to ignore how her petite body feels against mine for what feels like the hundredth time today. Right before we reach the pavement she leans over and whispers, "By the way, Theo, I think there's something we left unfinished today," biting her bottom lip.

With that, she rushes off to help the other girls, and I stand there wondering what the fuck just happened.

CHAPTER SEVENTEEN
CAROLINE

Hannah: Are we on for Margarita Monday tonight ladies?

Me: Is that even a question?

Margaret: Oh my god, I am so down.

Me: Y'all one of my juniors just asked where in the United States Brazil is. I'm gonna need a marg with an extra shot of tequila tonight.

Hannah: ^^^ I couldn't agree more.

Margaret: Bless your souls. Well I just left the building for my bakery. I am worried it's a little more run down than the pictures made it seem. I'm never gonna get everything done. Plus they said I can't start work until the new year because of something with the old owners.

> Me: Oh my goodness no! We'll help you figure something out!

> Hannah: Already on it. You know Seth teaches construction here at the school. I already threatened to tell his momma about his piercings if he didn't help you. He said he was happy to.

> Me: HANNAH! You can't tell Mrs. Gloria about that!

> Margaret: Oh my gosh, you are the best. And I didn't know Seth had an earring. How does he hide that?

> Hannah: Who said we were talking about his ears?

> Margaret: OH MY GOD!

> Me: This is a conversation for tonight. I'll see you soon ladies.

It feels like it's been weeks since I left the beach instead of days by the time I slide into our favorite booth at Maracas. I haven't been able to get Theo out of my head since we got home Saturday night.

I go through my usual routine of ordering my peach margarita and queso while I wait for the girls to arrive. I've only made it a few pages into my latest cowboy romance when Margaret slides into the booth across from me.

"Hey Caroline! Sorry to leave you waiting. I made Theo drop me off tonight. He wanted to come in, but I told him that Margarita Mondays are sacred girl time. I think I could drink a whole pitcher tonight after the day I've had," Margaret says slumping her shoulders down and looking dejected.

"Oh, you're good, girl. I haven't been here long," I say while putting my Kindle on standby mode. "And oh no! I am so sorry. The drama with your building?" I ask her sympathetically.

"Yes! I know buying the building before I saw it wasn't the best idea in the world, but I couldn't move here without a plan. The pictures looked so nice online. But it just feels a lot more run down than I'd hoped. It's nothing too major, but the counter area is probably going to have to be gutted to get the look I'm going for," she tells me with a sigh.

I think about the building she's referring to, and I understand what she's saying. Mr. Smith had kept it up well until he died several years ago, but since then the family had been trying to sell it. Since they didn't live locally and we didn't have an influx of people opening new businesses in Springside, I don't doubt that there is considerable work needed on the storefront.

"It's all gonna be fine!" I tell Margaret, trying to pull her out of the slump I can see her slipping into. "Don't stress. You have us and the boys. We'll all pitch in!"

At that moment, Hannah slides into the booth beside me and chimes in, "Hell yeah we will. Plus Seth is a literal mastermind with this kinda stuff. He'll have you up and running in no time."

Margaret lets out the first laugh I've heard from her today. "Y'all are the best. Also, I need some context from your text earlier today. Did you mean what I think you meant?" she asks with a blush.

"Damn sure did. He's a real momma's boy, and Mrs. Gloria thinks he hung the moon. But she also thinks he's the most innocent lil thing to exist. Little does she know he has three piercings on his dick. I think she'd faint if she found out," Hannah says with a loud laugh.

Margaret and I laugh along with her until Margaret pauses. "Oh my god, how do you know that? Did y'all hook up?"

At that Hannah and I make eye contact and dissolve further into a fit of giggles. "Hell no!" Hannah barks out a bit louder than necessary. "The four of us went out line dancing one night at the Boot Scooter right after we all moved back home. Seth had too much to drink, and he and Will made a dumb bet. The boys heard us discussing one of our books we'd read with a guy that had a dick piercing, and they decided the loser had to get one. Well, when Seth lost, he got Will to agree to triple or nothing. He lost again, and we found ourselves in a sketchy tattoo parlor in Saddle Ridge."

Margaret squeals with laughter before exclaiming, "Oh my God, that's epic."

"It was quite the night," I say with a giggle.

"Anyway, Seth said he'd help you with whatever you need. He said he would help without my threats, but it doesn't hurt to keep him on his toes." Hannah says with a shrug. "He is going to get with you about a budget for the project and start drawing up some plans so they're ready whenever you get the green light to start working."

Margaret sobers and looks close to tears of gratitude. "I don't know what to say. I can't believe y'all are being so nice to me. I didn't know what to expect when I decided to move to Springside, but oh my God, y'all are the best. I would feel enough stress about making this perfect anyway, but I used what was left of my parent's life insurance money on this project. I know it's silly, but it feels like if it's not perfect, I am disgracing their legacy or something."

Hannah and I exchange a silent look before I start, "Oh my gosh, Margaret, no way. They'd be so proud! You are going to have the most amazing business. One bite of those cookies and the whole town will be eating out of your hand."

"Of course they will," Hannah jumps in. "I am so sorry you're dealing with this, but I know your parents would be so incredibly happy that you're living your dream!"

Margaret looks at us, and I notice she has tears in her eyes. "God I am a mess. I'm sorry. Clearly, it's been forever since I had girlfriends, and Theo just shuts down when I try to talk to him about them. I just really miss them. It's been fourteen years, and sometimes it still feels like yesterday."

I reach out my hand to lay it over hers. "Well, you have us now. And we're here if you need to talk."

Margaret smiles lightly and squeezes my hand. "Y'all really are the best. I try not to dwell on the past but this whole process just has me thinking about them more than usual. Dad and my brother Jake would have spent every spare moment working on the building with Theo while Mom and I tried new recipes. She's the one who taught me to bake, and she made the best cinnamon rolls you've ever tasted. Maybe one day, I'll figure out a way to live up to their memory."

My heart breaks for my new friend, and Hannah gives Margaret a small smile. "I know what you mean. I know our situations are different, but my parents left years ago, and I haven't heard from them since. Caroline has had to pull me out of a funk so many times I can't even count. We can't bring your family back just like we can't make mine care about me, but we just have to keep going. Better days ahead, right?"

"Better days ahead," I chime in lightly and Margaret smiles.

"You're right. Okay, enough of that for now. But speaking of my family, Caroline, did I notice you and my brother hitting it off this weekend?" she asks me.

I let out a surprised giggle before gaining my composure. I don't know what to say. I kept waiting for him to make a move, but it seems pretty obvious he's not into me. He's clearly just trying to make sure we're on the right track after the fire drill fiasco. I am sure I have way too many curves for someone that looks like him. "Oh my gosh, stop. He was just being nice."

"Uhh, have you met my brother? I love him to death but

nice isn't exactly the adjective that I'd use when it comes to him," Margaret exclaims.

"What she said. I have decided not to hold the fire drill incident against him, but I saw y'all eye fucking each other all day on Saturday. Those were not sympathy eye fucks," Hannah chimes in.

I try to quell the rush of hope I feel in my chest that they think he might be interested in me and feign indifference. "I think y'all are full of it. So, who needs more margs?"

CHAPTER EIGHTEEN
THEO

By the time Tuesday afternoon rolls around, I am exhausted. The day has been brutally hot thanks to some A/C issues, and I leave the station craving a beer and a hot shower. I'd spent the day at work going through a log of local businesses and trying to make sure the fire protocols were up to my standards. Zach had stopped in to check on me, but other than that it has been a quiet day. But after football practice in the Alabama heat, I'm covered in sweat and dust. I am throwing my stuff into the backseat of my truck when my phone pings with a text.

Margaret: Hey, are you on the way home yet?

Me: Yeah, just got to the truck.

Margaret: Okay I need you to reroute. Hannah needs our help.

Me: With what?

Margaret: I'm not positive, but she sent out an SOS for help at her farm. Caroline texted me separately and said this never happens, so we think it must be something serious. Hannah's pride won't let her ask Will for help, and Seth had to go to Crestview to get some things for the project he's working on. I told them I would bring you for some muscle. I'm on the way there now.

I blow out a breath. So much for that shower and beer I had been dreaming about. But this does mean I'll get to see Caroline, so maybe it won't be all bad.

Me: Text me the address.

Fifteen minutes later, I am pulling up at Hannah's farm, and it becomes immediately obvious what the problem is. There are cows everywhere. I am not talking about two or three, but dozens of cows and calves standing around on the driveway to the house. I may not have grown up on a farm, but I am certain that this is not a good sign. I look over to see the girls about a quarter of a mile up the drive surrounding a massive hole in the fence. I reach into the back seat where I keep my dad's worn cowboy hat. Driving over, I jump out to join them in examining the gap.

"Evening," I say simply, momentarily distracted by the view of Caroline in a pair of tight leggings and an oversized shirt. Every time I see this woman, I swear I become a little more obsessed with her.

"Hey, Theo. Thank you for coming," Caroline says with a smile.

"You're welcome," I respond before turning to Hannah, "what can I do?"

She blows out a frustrated breath. Hannah has always given the illusion that nothing gets to her, but I can see this moment is overwhelming her. "Well we need to get all the damn cows back in the pasture and then we need to fix the fence."

"Clearly," I reply on instinct before realizing I definitely shouldn't have said that out loud. Three angry sets of eyes find me, and I can tell my sister is about to explode on me. "Sorry. We still have a few hours of daylight. We'll get them back in and rig something for today before it gets too dark.

Caroline chimes in, "Theo's right, Hannah. It's gonna be fine. Theo will get started moving the cows back while we go look for the fencing stuff in the barn. Right, Theo?"

"Sure," I respond quickly.

The girls turn and start walking towards the barn in the distance. Once they're gone, I give myself a moment to figure out what the fuck I just got myself into. Oh well, yee haw I guess.

I jump back into my truck and ride back to where the cows are lazily gnawing on the grass beside the driveway. They blink at me, waiting to see what I'm going to do. I look around and see a cattle prod leaned against the door of the house. I run up to grab it and walk back towards the stray cows. I carefully avoid the momma cow as she tucks her calf under her, not in the mood to get trampled today. I yell loudly for them to come on, and wave the prod in the air so they can all see it. It takes a minute, but finally, a few of them start moving slowly towards the opening of the gate. I look up to see Caroline leading a large American Quarter horse my way.

"Thought Merle here might make your job a little easier," she says as she holds out the reins to the large horse for me to take.

I grab them from her hand and slowly move to pet the horse's nose. I haven't been around horses since I lost my family, but I remember my grandfather teaching me how to make them comfortable before jumping on their back. The large animal blows softly before nuzzling my hand lightly. I make sure the saddle is secure around his middle before hoisting myself up while Caroline watches. "Thanks, Sunshine," I tell her with a small smirk before riding off on Merle while Caroline treks to an old farm truck. She hoists herself into the lifted cab before pulling off, driving through the new hole in the fence, and making her way to the barn.

I work as efficiently as I can moving the cows back to their rightful place. My normally jumbled thoughts have silenced as I focus on the farm, and I try to enjoy the blessed silence. I haven't ridden a horse in years, but it catches me off guard how easily the movements come back to me.

I haven't worked with cows before, but the longer I work, the more I realize I don't hate it. Why are animals so much easier to work with than humans? Out here, none of them think of me as the asshole fire chief or the poor little foster boy like some of the locals in my old hometown, and I find myself relaxing more than I have in years while I work.

I gaze out at the vast pasture as I work, and it hits me how amazing this scene is. The cows that have returned are grazing in the pasture while the sun starts its slow descent towards the horizon. The sky's alight with vibrant colors, and I realize in this moment that I really enjoy the farm work. It's definitely not all fun, as evidenced by the events of today, but I feel accomplished and in control after working with the animals for about an hour.

About five minutes later, all of the cows are back in the pasture, and I am standing guard in front of the opening to block it off. I see the farm truck Caroline took to the barn making its way towards us, and it pulls to a stop beside me. Margaret sticks her head out the window and yells, "We rounded up everything we'll need to fix the fence for the night, but we couldn't pick up the barbed wire roll. I swear it weighs about a hundred pounds. Will you take the truck back up there and help Caroline?"

"Sure thing," I shout. I pat Merle's head before swinging myself to the ground. I hold out the horse's reins and my sister takes them from me. "I'll be back."

I jump into the truck and start the bumpy ride back to the barn where Hannah and Margaret had just come from. Once I throw the truck into park, I leap out and make my way inside. "Caroline? Where are you?"

"Over here!" she responds. I track her voice to the back of the hay barn. Both the rolling doors are open and I look out at the most incredible sight I've ever seen. The rolling green hills of the pasture below stretch for as far as the eye can see, and the sunset's colors of pink and orange blend beautifully. The cows I had just relocated graze lazily in the distance, and Caroline stands in the middle of it all looking out at the view. Her brown hair gleams in the light and her leggings show off every inch of her luscious curves.

"Isn't it the most gorgeous thing you've ever seen?" she asks breathily.

"Yep," I say simply, not taking my eye off of her. I tell my feet to stop as I make my way closer and closer to her, but it feels like my brain has turned off as I act purely on instinct. When I get close enough to her, I reach out my hand and run it gently down her arm. She shivers, but she doesn't pull away. My brain warns me to move further away from her, but I ignore it and move closer. I continue closing in on her until I have her pressed against a hay bale by the door, and my body is pressed against hers.

I look at her expression, trying to gauge her reaction to me. I expect to find apprehension in her eyes, but there is nothing hinting that she doesn't want this as badly as I do. I move in closer to her until my lips are hovering over hers and pause, giving her time to stop this.

She reaches up with her hand, and I prepare myself for her to push me away. Instead, she runs her finger lightly around the brim of my cowboy hat and looks up at me to say, "Well cowboy, are you gonna kiss me or not?"

Fuck.

There's no way I can say no to that even if I wanted to. I reach my hands above her head, caging her short frame against mine, and move in to kiss her. Our lips meet and it is a frantic kiss. She grabs the hem of my shirt while I suck on her bottom lip until she moans, reaching under the hem to rub any part of my skin she can get her hands on. I feel myself lengthen in my jeans as she presses her center to me and rubs her hand up and down my chest.

I feel her tongue press against mine, and I kiss her back as ferociously as she kisses me. We are a jumble of hands and tongues and lips, unable to stop. I move my hands from beside her face to reach around and grab her hips, picking her up and letting her wrap her legs around me. She lets out a loud groan as her hips line up with mine, and she feels my cock press against her.

"Theo, oh my God," she moans out as I nip and suck at her neck.

I open my mouth to tell her how damn beautiful she is and how I want to see what she looks like when she comes. But all of a sudden we are interrupted by her cell phone ringing loudly from her pocket. She looks annoyed, but reaches to grab it. I sit her down so she can get to it more easily, and go to take a step back. When I do, she steps closer to me as if she isn't ready for the distance while she answers the call.

"Hey, Hannah. What's up?" she asks calmly, running her hand up and down my arm as she talks like she isn't driving me fucking crazy. I can't hear what she's saying, but she lets out a small laugh. "Yes we're coming, and I'll grab an extra pair of work gloves. See you in a sec," she says before hanging up and putting her phone back in her pocket.

"Come on. We gotta go," she says with a wink.

What. The. Fuck.

As we load up the rolls of fencing and barbed wire in silence, all I can think is what the hell just happened.

There is no way I am anywhere close to good enough for this girl. The more she gets to know me, the clearer that will become. She is going to come to her senses sooner or later. What happened to us being just friends?

We get into the truck and I'm about to shift it into drive when Caroline leans over and puts her hand on my leg. "Easy cowboy." She swoops in and presses a quick peck to my cheek before saying, "So, what do you say we go fix this fence?"

CHAPTER NINETEEN
CAROLINE

Oh my GOD. What the hell is happening?

We arrive back down at the fence and set to work fixing the gaping hole. We work together to cut off the old wire that was completely trampled by the cattle and throw it into the bed of the truck. Once that's done, Hannah holds up the new wire while Theo makes quick work of cutting it to the proper size and snipping it with the wire cutters. Margaret hands me the ties we're using to hold up the replacement fence until we can help Hannah figure out a more permanent solution.

We work in silence, ensuring that the new wire is secured well enough to keep the curious calves in and finish as the sun is slipping behind the horizon.

When we finish, Hannah breaks the silence, "Thanks. I really don't know what I would do without y'all. I'm sorry this craziness interrupted your evening. I know the whole damn fence needs to be replaced, but the last quote I got was outrageous. They said it would be twenty thousand dollars to fix it all. There's no way I can pay for it right now."

I open my mouth to comfort my best friend, when Theo pipes up, "Who were you gonna use?"

"Uhhh, I talked to Ray in town. He's a nice guy, but everything is just so expensive right now," Hannah says, looking a bit bewildered.

Theo just gives a silent nod while turning back to the truck loading up the remaining supplies. Hannah turns back to us saying, "Okay, but really. Y'all are the best. Margaritas on me this weekend at Boot Scooters. Now, let's grab some dinner. After today, I need a beer or-"

She stops talking and squints toward the animal pen on the other side of the driveway before cursing loudly. "Fuck. Little son of a bitch. Leroy get your hairy little ass back in that fence!"

Margaret looks bewildered, and I finally burst into laughter. "Looks like Leroy is in trouble again. Let's go," I tell her, and I notice Theo following us also.

We make our way over to the pen Hannah's grandfather had built close to the back door of the house. I swear it's no wonder Leroy thinks he's a dog. His pen is complete with a small water trough, a "pig house" with lots of hay, and a dog bowl with "Leroy" embossed into the side. I am pretty sure if Hannah thought she could house train him, she would let him live inside. She even had a collar custom made so that she can walk him on a leash. I note where Leroy bent back the pen to make his getaway. Hannah chases him as he makes his way to a mud pit across the field. I see his leash lying up on the porch, so I hurry to grab it before turning back to Margaret and Theo, who both look completely confused.

"Come on guys, we have a pig to catch," I tell them, thankful I wore my junky tennis shoes before starting to run across the grass in the direction of Hannah and Leroy. I hear Margaret laughing as she and Theo join me in our sprint towards the pig. When I reach Hannah, she is ankle deep in the mud. I drop the leash beside the pit and charge in after her.

"Leroy, come here little piggy," she yells before reaching out to get him. Instead, he dodges her advances, and Hannah loses her balance, falling into the mud. The animal then turns to me, and I swear the booger winks at me before charging at me.

"I got it," I holler as I dive to grab him, but the mud covering his large body makes him impossible to hold onto. I collapse into the mud and laugh loudly as Hannah and I both fight to regain our footing. I look up expecting Margaret and Theo to be standing at the foot of the hole watching us, but I'm surprised to see they both made the trek into the mud as well.

Theo looks determined to make sure Leroy doesn't slip by him, and he assumes a football-like defensive stance. "Oh you aren't gonna get past me big guy," he says.

As Margaret makes her way to Hannah and me, the three of us dissolve into a fit of giggles. "Here let me help you," she says, holding out her hands to help us up. We each take one, and Hannah and I look at each other before pulling her down into the mud with us. At the same time, Theo charges at the pig, who has decided that this is a fabulous game of chase. Theo gets his arms around Leroy but is unprepared for how incredibly heavy the animal is. Leroy wiggles out of his hold, and Theo joins us in the mud pit. The three of us look at each other before bursting into laughter again.

"Thought he wasn't getting past you," Margaret taunts her brother. She grabs a handful of mud and lobs it at him, hitting him squarely in the chest.

Theo looks at the place where she hit him and back at her with a frown on his face. "The hell was that for?" he asks.

"Just because I can. Loosen up brother," she responds, slinging another handful of mud in his direction. Leroy has started rolling in the wet dirt, and we have all forgotten about our quest to capture him.

The sun has set, and I can mostly see the outlines of my friends in the dark. However, I don't miss the quick malicious smirk that touches his lips before he grabs two handfuls of dirt and lobs it back at his sister. Unfortunately for him, he misses thanks to the moonlight, and ends up hitting Hannah in the face.

"What the fuck?" she screams before deciding to forego the handfuls of mud and launching herself directly at him. She misses and once again skitters into the mud where Leroy comes over to check on her, rooting his snout into the crease of her chin. She lets out a laugh before grabbing another handful of dirt and lobbing it at me. After that, we are all a mess of limbs and mud, chasing each other in the darkness and laughing as we take turns slipping and falling. By the time we call it quits, Leroy has fallen asleep in the mud and the four of us are completely coated.

Hannah leans down to Leroy, attaching his leash and gently petting him to wake him from his slumber. Once he is secured, she turns back and smiles before saying, "See I told you. Brighter days."

After Hannah puts Leroy in his cage and blocks off his escape route, she and Margaret go inside to find some towels while Theo and I make our way over to the water hose. There's no way we can drive home covered in mud, so I turn on the spigot and allow the cold water to run over my muddy skin.

Without giving it much thought, I whip off my shirt, knowing there's no way I'll get the mud out without a good soak. I feel my nipples harden as the frigid water runs down my body, and I see Theo's gaze darken as he looks down at my chest where my thin, white sports bra is not hiding much of anything. Whoops.

"Damn," he growls, and with that, I saunter over to where he is standing watching me and grip his shirt. Whipping it over his head and catching him off guard, I admire his chiseled abs and tanned skin.

I graze my fingers over his chest and skim my lips lightly across his before turning the cold water on him without warning.

As Theo snaps out of his daze, he lets out a stunned shout as the water hits his chest before moving to grab the hose from my grasp. He turns it on me and holds it over my head while I scream and try to climb my way up his tall body to regain control of the water he's holding out of my reach. We are both slick with water and mud, and neither of us can hide the giggles coming out of us as we wrestle.

After a minute of wrestling and feeling me rub against him, Theo mutters, "Fuck this." With that, he throws the water hose on the ground and pins me against Hannah's farmhouse. I feel the cold water hitting my feet, but I ignore it as I wrap my leg around his large frame to drag him closer.

We are both frantic between the playful tension of the water fight and the interrupted moment in the hay barn. He runs his hands over my hips and gently grinds against me, his cock very evidently straining against the jeans he's still wearing. I let out a low moan of desire, and fight to remind myself that Hannah and Margaret will be back any moment.

Theo seems to read my mind because he attacks my mouth with one more slow kiss before pulling back and whispers, "Swear to God, Sunshine, if I ever get you alone, we're not stopping until you're begging for it and screaming my name." With that, he steps back and grabs the water hose right as Margaret and Hannah make their way outside with their arms full of old towels.

Damn. It looks like I've found something to fantasize about tonight.

CHAPTER TWENTY
THEO

I feel like a walking zombie on Wednesday as I try to make it through the day. I'd never managed to find sleep last night after taking three showers to get all of the damn mud out of my hair. Every time I'd start to doze off, I began thinking about the kiss Caroline and I had shared. I have never met a woman I wanted more than I want her. I'm a selfish bastard, but even I know I'll never be good enough to have her.

I'd joked around calling her Sunshine this weekend, but the more time I spent with her the more I realized it was yet another reason that I should stay away. The nickname was a reminder that eventually, the darkness inside of me would always overtake her light. Just like the sun always slips under the horizon, she would eventually slip away from me too. I've been burned by losing the people I loved enough for plenty of lifetimes, and I didn't know if I could survive another round.

I manage to keep my eyes open at work as I tackle paperwork, feeling grateful football practice has been canceled thanks to a mandatory faculty meeting for the other coaches. I agreed last week to meet the mayor for a drink at Maracas, and with any luck, I should be able to be in bed in a few hours.

Around three o'clock I am sitting at my desk working when I hear music blasting. Needing a break from the monotony, I stand from my desk and walk through the station, looking for the source of the noise. As I walk into the kitchen, I see Zach and a couple of the younger guys leaning over a cell phone and laughing.

"What are y'all up to?" I ask, unable to hide my curiosity.

The boys all straighten and turn to me, before looking at each other as if they're trying to decide who is going to explain their odd behavior.

Finally, Zach laughs and says, "Afternoon, Chief. We are just working on our next post."

"Post?" I ask and I know everyone in the room hears the confusion in my voice.

"Well, yeah. You know, for TikTok or Instagram? We started our accounts when Huey was here, and we're trying to figure out how to keep it going without him. We have over five hundred thousand followers, but most of those were because even the internet became obsessed with Huey. We would film him talking about fire safety or trying new recipes in the kitchen and post them. We even turned his recipes into a cookbook and sold it as a fundraiser for the station. By the end, we sold over ten thousand cookbooks last year. But without Huey, all we know how to make are thirst traps and scrambled eggs."

The boys grunt in agreement and I just shake my head. "So, what did y'all post last?" I ask, fighting to keep the amusement out of my voice.

Zach turns the phone around and I see a video of him and two of the other men at the station dancing to "Pony" by Ginuwine. The performance is pretty tame but I shake my head at their thrusting and ab shots. I take the phone and click on the comment section to see comments are flooded already with women asking about their next "show" and their availability for upcoming bachelorette parties.

I shake my head at the men and grunt, "Well, I think they think we're a strip club, gentlemen."

"What?" Zach asks, his eyes widening in shock.

After reading the comments he lets out a groan and rubs his hand over his face. "Not quite the image we were going for."

"I have to agree with you there. Let me talk to my sister and see if she's willing to help with recipes once she gets her bakery going. For now, maybe press pause on the posts," I say with a small grin.

The other gentlemen laugh before saying, "Got it, Chief." I nod at them and head back to my office shaking my head.

I have to say, there's truly never a dull moment in this little town.

AFTER FIVE O'CLOCK HITS, I grab my bag and make my way to my truck. I make the quick drive over to Maracas and throw the truck in park. The restaurant looks like it could use some updates, but the parking lot is overflowing. It's clear they aren't hurting for customers.

I walk through the bright green front door and take in the yellow and blue walls. There are neon signs everywhere, and all the tables are already packed. I scan the room looking for Brian, and I find him sitting in a corner with an older man sitting across from him.

I blow out a breath and make my way over to his table, unsure what to do. I am not in the mood to get chewed out by another local that feels the need to call me an asshole. As I get closer, Brian notices me and waves me over. He stands to shake my hand before saying, "Hey, Theo. Welcome. I was waiting for you when Huey found me and needed to talk about the mentor program. You don't mind if he joins us, do you?"

Damn it. So this is the guy I talked shit about. Great. This shouldn't be awkward.

Left with no other option, I stick my hand out and shake his. "Theo Johnson," I mumble under my breath, preparing for him to have some words for the way I talked about him last week.

Instead, the old man's face breaks into a wide grin. "Huey Smith. Well, son, I gotta say, you know how to make an impression in this town don't ya," he says, letting out a loud laugh.

I blink at him, unsure of what to say until he pats the seat beside him and says, "Come on and have a seat. I know this town can be a bunch of assholes when they want to be, but we're good. I'm not saying you couldn't have maybe handled the school situation a little more discreetly, and yeah you were an asshole. But I can also admit you weren't wrong. There's a reason I decided to retire. I knew I was getting too complacent. So, what do you say we have a beer and put all this shit behind us."

Across the table, Brian is fighting a smile, so I glare at him before sitting down and nodding at Huey. The waitress comes over, and I order a beer while trying to ignore the fact that half of Springside is staring at our table.

"So, Theo, Brian told me you bought the old Wilkerson property. That's a whole lot of land. Are you planning on purchasing any livestock or do you have other plans for the property?" Huey asks me before taking a long swig of his Busch Light.

Brain lets out a laugh before adding?, "Yeah I was curious about that too. Mrs. Sally was telling everyone in town yesterday that you bought the land to build a mega mall because you want to destroy the town's economy. I swear that woman has watched one too many Hallmark Christmas specials. Any business ventures I should know about?"

Huey lets out a gruff bark of laughter that once again

attracts the eyes of everyone in Maracas. "That damn woman is always so full of shit."

I blow out a breath before mumbling, "Great. Damn it. That woman completely hates me. But no, the mega mall rumors are definitely not true. I am really considering getting some animals of my own though."

Brian responds quickly, "Oh yeah? I heard you were a master in the art of pig capturing."

I glare at him in confusion before it clicks what he could possibly be talking about. "How the fuck do you know about that?" I ask, shaking my head.

Brian lets out a laugh and says, "Apparently your sister was talking to someone on the phone at the Piggly Wiggly today. She told them the story while standing in the produce section, and Mrs. Sarah Beth overheard. She sent it out to the STS so it's common knowledge now. Pretty sure the subject was 'Asshole Fire Chief Tries to Trample Beloved Pet Pig.'"

I blink at him. "The hell is the STS?" I ask incredulously.

Huey and Brian break into yet another round of laughter at my expense before Huey explains, "Damn kid. You have a lot to learn about this town. STS stands for Small Talk of Springside. It's an email chain that a bunch of the old ladies in town swear by. It started as a Sunday school class prayer chain and eventually, the gossip overtook the prayer requests. Now anytime one of the ladies hears a piece of small talk, they send it out to the group."

Brian nods, "Yeah, how do you think so many people heard about the fire drill incident? Apparently, the Wi-Fi all over town moved slower than normal last week because everyone was trying to get in on the drama."

I shake my head. "This fuckin' town," I mumble under my breath. "But anyway, yes I am thinking about getting some animals. I have been looking around online trying to find some cows and horses to start, but I haven't found anything yet."

Huey nods his head. "Gotcha. If you're interested I'll make some calls for you tomorrow."

Damn. This man really is as nice as everyone has said. "Thanks, I'd appreciate that," I respond with a nod.

Huey nods before taking a sip of his whiskey. He returns the glass back to the table and grabs his menu saying, "Alright gentlemen, let's eat."

CHAPTER TWENTY-ONE
CAROLINE

Thursday morning rolls around and by the time I walk into the high school, I am feeling like I should have stayed in bed. I slept through my alarm, and when I went to put on my favorite dress, it wouldn't zip. Because of my frantic morning, I didn't have a chance to grab my coffee again, and I am praying I left an energy drink in my classroom refrigerator.

Part of the reason I'd overslept was that I had tossed and turned thinking about Michael returning to school today. I know I need to try to give him a clean slate, but the thought of dealing with another outburst like last week fills me with dread. I send up a silent prayer that today will go smoothly as I unlock my door and set to work making sure everything is ready for the day.

After running quickly through my morning routine, I reach into my classroom refrigerator and pull out a creamsicle flavored energy drink. I pop the tab and take a few sips at my desk trying to prepare myself for the chaos of the day. I hear my phone vibrate in my bag and grab it out, noticing the group chat is off to an early start today.

Hannah: Sending you hugs today, Caroline. If you need backup just holler. You got this!

Margaret: The kid comes back today right?

Hannah: Yep

Margaret: Oh dear. I'm baking cookies. Sending you love, Caroline! Do y'all want to come over for dinner tonight. Theo has plans, and I hate cooking for one!

Hannah: Hell yes!

Me: Thanks guys. It's gonna be fine! And I'm down for dinner! Just let us know what to bring!

Margaret: Yourself! I have some recipes to test. Just come whenever you're ready!

The bell signaling the start of the school day rings loudly, so I throw my phone in my desk drawer and grab my energy drink before making my way to my spot outside the door to welcome students in.

"Good morning! Happy Thursday! Let's take that hood off before you go in please, Josh. Hey guys," I say as several of my students trickle into my room.

"Good morning Miss Caroline," one of my students named Ty says as he stops in front of the door. "How are you this morning?"

"I'm good, Ty. How are you?" I ask him, trying to make sure the smile stays firmly on my face.

"I'm okay. I just wanted to check on you. We all know Michael is supposed to come back today," he says, letting the end of the sentence hang in the air like he's waiting for me to comment.

"Now Ty, you know I can't discuss another student with you," I respond, knowing what the six-foot-two linebacker is about to say.

"I know Miss Caroline, and I don't want any trouble. Coach would have my as-, uh butt. But I just wanted you to know we've got your back," he says with sincerity in his eyes.

"I appreciate that Ty. But I am gonna be fine!" I tell him, putting on a wide smile.

"I know. But we're all worried. He's seemed off and we don't want anyone to get hurt," Ty says sheepishly before walking into my room and sitting at his desk. I don't have assigned seating as long as my classes behave, and I notice that the athletes who have sat together since we started school have spread out throughout the room.

I feel a bit of anxiety zip through me since everyone seems on edge today, but I try to push it aside. It's all gonna be fine. Michael's just a kid that made a mistake, right? I've made mistakes. It doesn't define him and today's a better day.

My inner pep talk is interrupted by the sound of a locker slamming across the hall. I look over and see Michael making his way towards my room. He's staring at me and his face turns into a menacing sneer the closer he comes down the hall.

"Good morning, Michael," I say, plastering a smile on my face.

"Whatever," he grunts as he walks past me and slides into one of the desks by the door.

I blow out a breath and walk back into my room. I am introducing Transcendentalism with a mini escape room today, and it has become one of my favorite activities of the year. I stayed late yesterday to make sure all of the activities were correctly set up throughout the room and printed the digital code sheets my students would need to participate. I grab them off my back shelf before making my way to the podium to introduce the activity.

"Alright, good morning guys. I told you we were going to start our Transcendentalism activity today. I have ten stations set up around the room and your job is to work through all of them. You can use your Chromebooks if you get stuck, and we will discuss everything you learned tomorrow. You can break into groups or work on your own. The first three people to 'escape' get bonus points. You'll turn in your work today for a minor grade. You can start," I tell them after ensuring they all have a code sheet.

I watch as most of my students jump out of their desks and get to work. I walk around for the first few minutes checking on their progress before realizing that Michael is still sitting at his desk glaring at me.

A chill runs through me briefly before I shake it off and make my way over to his desk. I can instantly feel a shift in the room as everyone stops moving to watch the interaction. I notice some of the boys seem to inch a bit closer to me as I walk across the room.

"Hey Michael, I need you to participate today. The activity is a grade and I don't want you to fall behind," I say through a smile once I am beside his desk. I know the best way to handle the situation is to try to diffuse it, so I continue smiling and keep my body posture as relaxed as possible.

"Nope," he says with his arms crossed across his chest.

"Well I will need you to sign a refusal to work paper if you don't want to submit it, and I'll have to notify a parent. That's the county policy. Is that okay with you?" I say quietly enough to keep the rest of the class from hearing.

"I don't give a shit what you need!" Michael yells loudly as his eyes blaze with anger. "Take your goddamn paperwork and your stupid as fuck activity and choke on it."

I blow out a breath and calm myself before responding.

"Michael, I-" I say before he jumps out of his desk and gets in my face. I feel several of my students start to make their way towards us, but I point at them to stay where they are without taking my eyes off Michael.

"Why are you such a fucking bitch?" Michael asks. "You sit up here on your damn high horse with a fucking smile on your face like life is rainbows and butterflies while you drone on about dead dudes and act like any of this shit matters."

"Michael, I understand you're upset, but I need you to calm down. You are not going to speak to me like this," I say as calmly as I can.

"Fuck that!" he yells loudly. "I'll save you the trouble of calling the office. I am getting the hell out of here!"

With that Michael turns around and heads towards the door. He stops beside it and kicks over my rolling cart I keep stocked with paper and pencils for students to grab. He pushes open the door and slams it so hard I am surprised the window doesn't break.

"Miss Tyler, are you okay? Do you want us to go after him?" Ty asks me, anger shining in his eyes.

"Absolutely not. Y'all get to work. I need to call the office, and I'll be there to help you as soon as I am finished," I respond as I try to keep my voice even and calm.

I hear a chorus of "Yes ma'am" as I make my way to my classroom phone to call Mrs. Bess and pretend like I don't notice the way my hand is shaking.

AFTER NOTIFYING the administrators about the incident this morning, I did a quick write-up of the event to keep for my records and try to focus on my classes. Once again, by second period the news has spread throughout the school, and I hear my phone buzz as I run through the attendance. After making sure that the class understands the activity, I open the drawer where I threw my phone and quickly check my messages.

> Hannah: WTF. Caroline, are you okay? My kids just told me and one of them showed a Snapchat video someone recorded. Do you need anything?

> Margaret: Wait someone fill me in. What happened?!

> Hannah: The kid got in Caroline's face and cussed her out after he refused to work. Then he trashed her student cart.

> Margaret: Oh my GOODNESS! Caroline, what do you need? Are you alright? What can we do?

> Hannah: I've never seen anything like it. Surely that's his last strike right?

> Margaret: I would really hope so.

I take a deep breath before responding to their messages. Bless my sweet friends. I can feel their concern through the phone and try to settle my nerves.

> Me: Hey girls. I'm good. It's gonna be okay. I don't know what's gonna happen.

> Margaret: I am so sorry girlie. I am whipping up lots of comfort food tonight. I think you could use it.

I smile at the message from her, realizing that while we've barely known her for two weeks. Margaret has become a big part of our circle, and I am really not sad about it. I hear my phone buzz again and check it expecting a message from Hannah. Instead, I see a number I don't have saved on my phone. I go to delete it, but I instantly stop when I see Theo's name in the first line.

Theo: Hey Caroline. It's Theo. I just heard some of the guys at the station talking about your morning. I pestered Margaret for your phone number because I wanted to check on you. Are you okay?

Me: I am good. Thank you so much for checking on me. And remind me to tell Margaret thank you :)

Theo: I will check on you again after school Miss Tyler.

Me: I look forward to that, Mr. Johnson. Talk to you soon!

I drop my phone back into the desk and take a sip of my drink before making my way back over to my students. This morning might have been a shitshow, but the texts I just got seemed to have settled me. Maybe this day won't turn out to be that bad after all.

CHAPTER TWENTY-TWO
THEO

Halfway through Thursday morning, I was working on making sure our equipment was up to date when I heard a few of the guys talking about an incident in Caroline's classroom. That was two hours ago, and I haven't been able to focus on working since. I thought I'd feel a bit more settled after Margaret broke down and sent me Caroline's number, but instead, I am feeling more anxious. I know she said she was fine, but is she really? I've become a pro at ignoring my issues, but I don't want the light I see in Caroline to be extinguished the way mine has.

My thoughts of Caroline are cut short by the screech of the fire alarm in the station. My radio blares with the call for a house fire. I jump to my feet and feel the familiar shot of adrenaline hit my system. It's been two weeks since I started working in Springside, and this is the first emergency call I've heard come in. Most of the time, the calls we receive are for medical backup and fallen trees. I run over to my truck as Zach and a few of the other firemen jump into the fire engine. Throwing the truck into gear, I follow the fire truck as it weaves through the roads of Springside with the sirens blasting.

After five minutes of frantically racing through the country roads, the firetruck slows to a stop at a small farm on the outskirts of town. I look around quickly for signs of smoke or distress, but I don't see anything.

"This is Miss Mabel's house," Zach explains to all of us. "She lives alone and is in her seventies. The call center said she called in and reported smoke in her house."

Zach may be the youngest guy at the station, but he knows this community better than anyone. I appreciate him clueing me on what we are walking into. I nod in acknowledgment, and we quickly make our way to the door. It's obvious the home was once a beautiful white cottage with a lilac door, but time has not been kind to the farmhouse. The paint is chipped and some of the wood is beginning to show through along with some obvious cracks in one of the windows. Weeds have started to creep up the house in addition to completely taking over the yard. The grass in the yard is up to the middle of my knee, and the walkway to the door is so uneven it's almost impossible to walk on.

"Miss Mabel?" Zach yells loudly as he bangs on the door. I hear a bit of shuffling inside, and a second later an elderly woman with a kind smile opens the door.

"Oh my goodness, Zach! Samuel! Derrik!" Miss Mabel responds, naming each of the men from the station. "Please come in! I was in here cooking lunch and saw smoke from behind the oven. I got worried so I thought it was best to call it in," the elderly woman explains as we make our way to the kitchen.

I notice that there are casseroles, vegetables, salad, and a pound cake on the counter as we walk over to the oven. Zach and Derrik make quick work of pulling the oven out from the counter so that we can look behind it. There is no sign of smoke, and everything looks normal. The guys talk quietly making sure they haven't missed anything while I notice Miss

Mabel grabbing out plates from the cabinet before grabbing some silverware.

After the guys have checked the wiring to the outlet, Zach stands and walks over to Miss Mabel. "Miss Mabel, we weren't able to find anything. Are you sure it came from behind the oven?" he asked the woman who was now filling cups with ice and grabbing a pitcher of sweet tea out of the fridge.

"Oh, I could have sworn I saw something. But oh well, you know these old eyes. Either way, y'all come eat. I've fixed enough poppy seed chicken, noodles, broccoli, salad, and corn-bread for everyone. Y'all grab a plate for the inconvenience."

I feel my temper start to rise as I open my mouth. "Miss Mabel, we can't stay here and eat. Fire safety is not something to play with. We thought you were in danger!"

Miss Mabel's eyes widen, and I think she's about to burst into tears. "Oh, I am so sorry. I wasn't trying to upset anyone!" Her old hands start to shake, and I immediately feel like the world's biggest asshole.

Before I can say anything, Zach is by Miss Mabel's side and leads her over to a chair at the table. "It's okay Miss Mabel. You're okay. You have a seat and Derrik over there will bring you a plate, okay?" Zach makes eye contact with Derrik who nods and immediately sets to work fixing Miss Mabel a plate. "Chief Johnson, can I speak to you for a minute?" Zach asks after making sure that Miss Mabel has calmed down.

I jerk my head at a loss of what to say. Once again, I couldn't keep my mouth closed and I made myself seem like a jerk. I step outside the kitchen behind Zach who turns around looking sheepish.

"Listen Chief, I don't mean any disrespect, but I think you need to know the whole story. Miss Mabel lost her husband this time last year to cancer. They were high school sweethearts and had spent the last sixty-two years together in this house. Her kids are being little shits and refusing to help take care of it. They want her to go into an assisted living home in Hunts-ville, but she says this house is all she has left of Mr. Ralph.

"I know the way she handled it was wrong, and we should talk to her about that. But I do think she's just really lonely. Plus I think having lunch with her could help your image. Yelling at old ladies isn't really the way to go about winning the town over you know?" he says, looking a bit uncomfortable. "We have our radios, so if there's an emergency we can leave."

I look at him as he shifts from foot to foot. He looks nervous, like he's worried I am going to chew him out, but I realize he's right. "Okay, you're right. I need to apologize to her anyway. Hell, this is gonna be bad if it hits the STS," I tell him. Zach lets out a laugh, and we make our way back to the kitchen where Miss Mabel is talking away to Derrik and Samuel.

"Hey, Miss Mabel," I say, making my way over to the elderly woman and bending down so that I am level with her. "I am really sorry for getting frustrated with you. We got off on the wrong foot. It's something I am working on. If you still want us to stay, we would be honored."

Miss Mabel smiles at me before saying, "Chief Johnson right?" I nod at her, and she laughs. "Oh, I've heard all about you. What an entrance to Springside you made! I appreciate the apology. You were right, I shouldn't have made it sound like an emergency. I am sorry, I'm just so damned lonely. I'd love for you to stay so I can find out if you are really as horrible as everyone seems to think," Miss Mabel says as she lets out a loud laugh.

I smile awkwardly before turning back to the men. "Well you heard Miss Mabel, let's eat gentlemen."

CHAPTER TWENTY-THREE
THEO

By four o'clock, I am still stuffed from the lunch Miss Mabel cooked as I pull up to the football field where the team is getting ready to start practice.

It had turned into a nice afternoon, despite her deception in getting us there. Her cooking was incredible, and I couldn't help but smile as she told us stories about her late husband. He sounded like a character, always getting into more than he could handle around the farm and having to call her for help. She swears he did it on purpose so that she would have to spend time with him, but the smile on her face told me she'd never minded much. Before we'd left, Zach had given Miss Mabel his cell number and promised to come take care of her yard next week. My initial irritation at the woman had completely dissipated, and I had to admit, it felt good to not be seen as the villain in Springside.

I am halfway to the field when my phone rings. I glance at it quickly and see a number I don't have saved. I would normally let it go to voicemail, but since I don't have many numbers in town I slide to answer it just in case. "Hello," I say leaning against the entrance to the football stadium.

"Theo? This is Huey. I got Brian to send me your number, I hope that's okay. How are you?" the familiar voice explains over the phone.

"I'm good. How are you?" I say back.

"Good as gold. I heard you had quite the afternoon with Miss Mabel," Huey says and I don't miss the hint of laughter in his voice.

I let out a small laugh and sigh. "What do you mean you heard? It's barely been two hours since I left her house."

"Well, son that may be true but Miss Mabel is best friends with Mrs. Sarah Beth. Remember we told you Mrs. Sarah Beth runs the STS. Y'all weren't out of the driveway before Miss Mabel called her to tell her all about her afternoon with the fire chief. Good news is she sang your praises and said that even though you almost made her cry you were a good man. It all went out to the chain about an hour ago. I don't know that you're completely out of the dog house with the town yet, but I'd say today was a good start," Huey tells me, and I can tell he is trying to keep the laughter out of his voice.

"This damn town," I mumble under my breath as I shake my head.

Huey laughs again before saying, "Anyway, that's not why I called you. I made some calls for you on the animal front. Mr. Willy owns a farm out on Highway 137, and he is looking to downsize since he's gotten older. I talked to him this morning, and after convincing him that you're not as bad as Mrs. Sally has made you out to be, he said he'd be interested in talking to you. I am going to text you his number, and he said to call sometime this weekend."

I swallow, suddenly feeling a bit uncomfortable. It's clear my initial response to Huey was completely wrong, and I can see why he is so beloved by the town. Shaking away my discomfort I say, "Oh, awesome. Thank you, Huey. I really appreciate it."

"Not a problem, Theo. If I hear anything else I will let you know. Have a good afternoon," Huey says before disconnecting the call.

Slipping my phone back into my pocket, I make my way to the other coaches standing on the sideline while the boys stretch on the field. "Hey, Theo," Will says before returning to his conversation about next week's game against Saddle Ridge. The town was so close that this game had become a pretty big rivalry over the years. "Just a reminder, y'all are welcome to come over tonight. I'm going back over their film from last year, and I'll order pizza. Theo, how are the wide receivers looking?"

"Pretty good. Wesley and Bobby are making really good progress. I think TJ and Ty will be ready too after I run some more footwork drills with them. Their routes are much cleaner and faster than when we started," I say confidently. Will nods at me and I look over to the boys who are getting ready to run through the plays for the day before we break off into groups to run drills.

A flash of brown catches my eye from the gate at the end zone furthest from me, and after looking closer I realize Caroline is leading her squad onto the turf. About that time, Will calls the team over and says, "Okay gentlemen, we're gonna run through the new plays we introduced earlier this week. I want to make sure everyone knows what to do. Also, the cheerleaders have asked to practice on the sidelines to make sure they are ready for the game next week. We are going to stay out of their way, and if any of you cause them any issues your ass will be running until you throw up, clear?"

A chorus of "Yes, sir" and "Yes, Coach" comes from the boys and Will claps his hands. "Perfect, alright gentlemen, let's get to work. We're gonna start today with Navy-76." The players jump into action lining up in the play that Will had introduced on Monday. I had to admit that Will is a talented coach, and I can see how he got the job over men twice his age. The players respect him, and the plays he creates have a real chance at securing us a state championship this year. After looking over a bit of their film from last year it seems like he always manages to do the opposite of what is expected, and despite my initial reluctance in coaching the team, I am happy I've been given a chance to be a part of this.

The center snaps the ball to the quarterback, and Wesley runs the slant route we've been perfecting over the last week. The quarterback, a junior named Blake, rares back and throws a perfect spiral to Wesley who catches it and sprints to the end zone, dodging three defenders on the way in. I let out a loud whoop and run the length of the field to Wesley, who is hollering and waving the ball around. I slap his helmet and he turns to give me a high-five. I let out a loud cheer again, before I take a breath and turn to see the rest of the team and the cheer-leaders standing there watching our interaction.

"I'll be damned, Coach J can do something other than scowl," Bobby, one of my other wide receivers, jokes. Everyone goes still for a moment before I break out into a laugh, and Will brings the team over.

"Okay guys, that is what I want to see! Wesley, hell of a catch! Coach Johnson said you were working hard at drills and that work is showing off. Let's run it a few more times." Will says, and all of the boys move to take their positions.

As I watch the boys alternate through to the second string, I feel my phone vibrate in my pocket. I pull it out and try to keep from smiling when I see Caroline's name on my screen.

> Caroline: Well what do you know? I didn't know the grumpy firefighter could smile like that.

> Me: Oh I don't know about that. I was smiling pretty good in that hay barn.

Caroline: Chief Johnson, you're making me blush.

Me: I can think of some other ways to make you do that…

Caroline: Can you really? Interested in sharing any of them?

Me: I think I would rather show you.

Caroline: Hmmm I think I would like that too.

I look over to where the cheerleaders are running through cheers on the sideline and see Caroline smiling at me. I smirk at her and she grins broadly before turning back to Hannah. She and Hannah laugh loudly at something Caroline says and I watch as she pulls her phone back out and typing something quickly before I feel my phone buzz again.

Caroline: I guess not everything in Springside is as bad as you thought huh?

Shaking my head and fighting a smile I type back.

Me: Yeah, Sunshine. I think I might have found a few things I like a lot more than I planned.

And damn if that wasn't the truth.

CHAPTER TWENTY-FOUR
CAROLINE

I know that I should be focused on the cheerleading practice happening in front of me, but all my brain can think about is the gorgeous man standing across the field smirking at me every time I look over. I call out for the girls to run through a few more chants before I make eye contact with Hannah.

"Girl, you look like you just got done reading something dirty," she whispers to me quietly.

I let out a small laugh before I respond. "Well girlfriend, I've read a whole lot of smut but the fire chief still has me blushing."

Hannah lets out a small squeal that has the girls stopping their cheer and looking up at us. "Sorry girls. Go ahead. Defense, Defense!"

I try to contain my smile while she turns back to me and gives me a knowing look. "You like him, don't you? Has anything happened yet?"

I stare at her for a minute before she pokes me in the side. "Oh my GOD!" she yells loudly. This time she attracts not only the attention of the squad but the football players and coaches who are all huddled up on the field, making them turn to look at us expectantly.

My face breaks into a bit of a blush but Hannah just looks around and yells, "Let's go Springside! Whooooo!" I break into a fit of giggles at her antics before making sure the teams are both going back to their practices before I answer her. I can feel Theo's eyes from across the field as they blaze into my skin and I wonder if he knows that we're talking about him.

"Okay, you can't tell anyone. The old ladies would have a field day buuuttttt," I start and let the word draw out to tease my best friend.

"Caroline if you don't tell me right now I am going to tell Mrs. Sally you have a crush on her husband, I swear to God!" Hannah loudly whispers, impatiently.

Laughing again, I say, "Okay, okay! There's no need for all of that! Well if you must know we miiiigggghhttt have kissed Tuesday when we went to grab the stuff for the fence."

"WHAT," Hannah screeches, once again attracting the attention of everyone inside the stadium.

I elbow her sharply in the side before I whisper, "One more outburst and I swear I am not telling you another thing until tonight!"

She shrugs her shoulders before saying, "Okay sorry! You can't just give me information like that and expect me to NOT react. I need you to tell me everything! You've been holding out on me!"

"I haven't meant to. We have just had a lot going on between your escape artist little piggy and all the school drama. But Hannah, I swear to God I've never felt anything like it. We were up in the hay barn and he pushed me against the hay bale. I thought our romance books were full of it when they described a kiss as being *devoured*, but he damn sure did it. I have never been so turned on in my life," I tell my best friend as I feel a blush spread across my cheeks.

"Hell yeah, girlfriend!" Hannah says somewhat quietly compared to her other outbursts. "You should ride that man like a horse! You are totally going to get to live out your cowboy fantasies with the fire chief!"

"I hope so, but I don't know. It could have been a one time thing. I haven't gotten to really talk to him about it," I say, trying to keep from getting my hopes up.

"Caroline, are you for real? That man is looking at you like you're a five-course meal and he hasn't eaten in weeks. I'm pretty sure he'll let you saddle him up," Hannah says quietly with a laugh.

I let out a chuckle at the thought before shrugging and saying, "I guess we'll see." I turn my attention back to the cheerleaders and shout to Maggie, "Hey, is that all of the chants we needed to go over?"

The captain looks up at me before replying, "Yes ma'am! Are you ready for us to run through our halftime cheer?"

I nod my head and say, "Let's do it, ladies!" I reach over to the bleachers beside me where the cheer signs for the performance are sitting and lean over the side of the railing to hand them to Maggie. She passes them out as the girls transition into their formation.

Once the stunt groups are set and the girls in the front have their signs ready, Maggie calls out, "Let's Go Blue!"

The rest of the squad joins in with "Springside, you know what to do!" as the stunt groups load in and press up to single base extensions. "Yell it out, Let's Go Blue!"

Hannah and I yell along with the squad as they continue through the cheer and take notes on any problems we may need to fix before next week. Overall, I am proud of their performance. All of the fliers look solid in the air, and the sign girls in the front are hitting their marks right on time. Once they finish and the stunts have cradled down to the ground, I smile widely at the girls standing in front of me. "Great job ladies. Let's work on making sure we don't lose our volume during the stunt transitions. Top girls, I know you have poms, but make sure you are still making those motions really sharp. Let's run it a few more times before we call it."

The team nods and gets set to run through the cheer again. After three more times, I bring everyone up to the bleachers to sit with Hannah and me. "Great practice today ladies. This is our last week without a game until December if the team plays as well as they should. I hope you are all ready to buckle down. Maggie, do we have a theme for the first pep rally?"

"Well Crestview's mascot is the Colts, so we were thinking about making it a cowgirl theme. We could do a line dance mashup with 'Cotton Eyed Joe' and 'Copperhead Road'. Plus bandanas and cowgirl hats will look so cute with our new uniform," Maggie replies.

Hannah looks at me and winks, knowing my mind immediately went to our conversation about Theo. I shake my head at her and turn my attention back to the squad. "That sounds great. Type me up a tentative schedule before Monday's practice so I can make sure that we are ready to go."

Maggie nods her head, and I run through the schedule for next week before saying, "Okay ladies, I think that's everything. Does anyone have any questions?"

One of the sophomores named Samantha raises her hand. "Okay Miss Caroline, don't kill me but why is the new fire chief staring at you? I am pretty sure he hasn't stopped looking at you since we got here."

The squad breaks out into a chorus of giggles before Sarah, one of the youngest members asks, "Yeah, is he your boooyyyff-frriiieennnddd?"

I manage not to laugh at their silly antics and bite my lip to compose myself. "Ladies, this is inappropriate. Chief Johnson and I are friends. He's a coach so the same rules will apply to him as Coach Will. If I hear any more of this, y'all will earn a whole practice of conditioning."

The girls laugh, remembering the time last year Hannah and I had gotten so sick of hearing the girls talk about how dreamy Coach Will was, we'd created a killer workout circuit. Between the burpees, sprints, planks, and mountain climbers, we hadn't heard much else about the coach.

"Okay, ladies. Good work today! We will see you on Monday! Have a good weekend!" I say as the girls huddle up to end practice. I make eye contact with Theo again across the field and a shiver of desire runs through me. I know I just told the girls he and I were friends, but the thoughts I am having about the man standing across from me are way more than friendly.

IT's close to seven that evening before I pull up in front of Theo and Margaret's farmhouse. I'd run home after practice to shower and change clothes, and it seemed like the weight of the day had decided to settle in over me. Between the confrontation with Michael this morning, a full day of teaching, practice, and the texts from Theo, I was feeling a bit overwhelmed. I couldn't help drying my hair and throwing on my favorite shorts even though Margaret had already said her brother wouldn't be home tonight.

I grab my phone out of my bag and shoot Theo a text before going inside.

Me: Having dinner at your house without you… Don't worry, I'll give Bear lots of kisses for you

Theo: Bear is such a little bastard. I can think of some better places for those lips of yours.

Me: Is that right? I can't imagine what you might be talking about.

Theo: If you're still there when I get home I'll show you.

Me: Yes sir ;)

Smiling to myself I throw my phone into my pocket and make my way inside. Bear meets me at the door and gives me a small tail wag when I bend down to pet the pup beside his ears. As I make my way into the house, I'm hit with the most incredible smells. I follow my nose into the kitchen and find Margaret with an apron on, pulling out a pan of her cookies from the oven. A large pan of chicken spaghetti sits on the counter, and there's a tray of garlic bread sitting beside it. My stomach growls as I take in the meal Margaret has pulled together.

"Hey, friend!" She takes her AirPods out of her ear and smiles at me. "Oh my God, it smells amazing in here," I tell her, snagging a piece of bread off the top of the pile.

Margaret gives me a wide smile before she responds, "Oh thanks, girl! I am so glad y'all could come. Theo is over at Will's watching film for next week, and I hate cooking for just me. Have a seat and I'll grab you a drink while we wait on Hannah." She turns and digs through the fridge before pulling out a bottle of peach Moscato. She pops the top and pours me a small glass before asking, "How are you holding up?"

I collapse onto the sofa that is on the other side of the bar, and Bear immediately jumps onto my lap and rests his large head on my leg. I blow out a breath and grab the glass Margaret's holding in my direction. "Girl, it's been a day. But I am okay! I just wish I could figure out how to help him," I tell her. I know without saying anything that she knows I am referring to Michael. "People are always telling teachers we can't save them all, and they are totally right. But I can't stop asking myself, what if I'm supposed to save this one?"

Margaret takes a sip of wine and says, "You know I haven't known you that long, but I am starting to think you have a way with broken things."

One glance in her direction clues me into the fact that we aren't talking about Michael anymore. "Margaret, I -" I start to say but she lays her hand over mine and interrupts me. The motion stops the mindless petting I was tracing across Bear's head, and the pup lets out an annoyed huff.

"I know. Theo has been the only family I've had for the last fourteen years, and the last few days with you it seems like he's finally living again. I can't tell you how much that means to me. But go easy on him for me, please. He has a really hard time letting people in. And I think you could be the one to remind him that hearts don't stay broken forever," she says. A stray tear has collected in her eye, but she smiles at me through her emotions. "And just remember no matter what happens with y'all, you still have to be my friend. This town is too damn small for any other option."

A small laugh bubbles out of my lips, and I squeeze the hand Margaret has over mine before responding, "Oh, I promise."

I lean over to hug her as Hannah walks through the door, "Shit, what'd I miss? You both look pretty damn depressed," she calls out grabbing the wine glass Margaret had left out for her.

"Oh, not much. Just talking about Theo," Margaret responds.

"Oh my God, did she tell you about the kiss?" Hannah yells.

Margaret looks like her eyes are going to pop out of her head before she screams, "Y'all KISSED?! Oh my GOD!" I look at her face for a hint of anger, but instead, she looks completely excited. "Yep, we're totally gonna be sisters-in-law," she says with a huge smile, and with that, we all dissolve into a fit of hysterical giggles.

Yep, I think tonight is just what I needed.

CHAPTER TWENTY-FIVE
THEO

Damn, Caroline and her flirty texts.

I hadn't been able to focus on another thing since my phone had lit up earlier. Our kiss this week has been on a constant loop in my brain, and seeing her at practice has done nothing but heighten my desire for her. I tried to focus on the film Will called us over to watch, but all I'd been able to think about was the way she responded to my touch.

As I pull into the driveway, I feel a shot of excitement run through me when I notice Caroline's car is still parked outside. I pull up beside her empty vehicle as I see Hannah walking towards hers. She stops at my window and waits for me to roll it down. "You hurt her, and I'll make sure they never find your body? She's my best friend and she deserves endless orgasms and a man that doesn't fuck around. Got it?"

I give her a nod before saying, "Yes ma'am." She walks off without another word, and I can't help but smile at Caroline's best friend. I know it isn't the most normal response to a death threat, but I like knowing that Caroline has someone who loves her so fiercely. I also make a mental note to not piss Hannah off because I am positive she wouldn't hesitate to carry out her threat.

I lock the door to my truck and make my way inside. Reaching the living room, I see Caroline sitting on the sofa with my dog in her lap. The little traitor has his head resting on her chest, and he's looking at her like she hung the damned moon. *I feel you, bud,* I think to myself. Caroline moves to fold the blanket she had thrown over her legs, trying not to disturb Bear as the end credits roll on screen to *Sweet Home Alabama*. Her back is to me, and I take a moment to watch her before my sister says, "Hey, Theo."

Caroline jumps slightly, and Bear lets out a frustrated huff before jumping onto the floor and collapsing. Without the additional ninety pounds of mutt, she's able to twist around and make eye contact with me. "Oh, hey Theo," she says with a smile.

"How was y'alls night?" I ask them, unable to take my eyes off the way Caroline's shorts hug her curves. She looks cozy enough to crawl straight into bed.

"Like anyone could have a bad night with Melanie Smooter," Caroline replies. "Thank you so much for dinner, Margaret. I still have to work in the morning so I should get going. I'll see you tomorrow afternoon for Boot Scooters right?"

My sister nods. "Yep, wouldn't miss it. Our DD and I will pick you up around seven?"

"Yep, sounds like a plan. See you then!" Caroline says before turning her attention to me like she's trying to decide what she should do.

"I'll walk you out," I say, not missing the way her eyes heat at my words. I hear my sister mumble under her breath something along the lines of "Of course you will", but I ignore her as I follow Caroline outside.

We make our way to her car in silence for a few moments before she says, "How was film night?"

"It was fine, but I must admit I was pretty damn distracted, Miss Tyler," I respond. By now, we are standing beside her car so I move in closer to her as she leans against the door.

"Oh really? That's terrible. What were you thinking about Chief Johnson? New fire safety protocols?" she asks, leaning into me.

I step closer, erasing the space between us before replying, "Not quite ma'am. I was actually thinking about pushing you against that hay bale again. But I thought next time we could see how much you like it when I kiss a different set of lips."

Even in the dark, I can see a small blush creep up her neck before she responds, "Oh is that right?"

I don't break eye contact when I respond, "Quite. I haven't been able to get the image of your pretty little legs wrapped around my face while I run my tongue up and down your slit until you moan my name loud enough for the neighbors to hear out of my head." I feel her breath catch as she pushes her body in closer to mine, so I continue, "I bet you'll sound so damn good when you come for me, Sunshine. Thinking about your breathy little moans has had me so hard I can't even think straight."

Caroline's lust-filled eyes blink up at me until she says, "Theo, I swear to God if you don't kiss me right now I'm gonna-" I don't give her time to finish her threat before I close the distance between us. I kiss her hard, reaching for her hips and maneuvering her until she's sitting on the side of her hood with her legs wrapped around my waist. Her fingers slip into my hair, and she gives it a tug causing me to let out a growl. I swear I didn't think it was possible for my cock to get harder than it was, but I'm proved wrong as she moans into my ear.

"Oh, my God," she whimpers in my ear as I lightly skim my fingers over her center through her shorts. "Theo, oh my, that feels so damn good."

I pull back slightly, running my hands up her sides before

running my thumbs over her breasts. I know if I don't stop this I'll end up taking her on the side of her car, and while my cock is certainly fond of the idea, I don't want to rush this and mess it up. "You're so beautiful. And while I would love nothing more than to kiss you all night, it's late and I'm really trying to do this right."

She smiles at me before leaning in and kissing me hard. After a few minutes, she pulls back and says, "Well, Cowboy you are full of surprises, but you're right. I'll see you tomorrow."

I nod and lean in to kiss her again. I'd meant for it to be a quick kiss, but this girl has destroyed every bit of my self-control. She tugs on my hair again while she nips at my neck. Feeling my last bit of restraint slipping, I wrap my hand around her throat and pull back so she's forced to look into my eyes before saying, "Caroline, you've got thirty seconds to get your pretty little ass in the car before I change my mind and haul you inside. But something tells me you don't want your new friend to hear you beg for my cock tonight."

Her eyes heat before she laughs. "Point well made. Goodnight, Theo," she says as I open the door and she sits in her car.

I lean down so I'm level with her, and say, "Goodnight. Sweet dreams." With that, I close the door and wave at her as she backs down the driveway. Yeah, like I'll be dreaming of anything other than her in my bed tonight.

By the time Friday afternoon rolls around, my cock is pissed and wishing I hadn't chosen last night to be a gentleman. After tossing and turning all night thinking about how good it would feel to sink into Caroline's tight pussy, I'd finally given up on sleep and went for a run around the time the sun was coming up. The farm property I purchased needs a lot of work, but I can see a ton of potential in the land. Something about the stillness of my new home makes me feel incredibly close to my family out here after all the summers we'd spent on my grand-father's ranch.

We had an uneventful day at the station, and after a quick shower and cup of coffee, I was getting ready to head out for the evening. Caroline texted me earlier to make sure I was still willing to serve as their driver, a result from our bet last week-end. I confirmed and had to admit I was looking forward to seeing her today.

Throwing on an old pair of jeans, a plain black shirt and grabbing my favorite hat, I walk out of my bedroom and down the stairs. Bear is sitting on the sofa, and I sit down beside the large lab. I reach out my hand to pet him but before I can touch his head, he stands and hops onto the floor. Taking a few steps away from me, he collapses into a ball on the rug and lets out an annoyed huff at me. I roll my eyes at his antics before muttering "asshole" at him under my breath.

After checking the time I shout upstairs to my sister, "Margaret, are you ready?"

I hear some shuffling before she screams back, "Yeah, one more minute!"

I turn the TV on and watch a few minutes of ESPN while I wait for my sister to be ready. The commentators are discussing the upcoming start of the college football season. Living in the South, football has always been unavoidable this time of year, but I don't feel the familiar twinge of grief I usually do when thinking about the sport. I guess it's a result of my work with the Saints, but instead of missing my brother, I feel a bit of the excitement he used to feel about this time of year.

About twenty minutes later, Margaret finally comes down-stairs dressed in jean shorts and an old George Strait concert tee. "Alright, Theo. Are you ready? We're gonna grab Caroline and Hannah at their houses and then head to Boot Scooters.

Sound okay?" she asks, sitting down to throw her cowgirl boots on.

"Yeah, that works for me. What's the bag for?" I ask, eyeing the overnight bag she has sitting beside her.

"I am going to stay at Hannah's tonight. I know she needs some help with some things around the farm, but she's too damn stubborn to ask. I asked her if I could stay over tonight, and I am going to figure out how to help her tomorrow," Margaret replies.

"Does Hannah know you're staging this intervention for her?" I ask shaking my head at my sister.

"Nope. I just told her I needed a sleepover and promised more muffins in the morning," Margaret says, reaching down and pulling out a bag of muffins she's tucked into her overnight bag.

That causes me to laugh before I ask, "Got it. Is Caroline staying over too?"

Margaret gives me a knowing smirk and says, "No. I texted her about my plan and she thought it was good. She's been trying to help Hannah for years, but we don't want it to look like we're ganging up on her. Plus Hannah's farm is on the other side of town, and I thought if last night was any indication, the last place I want to be is in the truck while you tell her goodnight." My sister wrinkles her nose at me in mock disgust, and I let out a small laugh.

"Come on sis, let's get going," I say, making my way to the front door after making sure that Bear has food and water in his bowl.

We load up in the truck, and Margaret makes quick work of fiddling with the radio until her phone connects to the speaker. She blasts a playlist of nineties country songs while I drive, singing loudly and dancing around in her seat. Her singing is terribly off-key, but I ignore it, just happy to see her smiling. The breakup she'd been through had hit her harder than she'd wanted to let on, and I was glad to see that Springside seems to have been the right move for both of us.

We are a minute away from Caroline's when she leans forward and turns the radio down. She looks at me for a moment before saying, "You know Theo, we've been through a whole lot of shit, but don't forget you deserve happiness too. I've seen the way you look at Caroline, and while it may gross me out a bit I still know she'd be lucky to have someone that loves as hard as you do."

I don't take my eyes off the road, feeling a lump in my throat at my sister's words. "Thanks sis. I am really glad you decided to move to Springside with me. I think Mom and Dad would be proud of us," I say.

Margaret smiles as I pull into a parking spot in front of Caroline's apartment before she replies, "Oh, I know they would." With that, she pops out of the front seat and motions for me to follow her. We make our way upstairs and knock on the door.

"Just a sec," Caroline calls from inside. After a moment, she swings the door open, and I am pretty sure my jaw hits the floor. Her brown hair has been curled and is wild around her face. She's wearing the tiniest pair of denim shorts I've ever seen and a light pink shirt that says "Should've been a Cowgirl" along with a pair of tall white boots.

"Hey Cowboy," she says with a wink before turning to my sister and squealing "Margaret, oh my god you look incredible!"

"Thanks! Let's go dance," my sister says before turning and walking back down the stairs.

Caroline grabs my hand and smirks at me before whispering, "Come on. I'm ready to have your hands on me on the dance floor."

Yep. I'm fucked.

CHAPTER TWENTY-SIX
CAROLINE

By the time we pull up to Boot Scooters, I am ready to maul Theo in the parking lot. Margaret offered me the front seat when we left my apartment, but being in such close proximity for the last hour made me hyper-aware of the man sitting next to me.

Margaret and Hannah chattered and sang loudly the whole way, but no matter how hard I tried to concentrate, all I could think about was how damn good he smelled. How his hands felt on me last night. How his tongue would feel as it slid up my leg to my-

"Come on ladies! Let's go find us a cowboy to saddle up tonight," Hannah yells with a laugh as she jumps out of the truck loud enough to attract the gaze of a handful of guys standing around in the parking lot. I'd been so lost in my daydream that I hadn't realized Theo already parked at the familiar dive bar.

As we make our way inside, I can't help but smile. Boot Scooters had become one of our favorite places for a night out when we moved back from college. I love the rustic feel and dancing with my friends under the glow of the neon lights. The dive bar is covered in quirky neon signs with the lyrics to nineties country music, and there is always a cover band playing songs by Brooks and Dunn or Shania Twain.

The sound of "Alabama" by Cross Canadian Ragweed greets my ears as we scan the small assortment of booths towards the back of the bar. We'd agreed on the ride over to grab some appetizers first since we'd all skipped dinner. Plus Boot Scooters has the best loaded fries around.

"Over there," Hannah screams, pointing at an empty booth tucked into the back corner before taking off in a full sprint. She barrels into a middle-aged man and I hear a "sorry" thrown out over her shoulder before she reaches the booth and dives in head first.

Margaret and I break out into a fit of giggles at her while Theo just scowls and shakes his head. "Come on, y'all," I say to them, leading them over to Hannah. I slide into the booth across from her, and Theo slides in beside me while Magaret slides in beside Hannah.

A waitress comes over to take our order and before she can open her mouth to greet us Hannah bursts out, "Hey, I promised these ladies a drink so we need three Scooter shots and an order of loaded fries on my tab, please. And it's been a hell of a week so can I get a Michelob Ultra too."

The waitress just smiles at Hannah while I roll my eyes at her impatience. Once she's finished writing Hannah's order she turns to me. "Hey, can I get the same thing without the shots?" She nods and moves to Margaret who orders the same thing and then to Theo who asks for a water and an order of the famous fries.

As the waitress walks over to put our order in, Margaret asks, "So what exactly is a Scooters shot?"

Hannah and I laugh loudly before she responds, "Well they're really a start for a great night, it's pretty similar to an Alabama Slammer shot. But in addition to the sloe gin, amaretto, and peach Southern Comfort they add Everclear, and they only come in a double."

Theo and Margaret's eyes widen and I giggle. "Remember the story we told you about what happened the time Seth and Will placed bets when they were here? We ended up in that piercing place because they both had at least three of them," I tell Margaret. "So just keep that in mind for tonight."

Margaret opens her mouth to speak but Theo beats her to it. "Piercings? I didn't notice either of them having their ears pierced."

"They don't. She's talking about-" Hannah starts but Margaret throws her hand over Hannah's mouth before she can finish. Her timing is perfect because at the same time, our waitress arrives with our beers and Theo's water.

"Here you go. I will be right back with your shots and food," she says without ever looking away from Theo before walking away. She isn't overly flirty, but I can tell she's admiring how sexy the man is. Considering she has perfect curves, and her dark hair is bouncy and shiny, I bet they'd make quite the couple. The thought makes me sad, but she is definitely beautiful and we have only shared a couple kisses.

I look over at him expecting him to be looking at her, but instead, he is looking at me. We make eye contact and he runs his hand along the hem of my shorts under the table while Hannah and Margaret continue chattering. I instantly feel warmth fill my body, and I reach for my beer to steady my nerves. He slides one finger closer to the inside of my thighs and I jump so high my leg knocks the leg of the table and shakes the beers.

"Damn Caroline, what has you over there feelin' froggy?" Hannah asks with a knowing smirk. I shoot her an ugly look and she just laughs while the waitress sits our food and the large shot glasses on the table before walking away.

Hannah grabs her glass and says, "Cheers ladies. To Leroy,

romance novels, and new friends." We knock back our shots, and I try not to laugh at Margaret's face as she sputters at the liquor. Hannah laughs loudly before saying, "Let the fun begin," with a laugh.

With Theo's hand trailing my thigh and the liquor now running through my system, I couldn't agree more.

AFTER SCARFING DOWN DINNER, Hannah, Margaret, and I rush out onto the dance floor, dancing to the band and singing at the top of our lungs. Theo neglected to keep our table, but I can feel his eyes on me as I swing my hips to the music. His gaze makes me feel like my skin is on fire with desire. He sits on a barstool in the corner with his signature scowl, but every time our eyes lock, the corner of his mouth tips up at me.

We continue dancing and singing to music by George Strait, Trisha Yearwood, and Reba while laughing until our sides hurt. When the band plays "Any Man of Mine" by Shania we scream the lyrics so loud I start to lose my voice, and Hannah and I work together to teach Margaret the line dances to "Boot Scootin' Boogie" and "Copperhead Road," which the bar plays at the top of every hour. Between the music, laughter, and Theo's gaze I feel like I am floating.

After an hour or two with my friends, Hannah leans over and whispers in my ear, "That man has been eye fucking you across the room since we got here. Do you intend to do anything about that?"

I smile sheepishly before responding, "I'm not sure yet. I was just enjoying the night with y'all."

Hannah rolls her eyes at me. "Girlfriend, I love you more than anything but I am not the one that's dying to explore your pussy. Plus I am pretty sure that if he sees you shake your ass again, the man is gonna explode. Go put him out of his misery!"

she yells leaning over and kissing my cheek before pushing me hard towards where Theo is sitting. I hear her and Margaret cackling as I regain my balance and walk towards the man who has completely consumed me the last few weeks.

"Hey, Cowboy," I say, walking over and running my hand down his shoulder. His eyes blaze and I can feel the desire rolling off of us in waves.

"Hey, Sunshine. You having fun?" Theo asks.

"Yeah, I am. You look lonely over here so I thought I'd come see if you wanted to dance with me. Wanna spin me around tonight?" I ask, smiling at him.

"Darlin', I would like to do a whole lot more to you than that, but I guess we can start there for now. I am not much of a dancer, but if I don't get my hands on you I am going to lose my goddamn mind," he responds while he stands up. As he rises from the barstool, he reaches over and lightly skims his hand up from my hip to my face. My breath gets caught inside my chest and all I can think about is how desperately I want this man.

I lead him to the dance floor while the band starts playing "Should've Been a Cowboy" by Toby Keith. I can't help but giggle before saying, "They have really good timing."

Theo rolls his eyes and grabs my hand. He pulls me close to the front of his body until I can feel him everywhere before wrapping his arms around me. We twirl around for several songs while Theo impresses me with how well he seems to know my body. Each time I spin around he brings me close enough that his lips barely graze mine, and his hands leave the lightest touches on my hips and my breast. He leans down and whispers, "Caroline, do you have any idea how badly I want you right now? I feel like a damn sixteen-year-old."

I look up into his blue eyes that seem to darken the longer we tease each other. "I think I have an idea," I say with a smirk before grabbing his hat off his head and spinning away from his grip. I slip his hat on my head and turn to smile about him, but before I can make it all the way around, he is on me.

We are in the middle of the packed dance floor, but it feels like we are the only two people in the room. Theo wraps his hand around my neck and brings my face close to his again. "You are pushing every damn button I have right now. All I can think about is you in nothing but that hat. I am trying to take this slow, but all I want is to take you outside and taste your sweet pussy. I can't stop thinking about you. Wondering what kind of sounds you would make if you let me push my cock into you. Imagining you spread open for me with your legs wrapped around my face until you scream my name."

I feel warmth flood my core and before I can stop myself I'm throwing myself into his arms and attacking his mouth. He catches me easily and our tongues tangle for a few minutes, both of us unable to stop ourselves. He nips at my chin while he kisses down my neck, both of us completely oblivious to the fact that we are still inside amongst the crowd. I am seconds from wrapping my legs around his waist and rubbing myself against his jean clad cock, when the band starts playing "Friends in Low Places" by Garth Brooks, signaling the last song of the night, and the jostling of the crowd jars us out of our fantasy.

As the song is about to end, a tipsy Hannah and Margaret make their way over to us. "Carolineeee!" they holler.

"You missed it. Some guy bought us two rounds of Scooter Shots after we beat his ass at pool!" Hannah screams, oblivious to the fact that she no longer has to scream since the band has stopped playing.

Margaret smiles at us before she says, "She's too busy thinking about my brother fucking her eighteen ways to Sunday." We all look at her in shock, and I briefly worry that she's mad at me. I open my mouth to apologize, but she must see the concern on my face because she cuts me off.

"I swear I am not mad. It's the first time I've seen him happy in over fourteen years, and that's all I care about. But let's be real. You're wearing his hat. We've all read Elsie Silver, so we know what that means. Gross but whatever. We're totally gonna be sisters-in-law." She looks at Theo before continuing, "Just so you know, I love you but if you screw this up, I'll help them go all "Goodbye Earl" on your ass."

Hannah bursts out laughing at Theo's confusion before breaking into a terribly off-key rendition of "Goodbye Earl" complete with a dance solo. Unable to contain ourselves, Margaret and I dissolve into giggles while Theo shakes his head at us.

"Okay now that we have that out of the way, let's drop these two off and go home," he declares with a wink. He turns to make his way back to the parking lot, but he turns after a few steps and shoots me a look that lets me know we aren't done with what we started on the dance floor.

Thank God.

CHAPTER TWENTY-SEVEN
THEO

After getting the girls loaded up, I throw myself into the front seat and drive like a bat out of hell back to Springside. Luckily since it's after one in the morning there is no traffic on the back country roads. I never go fast enough to put us at risk of crashing, but I am so desperate to get my hands on Caroline's body, I can't think straight.

Every few miles, I look over at the passenger seat and Caroline sends me a look with the same heat I am feeling. She is sitting on her hands while she talks to Hannah and Margaret like she doesn't trust herself to keep her hands to herself. I look down and see how tightly I am holding the steering wheel, and I can't help but feel the same way.

After what feels like forever; I wheel into Hannah's long driveway and pull up at her farmhouse. I barely put the truck in park before saying, "Alright, it's late. Let's go. Bye y'all."

Caroline and Hannah laugh, and Margaret rolls her eyes at me while she grabs her overnight bag. "Chill your tits dude," she says while reaching out to knock my arm. "You keep this up, and I'm gonna make you take me home. Then you won't get any time with Caroline. What do you think about that?"

"Sorry, sis. Love ya," I say faking a smile so she will get the hell out of the truck.

"I guess that's a bit better. Goodnight Caroline," my sister says, turning her attention to her friend.

Caroline makes quick eye contact with Margaret and I swear they have a conversation with just a look. "Call me in the morning if y'all want help! Goodnight ladies," she says. I can tell it's killing her not forcing herself on them with help on the farm, but I think my sister was right that Hannah will respond better to accepting a little help at a time.

Hannah proves my point by scoffing, "I am good. Margaret just bribed me with the promise of breakfast. Plus you have that new band dance to make up since they decided to add 'Radioactive' before the game next week. I'll talk to you tomorrow. I would say don't do anything I wouldn't do, but that's a pretty short list. Instead, I'll just say you two have fun." She winks and before either of us can come up with a comeback, the girls sprint from the car laughing.

I throw the truck into reverse, shaking my head at my sister and her new friends. "Ready, Sunshine?" I ask Caroline while throwing a smirk at her.

She leans over and runs her hand down my arm again before responding, "Let's do it."

We ride in silence for a few minutes before both of our phones buzz with an alert. She leans over to check the notification before saying, "Looks like we are about to be under a wind advisory and thunderstorm warning. I had no idea the weather was supposed to be bad."

"Me either," I reply before noticing that since we dropped the girls off the wind has picked up a good bit. The trees on either side of the county road are leaning and shaking debris into the road, and as we hit the city limits it's like someone opened the floodgates. Rain falls so hard it's almost impossible to see the road in front of the truck and lightning pops illuminating the truck every few minutes.

I'd been looking forward to taking Caroline to the farmhouse all evening, but I'm unwilling to risk driving the extra fifteen miles in a storm this bad. "You okay with waiting this out at your place?" I ask, and she nods just as a loud boom of thunder shakes the truck. I pull quickly into the parking spot in front of Caroline's door and throw the truck into park again, watching as branches snap in the small downtown park across the street.

We sit for a few minutes watching the rain. Neither of us speak, and the sexual tension is so strong it feels like we could combust into flames at any second. Finally, Caroline grabs her phone and checks something before saying, "Radar says this is setting in for the next few hours. Wanna make a run for it?"

I nod my head at her and throw my phone in my pocket. We make eye contact and she says, "Let's go!". With that, we throw the doors open and sprint to the front door of her apartment. Lightning cracks and the rain hits my face hard, but I can't help but think that this is the most alive I have felt in ages.

By the time we make it to her apartment door, she is laughing and we are both dripping wet. I look down at the wood floor in front of her front door where we're standing while she fumbles with the key and see we have left a huge puddle of water in our path.

"Come on in. Doesn't look like you're going anywhere any time soon," she says leading me inside. My cock grows hard with thoughts of what that could mean.

She walks through the tidy, colorful apartment and stops at the refrigerator, "You want something to drink?"

"Sure, water is fine though," I reply while I pull out a bar stool and take a seat. The tension is still strong, but both of us aren't really sure how to handle it now that we're alone.

"Here you go," Caroline says as she hands me a cup of water

and comes to sit beside me. "The storm looks pretty bad. There's no way you're leaving until it clears. But I don't have a guest room, so it's just my bed..."

"I can sleep on the couch if you want me to," I say quickly, feeling a bit of panic setting in. I haven't shared a bed with anyone since before the accident.

"Oh," Caroline says, and I don't miss the intense look of hurt that passes over her face at my statement. Fuck. This is why I will never be good enough for this girl.

Blowing out a breath, I know I am going to have to have the talk with her. I breathe through the panic I feel clawing at my chest. I haven't talked about that night with anybody except Margaret. But for the first time, the pain of talking about my past seems like a better option compared to the thought of Caroline thinking I don't want her more than anything I've ever wanted in my life.

"I would love to sleep in your bed, but I need to tell you some things if that's what you want," I say quietly. Her eyes meet mine and her expression turns serious before she nods.

"Go ahead," she says, reaching out and taking my hand.

I take a deep breath trying to figure out where to start. Caroline sits quietly beside me, running her thumb up and down the side of mine. I focus on the tiny movement and try to ignore the way that my heart feels like it's going to beat out of my damn chest.

"I know you've probably picked up a few things from Margaret and me, but there is a lot you don't know. I know Margaret has mentioned our foster parents but I am gonna have to start at the beginning. My family-" I start but pause when I feel my throat threaten to close up.

"Theo, you don't have to do this," she says, and I look up to see sincerity in her eyes.

"I know. But I like you a whole damn lot. And if we are gonna have any shot at anything happening, you need to understand what you're getting into. I need you to understand you're way too good for a man like me," I say and she jerks her head up and frowns.

"Stop that. It's not true. I-" She starts, but I cut her off.

"Fourteen years ago, I watched my parents and my brother die," I blurt out before she can say anything else. Her eyes widen and start to fill with tears, but I continue, "It was around Thanksgiving and my brother Jake was home on fall break. He was a star football player for Alabama, and he'd come home to see us for a day or two before he went back to Tuscaloosa for the Iron Bowl. The plan was for him to take me back with him for an official visit. I was sixteen and idolized Jake. I was on track to follow in his footsteps. I played Wide Receiver, and I led the state in touchdowns and receptions. I thought life couldn't get any better." I take a deep breath before continuing.

"Margaret had asked to spend the night with a friend next door, and my parents let her since we were out of school. We went out to dinner and came home to watch film. My parents were both of our biggest cheerleaders, so there was always a game on the TV. We said goodnight and went to our own rooms like normal. It was just a regular night until I woke up around three in the morning smelling smoke."

"Oh, Theo," Caroline says, moving closer to me and wrapping her arms around me. I am grateful for the connection because I can feel the ghosts of my past swarming me.

"It took me a minute to realize what was happening. When I woke up, I was just so damn hot. I tried to go through the door but the knob burnt my hand. I couldn't get to them. I jumped out the window and I'd planned to go around the outside to help them. But about the time I made it outside, the house collapsed. One of the beams caught my shoulder and burnt my skin which is how I got the scar on my back. When I got out, I saw Margaret standing outside. The neighbors next door where she was staying had run outside to try to help. For a minute, I'd forgotten she hadn't slept at home. I thought it meant we were all safe," I continue. Now that I've started talking, I don't feel like I can stop.

"I ran to her and held her, and after a few minutes the police and firefighters came up to us. They told us they were so sorry for our loss, and no one else had escaped the fire. Just like that, everything was gone. Our parents, Jake, the house, and every piece of a future we thought we had. The firefighters said there was some faulty wiring to one of the outlets in my parent's room. It sparked and there was nothing anyone could do. My parents were both only children and our grandparents were all dead. A couple that had gone to church with us were registered foster parents, and they petitioned to have us placed with them.

"They took us in and did what they could. They got us into therapy where I was diagnosed with PTSD. I decided to graduate early so I could start providing for myself, and I got a job at the fire station so I could try to do what I could to keep other people from going through what I went through. I hadn't touched a football again until I moved to Springside. I promised myself I would just help take care of Margaret and that would be it. I told myself I had too much darkness and too many broken pieces to do anything but go to work and help my sister. But then I met you. And I call you Sunshine because you've brought all of this light into my life. But here's the thing. Eventually, at the end of every day, the sun sets. The darkness comes in and takes over. And if you stay around me, that's what will happen to you."

"Theo," she starts, but I keep talking.

"I haven't ever talked about this with anyone. I quit going to the therapist after he diagnosed me. I am shit at feelings. But I haven't slept in the same bed with anyone since. I have night terrors. I have had the same dream every night for the last fourteen years. I wouldn't be able to live with myself if I accidentally hurt you," I say, trying to ignore the tremble in my voice.

"Stop it," Caroline says, and I am surprised by the fierceness in her tone. "I am so sorry for everything that has happened to you Theo, and I am incredibly honored that you decided to share it with me. But you aren't broken. You are one of the strongest, most incredible men I know. And I am not gonna sit here and let you talk about yourself like that because, quite frankly, it's bullshit."

"Caroline," I start.

"No, you listen. We are gonna take this slow because I think it's what we both need. But I want this. I want you, and I want us. If you don't I understand, but it better as shit not be because you don't think you're not good enough for me. Is that clear?" she asks.

"Baby, I would be a damn fool not to want you. I want as much of you as you'll give me. The thought of not having you makes me crazy," I respond, unable to argue with her when I want her so damn badly.

"So, we're gonna do this?" she asks looking into my eyes. "We're gonna be a couple and try this for real? Because if this is just sex, I need you to tell me now."

"It's not just sex, Sunshine. If you want me, I am yours," I respond even though it scares the shit out of me.

"Good," she says with a smile. "In that case, I am positively exhausted." She finished the statement with a wink before sliding her shirt off her body and walking toward her bedroom. "Come on, Cowboy. You comin'?"

Hell yeah.

CHAPTER TWENTY-EIGHT
CAROLINE

Oh my God.

This isn't exactly how I pictured tonight going, but I certainly don't have any regrets. I race into my bedroom, and I can feel his presence as he races after me. I stand on the other side of the bed as he enters the room. I didn't bother with turning on any lights in here, so aside from the dim light pouring in from the living room and the occasional flashes of lightning outside, it is pitch black in the room.

"Well, if you're sure you want this, let's see if you're as good as you've claimed to be." I slide my bra off my shoulders right as a loud crack of lightning strikes illuminating the room momentarily.

Apparently, the statement is the only encouragement Theo needs, because before I can move he's closing the space between us and pushing me against the wall. Once again he wraps his large hand around my throat and asks, "Are you gonna be a good girl for me? I want to see you in nothing but that hat. I want you to wear it while you wrap your sweet thighs around my face and grind your clit against my tongue. I can't wait to see how your sweet pussy tastes."

Holy freaking shit, the mouth on this man. "Yes sir," I say with a wink, testing the waters. His eyes blaze and his mouth attacks mine. He nips at my lips while he runs his fingers over my exposed nipples. I feel him smirk as he hears my breath catch.

"So damn sweet," he whispers as he kisses down my neck before flicking his tongue across one of my nipples. I whimper and wither against his touch desperate for more.

"Theo, please," I start but the words aren't even out of my mouth completely before he runs his thumb across my hip bone close to my shorts.

"I know, darlin'. Most perfect tits I've ever seen," he says as he runs his hands up and down my waist. I suck in a breath as he unhooks the button on my shorts and works his hand lower and lower until he hits my core. "So damn wet for me, Sunshine."

I feel his finger slide under my panties, and I can barely hold in the moan threatening to come out of my mouth. He works his finger in and out of me until I explode on his hand. "That's right baby, soak my fingers."

I collapse against the wall, and he just laughs, "I hope you know I'm not even close to through with you."

He slides down until he's on his knees in front of me, taking my shorts and pushing them down my legs until they pool at my feet. "Now step out of these, and climb up on the bed."

I scramble to follow his orders, and Theo mutters, "Such a good girl," before grabbing my waist and pulling me on top of him on the bed. "Go ahead and wrap your gorgeous legs around my face. I need to taste you."

The second his mouth touches me, I scream which only seems to encourage Theo. "Damn baby," he says before continuing to run his tongue against my clit. I grip his hair with my fingers and rub myself against him until I'm screaming again.

He pulls back after he's sure that I've finished, and I climb off him. I see a look of concern flash across his face like he's afraid I'm regretting what we just did. I smile at him before saying, "Alright, it's your turn."

Theo lets out a little laugh before I grab his belt loops and pull him up until he's standing beside the bed. I grab his belt and undo the buckle before pushing his jeans to the floor. I lean up and kiss his mouth while tearing his shirt off of him.

Once he's standing naked in front of me, I sink to my knees taking his cock in my mouth. I knew he'd be big, but I don't think I was fully prepared for his size. After running my tongue up and down his shaft, I pull back and place a kiss on the tip. Darting my tongue out, I collect the precum leaking from him with my lips before sucking his length into my mouth. He rocks his hips slowly at first, but his thrusts become quicker and more forceful as I run my mouth up and down his cock.

"I'm close," he warns as if there is any chance of me stopping. I reach one of my hands around and press my nails into his ass cheek, pulling him closer while I suck harder. He thrusts one last time into my mouth, and I feel his cum fill the back of my throat. After I'm sure he's finished, I run my tongue around him and swallow. He looks at me with a look of adoration in his eyes before winking at me. "Well Miss Tyler, you certainly are full of surprises."

I laugh and rise to my feet before leaning over to kiss him quickly and responding, "Back at ya, Cowboy."

CHAPTER TWENTY-NINE
THEO

It's after three in the morning before Caroline and I slide under her covers. We'd both been in desperate need of a shower after the events of the day, and since we decided to shower together, it had taken forever. I'd found it impossible to keep my hands to myself, and I'd ended up making her come two more times on my fingers in the shower.

After pulling the covers up over us, I remind myself to lie still as I wait for the anxiety to sink in. I haven't had a dreamless night in fourteen years. The thought of falling asleep beside her and not waking up in a panic feels like a fantasy. I figure if I can lay here for a couple hours I can get up early in the morning and avoid the possibility of scaring her with my inevitable panic.

She leans over and kisses me quickly before throwing her arm around me and saying, "Goodnight, Chief Johnson."

I can't help the small ghost of a smile from touching my lips before I say, "Goodnight, Sunshine."

Caroline burrows closer to my body and I wrap my arm around her. I've never slept in the same bed with a woman, and while I know I won't be able to sleep, I can't deny that it's nice to lay here with her in my arms.

I tell myself no harm will come from holding her, and I close my eyes and allow myself to imagine a future with this woman that I know will never become a reality.

~

"WELL, GOOD MORNING," I hear as a warm hand rubs my arm. I roll over until I am eye to eye with Caroline before it hits me that it is daytime outside.

"Good morning," I reply while reaching up to rub my eyes. "What time is it?"

"A little after ten. I didn't want to disturb you, but I got worried about Bear. If you want to go back to sleep, I'll go check on him," Caroline replies with a smile.

I blink back at her in shock. That can't be right. I haven't had a night without a nightmare since the fire. I'd worried that talking about the accident for the first time in fourteen years would leave me worse off, but right now I feel more well rested than I have in years. "Ten? Like in the morning? I didn't think there was any way I would fall asleep. I'll go check on him. I have some calls to make about the farm. But listen, Caroline-"

"You still mine, Cowboy? Or are you regretting everything that happened last night?" she asks, interrupting my internal freakout.

I take a breath before meeting her eyes. "I'm all yours, Caroline. For as long as you'll keep me, I'm all yours."

She leans in and smiles at me before saying, "Good answer, Chief Johnson."

I spend some time kissing her and trying to memorize the way her skin feels under my fingers before rolling out of bed to look for some clothes. "Bear already hates me. I'd better go before he decides to shred my mattress. But text me later. If we are gonna try this, I need to plan a real date for us."

I had never been on a real date, especially with someone as perfect as her. However, I figured if I wasn't sure I could keep her, I had to give it my best shot.

"Of course, let me know how your calls go. And thank you, Theo—for dancing with me, driving me home, and the multiple orgasms," she responds with a laugh.

Shaking my head I mutter under my breath, "My pleasure, Sunshine."

By Monday morning, I am walking into the fire station, but all I can think about is how desperate I am for more of Caroline's touch. I had spent the afternoon on Saturday working on the farm, trying to make sure it was ready for a new set of animal inhabitants after spending half an hour on the phone with Mr. Willy. I'd stayed close to the phone in case I got called in for help at the station after the storms on Friday, but none ever came.

The man whom Huey had connected me with had been skeptical about talking to me at first, but after he realized I was interested in his animals, he seemed to have dropped his guard. He'd stopped by yesterday on his way home from church to look at the land and make sure he was comfortable with moving his animals to my property.

After ensuring that the animals would be well taken care of, we agreed on a price and he told me I could come get my new animals later this week. I was the new owner of four horses and about ten cows. It was a small farm, but it was a start.

After Mr. Willy left, I'd spent the afternoon working on the old barn behind the house and texting Caroline. She'd offered to come help me, but I knew I wouldn't be able to focus on working with her here. As much as I would enjoy having her with me, I need the barn to be liveable. I'd set to work and been surprised at the sense of calm that had settled over me while I fixed broken boards and raked new hay into the stalls.

Since I lost my family, I have avoided anything that reminded me of what I lost, and that included the horses my parents loved so much. However, as I worked in the silence of the farm, I had to admit I was regretting that decision. The more I worked yesterday, the closer my family felt.

Despite the rough start I had in Springside, I can feel myself starting to heal. I didn't think it was possible, but the last few weeks have brought me more peace than I could imagine. I still could feel the loss of my family like a gaping hole in my chest, but I was starting to realize that Margaret was right when she told me that none of our family would have wanted me to punish myself the way I have been.

On top of all of that, I hadn't had a nightmare since the night Caroline and I spent together. After fourteen years of the recurrent nightmare, I never dreamed that I could sleep through the night. Without the nightly reminders, I was able to think a little more clearly.

As I sit down at my desk, my cell phone rings. I pull it out of my pocket and see that it's a call from Heather, my foster mom. I hit accept and lift the phone to my ear while saying, "Hello."

"Hey, Sweetie. How are you?" Heather asks and I can hear the genuine concern in her voice.

I blow out a breath and run my hand over my face before responding, "I am actually really good. How are you and Bobby doing?"

"We are good! You know he is ready for football season to get going. He has added an extra screen to the game room so that he can have ESPN and CBS going at the same time. I swear that man thinks it's a sports bar in there," Heather responds with a laugh. "We were actually talking about making a quick trip over to Springside soon to see you and your sister in the next few weeks. Would that be okay with you?"

I lean back in my chair before responding, "Yeah, that's fine. I might have someone I want you to meet."

Shit! Had I really said that out loud? Were Caroline and I really at the "meet the family" phase? Was this moving too fast? I am not cut out for this. It's barely after seven in the morning, and I am in desperate need of a beer already.

Amidst my internal freakout, I hear Heather let out a small squeak, but other than that, there is complete silence on the phone. I am about to check the phone to make sure the call wasn't lost until I hear a loud sob on the other end of the line. "Oh, Theo!"

I clear my throat, unsure of how to handle the sudden onset of emotions, deciding to sit quietly and hope she doesn't acknowledge my previous statement.

"I am so happy Theo. I just know your momma is dancing in heaven. Callie loved you so much, and all she wanted was for you to find someone who complimented you. I know these last few years have been incredibly hard, but I can't wait to meet the girl who's mended your broken heart."

Still unsure of how to respond, I breathe through the lump in my throat and settle with a, "Yes ma'am," for my foster mother.

Thankfully, Heather is used to my aversion to emotional topics, and she quickly shifts to making small talk before telling me she'd let me know when they planned to visit and hang up.

With that taken care of, I sit down at my desk planning to get to work but decide to send Caroline a text first.

> Me: So I may have accidentally signed you up to meet my foster parents…

Caroline: Is that right? Honestly I am flattered
Chief Johnson

Me: Well Heather might decide to hold you
hostage, so don't say I didn't warn you.

Caroline: Bring it on, Cowboy. You can't run
me off that easily.

SMILING, I am about to respond when Zach knocks on my office door. He looks worn out, and he almost collapses into the chair when I motion for him to have a seat.

"What can I do for you Zach?" I ask, looking over at the young firefighter. He reminds me so much of myself when I started working at the station. I've realized over the last few weeks that none of us are exempt from tragedy, and it strikes each of us differently.

"Well, Chief, I am really sorry, but I need to switch shifts for this week or something. I got the call from the doctor that they have an opening for Bethany, but I have to go with her to therapy from nine until two on Monday, Wednesday, and Friday for the next two weeks in Saddle Ridge to make sure we both understand how to use her equipment. I will do whatever else I need to do to make sure I can contribute. I used all my PTO with the accident, and I need my insurance, Chief."

I look at him and realize that his haggard expression isn't only due to physical exhaustion— Zach looks like he's carrying the weight of the world. I remember how I felt after the accident, and immediately feel a pang of sympathy for him.

"I'll tell you what Zach; I will need to run it by the mayor first, but I think he will be more than happy to work with us. If he agrees, I will assign you to the night call for the next two weeks. That way you're still working, but can stay home unless you need to be called out."

The Fire Department in Springside decided years ago that it didn't make sense to run two shifts since the incident rate was so low. The city had even debated shifting to a volunteer model since we were so small, but some of the local government appreciated having the perceived extra layer of safety of a municipal station. So, the other men in the station each take call one night a week along with a weekend every month. If anything major happens, they can call the rest of us in, but that hasn't happened for several years.

Zach looks like he is ready to cry so I clear my throat and say, "I'll figure something out. Your sister needs you. If you need anything else, we're here."

"Thank you, Chief. You sure aren't as bad as everyone seems to think. I really appreciate it," he replies with a laugh. I shake my head at him, hoping maybe he is right.

With that, he leaves my office and I start up my desktop, planning to start the day by checking my emails before calling the mayor. As I wait for the ancient Dell to start up, my phone rings again. Damn it, I am popular today.

I see Huey's name light up the screen and slide to accept his call.

"Hey, Huey," I say while furiously wiggling my mouse as if that will speed up the process.

"Good morning, Theo. How are you today?" the older man asks me.

"I'm good. I talked to Mr. Willy. Thank you for setting that up for me," I reply with sincerity.

"You're welcome, son. He may have been skeptical at first, but he called me after y'all talked and said you impressed him. If you aren't careful, people are almost going to think you like it here," Huey says with a laugh.

I just shake my head at him, but I can't deny that he's right.

"Anyway, that's not what I called you about," Huey says. "Now you can tell me to mind my own damn business, but I just wanted to share this with you. There is a PTSD support group that meets each week on Thursdays in Saddle Ridge. One of my friends started going after he got in a terrible car accident, and he swears it's changed his life. Now, I am not trying to overstep, but I know what happened to your family. At the station, I worked with grown men who held in their trauma until it ate them alive, and I don't want that to happen to you. Honestly Theo, I don't know anyone that could come out of that tragedy without some big feelings. I just thought it could be good for you. If you want to go, I will go with you, or you can tell me to buzz off. I just wanted you to know."

I feel my chest tightening for the second time in less than an hour, and we both sit in silence. After taking a deep breath I reply, "I appreciate it, Huey. I don't think I am interested, but if I change my mind, can I call you?"

"Of course. And hey, Theo, let me know if you need anything else," Huey says before clicking off the call.

Damn it. What a Monday.

CHAPTER THIRTY
CAROLINE

When third period hits, I still feel like I am flying in the clouds after the night I spent with Theo this weekend. Every time I heard my phone vibrate, I felt like a teenager as I raced to see what he had texted about. I'd known I was physically attracted to Theo, but damn that man knew what he was doing in the bedroom and I have to admit I am already desperate for more.

As my class walks in, I blow out a sigh of relief that Michael didn't show up today. The principal and I are completely mystified as to what is going on with him. We both attempted parent contacts last week, but they had been unsuccessful. I know Mr. Hale hopes one talk with the counselors will solve his behavior problems, but I know there's more to it than we can see. Over the last few years, I have learned that almost no behavior issue was truly random, and I want to try to help him the best I can. But it's clear that his presence also sets the rest of the class on edge right now, and I don't have it in me today.

I make my way through the room as I ask about their weekend or interests. I look over and see that Robby, a junior on the baseball team, looks uncomfortable. He sits at his normal desk, but he shifts awkwardly in his seat and keeps glancing between me and his backpack.

I briefly think that I need to pull him aside once class gets going to see what's going on, but the loudspeaker from the office clicks on announcing a meeting change for the Beta Club, and I lose myself to attendance and the bell ringer.

I'm grabbing my computer and notes to cast on my screen before we get started with the content for the day when I see Tilly, one of my cheerleaders, raise her hand.

"Uh, Miss Caroline..." she says as I continue making sure my slideshow is ready for the class.

"Uhh, why is Robby's backpack moving?" Tilly asks, and I immediately stop my setup and look over in the corner where Robby looks like he's ready to crawl onto the floor while reaching towards his bag.

"Robby," I start, already knowing something is really wrong. "What's in your bag?"

"Well, Miss Caroline, I didn't want you to" he starts, but he's immediately interrupted by a tearing sound.

One of the girls sitting closest to Robby lets out a blood-curdling scream, and I look frantically at her while she points at Robby. I move closer and see claws coming out of his bag until a small head pops out with its teeth bared.

"Is that a raccoon?!" the boy sitting closest to Robby asks.

I feel like my eyes are about to pop out of my head. I have sat through hours of training on curriculum and airborne pathogens, but nobody in professional development has ever talked about how to handle a wild animal in my room.

I run over to my phone and send an SOS text to Hannah. I know it's her planning period so as long as she isn't in a meeting she will come running. I dial the office, but after their track record the last few weeks I am not surprised I can't get any of the staff on the phone. They've been overrun with it being so early in the year. Oh well. Guess I'm gonna have to figure this one out on my own.

I glance up at my students and realize they've all climbed on top of their desks. The young raccoon pulls itself all the way out of the bag and looks around the room. As the creature turns, he takes off as though he just realized how outnumbered he is. He sprints around under the desks as he runs, which causes all of the students in the room to scream. Even Robby is standing on top of a table.

"Robby, is this yours? What is going on?" I yell over the screams.

Robby looks as though he is about to cry. "Miss Caroline, you have to believe me! I was on the way to school this morning, and this guy was in the road. I watched someone swerve at him, and I couldn't take it. I got out of my car and walked towards him before I realized he'd been hurt. His arm is all messed up. I couldn't just leave him, and it looked like something had knocked him out so I put him in my backpack so he could rest."

"Well, he's not resting now is he?" I hear one of my students yell.

I hear a knock at my door and rush over to let Hannah in. "Hey, I saw your text. What the heck is going on?" my best friend asks as she steps in and I hurry to close the door. "Oh my GOD holy shhhhhi-" she starts before she realizes where she is. "Shoot. Holy shoot. Is that a freaking RACCOON?!

"Yep. Indeed it is. "

Hannah and I make eye contact and she says, "Great," before she leans over and whispers, "What the hell Caroline. What are we gonna do?"

I stare at her before shifting my gaze back to the situation in the room. The little raccoon has realized how outnumbered he is, and is hissing at all of us.

"You are going to call Gerald over at Animal Control. He's helped us at the farm a time or two. Maybe he can send someone. I'll call the office again," I say as we finally jump into action.

"On it," Hannah says as she grabs her cell phone from her pocket while I walk over to the room phone.

"Okay, guys. Y'all just hang on. Y'all just stay away from it the best you can." I encourage my class as I dial the front office number. After three tries, I finally hear someone answer.

"Springside High, this is Mrs. Bess! How-," the secretary starts before I interrupt.

"Where's Mr. Hale? I need him now," I say frantically.

"Caroline?" Mrs. Bess asks.

"Yes. Where is he?" I ask, cringing at how blunt I sound.

"Oh well, I swear I saw him around here a minute ago. He was waiting on someone from the district to come by. You know they always like-" she starts and I know if I don't stop her, I'll be here for several minutes. The critter on the floor chooses that moment to dart from where he was hiding towards the other side of the room. Screams fill the room while students jump around on top of their desks.

"Mrs. Bess! I need him in my room right now. There's a raccoon in my room," I say, trying to remain calm.

There's silence on the line for so long I think she's gone, until I hear her whisper, "What?"

"Someone picked up a baby raccoon on their way to school this morning thinking it was injured. It clawed its way out of their bag and now it's running around with all thirty-two of us in this room. I need someone in this classroom please," I say, knowing this situation isn't her fault but feeling the frustration building nonetheless.

"Oh sweet Jesus. MR. HALE!!!!" I hear her shriek and I pull the phone away from my ear. I look over at Hannah who is still on the phone while the raccoon continues running around and hissing as it makes its way around the room. Hannah and I both jump on top of my desk when the animal heads our way, and I say a silent prayer that the desk will hold us both. Collapsing on the floor is the last thing I need to do today.

"Okay guys, it's gonna be okay," I exclaim trying to reassure them. I love animals but if someone gets bit or scratched by this chaos I will feel horrible.

Hannah ends the call before saying, "Gerald is sending someone. He said less than five minutes."

Great. Can't wait.

~

Hannah: Happy Margarita Monday ladies!

Margaret: Heck yes! I can't wait!

Hannah: Me either. After today I need the whole damn pitcher.

Me: YES! A full flavor flight is calling my name.

Margaret: Everything okay at Springside High?

Hannah: GIRL It's been a DAY!

Me: Two words: Animal Control

Margaret: Drinks are on me tonight. See y'all in an hour.

By the time I walk into Maracas, I feel like today should be Friday. I fall into our favorite corner booth and ask for the margarita flight and a large queso. The flight has smaller versions of their original, peach, raspberry, and blue margaritas in beautiful little colored miniature glasses that match the drinks.

While I am waiting on my drinks, Margaret arrives and makes her way over to me. "Hey, girl! Hannah just texted us. She parked her car at your apartment since she's staying over and is walking this way now."

"Sounds good! How was your day?!" I ask her.

"Good! I think it's safe to say, much better than yours," Margaret replies with a laugh.

"Girl, you have no idea!" I respond with a laugh.

The server walks over with my mini glasses on a wooden carved board and sits them down in front of me before taking Margaret's order. By the time she walks off, I look over and see Hannah coming through the door. She collapses into the booth before taking a sip of my blue curaçao margarita and laying her head on my shoulder. I lean my head on top of hers and Margaret laughs from across the table.

"Y'all look pitiful. I gotta know, what the heck happened?" she asks, looking both concerned and entertained.

"Oh my God, girl, it was complete insanity," Hannah exclaims loudly. A few of the other customers in the room look up at us, and I see one of the older ladies make her way towards us.

"Ladies! I heard y'all had quite a day, bless your hearts! After you called Gerald, he called Mrs. BettySue. Well, she called Mrs. Ruth Anne and since she and Sarah Beth are first cousins through her momma's side they spent an hour piecing it all together. You two got a full two-page write-up on the STS. I swear I don't remember the last time Springside had this much entertainment from you young people," Mrs. Dorthy says, looking at Hannah and me.

"Oh yes ma'am," we say in unison, smiling back at the older lady. I swear the way news travels in this town never fails to blow my mind.

"Y'all take care now ladies! Don't forget several of us are more than willing to give y'all some help on finding a man. Nice girls like y'all can't wait around forever. BettySue has a grandson that is gonna make somebody a fine husband!" Mrs. Dorthy says before walking off.

I look over at Margaret's eyes that look like they are about to pop out of her head. "Did she just basically call us old maids?"

Hannah and I roll our eyes before we both burst out laughing. "Yep," we say in unison.

"I didn't know if I was supposed to cry or say thank you," Margaret says looking genuinely confused.

"Welcome to Springside," I tell her with a laugh. "You're officially a local now."

"Great," she responds. "Okay, whatever, enough of that. What happened today?"

Hannah and I take turns sharing the attempts to capture the baby raccoon, as Margaret looks equal parts horrified and amused.

"So, since the only person that could come was brand new to the Animal Control unit, they didn't know what to do either. They finally found Mr. Hale almost twenty minutes after I'd called, and we had managed to slip the kids out. Our classes went to the gym and we tried to catch the darn thing," I explain.

"Yeah, the little shit was pissed and terrified. He managed to latch onto the leg of Mr. Hale's suit pants, and I thought he was about to strip right then. If it hadn't been for the injured arm, I think that's what it would have come to," Hannah says, shaking her head.

"No freaking way. You're making this up!" Margaret says as we all take big gulps of our drinks.

"I swear. It took almost two hours for us to get him in the cage for the animal rescue guy. The little thing was almost dead on its paws; it was so worn out," I say.

"He wasn't the only one," Hannah says with a laugh.

"I always joke that it's not a Monday morning without a little bit of chaos, but I think I have filled my quota for a bit," I say before grabbing some chips.

We continue chatting until finally, Margaret says, "So Caroline, what's the deal with you and Theo? I barely saw him this weekend so I didn't ask," Hannah giggles a bit at the question as she sips her marg, both of them waiting on me to respond.

"I really like him, y'all. We're together, and we're just gonna see where it goes. But I hope that won't affect our friendship, Margaret. I know you haven't been here that long, but I really love having you here," I say, suddenly nervous and hoping she can hear the sincerity in my voice.

"Of course it won't! I haven't ever had any real girlfriends and my brother does not get to take that away from me. Just be easy with him. He can be a real jerk, but he usually means well. But if he pulls another stupid ass move like he did with the fire drill, I will help you kick his ass."

I laugh before saying, "Deal."

"So, did you ride his bronco Friday night?" Hannah asks before erupting into a fit of giggles.

"And that's my cue to go to the bathroom," Margaret says while trying to look mortified, but I don't miss the hint of a smile on her face.

Once she's gone, I turn to Hannah who has a look of expectation. I blow out a breath before saying, "Not his bronco, but his tongue was pretty damn good."

Hannah lets out a squeal loud enough that everyone in the restaurant turns to look at us. She launches into asking a million questions when my phone buzzes and I reach over to grab it.

Theo: Come sneak out back. I need to see you for a minute.

My heart rate picks up as I look out the back windows of Maracas. Behind the restaurant is a large parking lot. The city hasn't replaced the lights out there yet after a hurricane came through last year and damaged the existing ones, so I know it's almost pitch black out there.

Hannah notices me looking at my phone and asks, "Is that him?!"

"Yeah. I'll be back in a few," I tell her, trying to keep myself from blushing.

Hannah notices my expression because she screams again before winking. "Go get him, girlie. We'll be here when you get back."

I make quick work of slipping out of the booth and almost running to the door. As soon as I slip out the front door and make my way around the building, I see Theo's truck parked in the back of the lot. If his headlights weren't on, I probably would have missed it completely. As soon as I walk up, he cuts the lights and jumps out.

"Hey, Sunshine," he says, reaching for my hand and spinning us until he has me pressed against his truck. It's so dark I can only see the outline of his muscular frame, but he's so close to me I am okay with it.

"Hey, Cowboy. What's going on?" I ask as he skims his hands up and down my waist.

"Well, Margaret asked me to pick her up tonight, so I ran some errands and have been out here waiting for the last twenty minutes. I started thinking about this weekend, and I had to see you," he says, easing his hands up my sides.

"Hmmm, no complaints here," I say leaning in closer to him, desperate to feel more of him.

He skims his lips lightly across mine, teasing me before he moves away. I let out a choked sound before saying, "Theo, please."

"Yes, darlin'," he says, rubbing his hands up and down my waist again but this time he lets his thumb skim across my nipple through my sports bra and tee shirt.

"I missed you. Please," I say, feeling desperate to feel his lips against mine.

He chooses that moment to grind his jean clad cock into my center. I open my mouth to let out a moan and he dives into me to devour my lips.

Between kisses, he says, "Damn. I... Missed... This... Perfect.... Mouth."

He grinds against me once more and I claw at his back. The fact that we're technically in public despite the darkness surrounding us has me even more desperate for his touch.

I savor the feeling of his mouth on mine as we kiss until I am breathless and desperately needy. Theo pulls back before kissing my forehead and saying, "I'm sorry. That's not what I called you out here for. I really just wanted to see if you were okay after your day. My guys couldn't stop talking about it at practice today. But I obviously got carried away."

"Me too," I say with a laugh. "And I'm good. I'm glad you called me out here. Also, just an update—Margaret asked about us and I told her we were together. I hope that's okay."

"Of course. I am not hiding us. I just haven't seen much of my sister since Friday. You having any regrets yet?" Theo asks. It catches me off guard because he says it like a joke, but I don't miss the way his body tightens as if he's preparing himself for a hit.

"Nope, none. What about you?" I ask, dropping a quick kiss to his lips.

"Sunshine if you change your mind you are gonna have to kick me out. I don't plan on going anywhere," he says, kissing me again.

"Good," I say, pulling away a bit and trying to make sure I don't look too disheveled. "Now, I am going to go back and finish my margaritas. Give me a kiss, and I will text you when I get home tonight."

"Yes ma'am," he says before kissing me again and pulling

back to straighten his cowboy hat. He reaches out and spanks my ass lightly before he says, "Go have fun, but later this week, you're mine."

"Yes, sir," I say, shooting him a wink and racing back towards the restaurant before he can convince me to do anything else in this parking lot. That damn man.

CHAPTER THIRTY-ONE
THEO

Like always, my first thought when I wake up is that it's much hotter than it should be. In my groggy state, I first think that the air conditioner must have broken, but I quickly realize that this heat is way different from a normal Alabama night.

It's dark when I open my eyes, but I can feel the heat on my face. I look around and notice the gap under the door shows a bright light and smoke is billowing up through the gap. Coming to terms with what's going on I scramble out of bed and start screaming for my siblings. Calling out for my parents. Looking for a way out of my bedroom. I grab for the door, but the knob burns my hand warning me not to open it. I cough and sputter still trying to yell out for anyone that could help me. But help isn't coming. My heart races out of my chest and I continue screaming "MOM, DAD. HELP ME! JAKE!!!! MARGARET!!!"

All of a sudden, I hear a small voice screaming, "Theo, please help me. Theo! Theo!"

My panic reaches a new level when I recognize the voice. It's Caroline.

"CAROLINE! Where are you?" I shout, coughing through the smoke filling the room.

"Help me, Theo!" Caroline screams again, and I see her form huddled on the floor across the room. I take a step to run after her, but as soon as I do, she and the rest of the house become engulfed in the flames, and I am in the dark.

"Theo! Theo! Wake up! Theo! I need you to wake up!" I hear as I jerk awake. As I come to my senses I realize Margaret is banging on my locked door.

I leap up and grab the door, and almost fall over when Margaret launches herself at me.

"Oh my gosh, Theo, are you okay? You've been screaming for forever! I thought I was going to have to break the door down," my sister says, and when she looks at me I see that she has tears in her eyes.

I blow out a breath and wipe the sweat from my brow while she scrutinizes me. "You were yelling for Caroline. Was this dream different?" Margaret asks, examining my face to make sure I am okay.

"Yeah," I say simply.

She nods at me and hugs me quickly before she says, "I am here if you need to talk."

With that, she wipes the tears from her eyes and squeezes my hand before heading back to her room.

I walk to the bathroom, trying to even out my breathing, and throw some cold water on my face. My heart is still racing and no matter how many times I tell myself none of that dream is real, I can't seem to calm down.

Feeling like I am out of options, I grab my phone, needing to hear Caroline's voice. Nothing has gone right this week. I've been desperate for more of her since teasing her Monday night, but our schedules haven't lined up thanks to me needing to make sure everything is ready for the new animals to come this weekend, and our sports schedules.

When I go to unlock the screen, I realize it's 3 a.m. on Thursday. I don't want to wake her, so instead I decide to go with another option. Without giving myself time to change my mind, I go to Huey's number and send him a text knowing he won't see it until after he gets up.

> Me: Hey Huey, if the offer still stands, I will meet you tonight.

Part of me still craves Caroline's voice, but the other part of me doesn't want to share this broken part of myself with her. What if she hears about the group and thinks differently about me? What if she realizes she's way too good for me? I know that she will come to that realization soon enough on her own, so she really doesn't need the help from me.

I decide to take a shower and try to push the nightmare far from my mind. After standing in the hot spray for a while, I get out and lay in the bed, watching the fan turn since I am afraid I will have the same dream again. Around five, I give up and decide to go for a run around the property. As I am lacing up my running shoes, I hear my phone buzz with a text.

> Huey: Sure. I'll pick you up at 6 tonight.

I sigh and tuck my phone into my pocket deciding to try to outrun my past for a little while longer.

BY THE TIME 5:30 rolls around, I have almost canceled on Huey six times. But every time I go to grab my phone, I remember why I am going to this group. I want to be the best version of myself that I can be for Caroline. She deserves a whole hell of a lot more than me, but I have to try.

I pace the halls where Bear is lying, and he gives me a series of annoyed glances. "Sorry, Bud," I reply to the dog who lets out a loud sigh and turns away from me.

I feel my phone buzz, and I grab it out to see a text from Caroline.

> Caroline: Look what song just came across my Spotify. Made me think of you.

Accompanying the text is a picture of a song by Jon Pardi that talks about his girl wearing nothing but a cowboy hat.

> Me: I like the way you think, Darlin'

> Caroline: Any desire for a repeat performance this weekend? I wouldn't complain…

Damn, this woman. I am fully convinced no one else could make me smile the way I am grinning at my phone. I am half hard just thinking about wrapping her thighs around my shoulders again while I lick her sweet cunt. I can't stop thinking about how good it would feel to slide my cock into her wet heat. How good she would look bent over in my bed while I spanked her tight ass for her smart perfect mouth.

I look up to see Huey pulling into the driveway. I pat Bear's head and walk out the door to sit in his passenger seat while putting my phone in my pocket. Not wanting Huey to know what I was thinking before he pulled up, I decide to text her back once we get to Saddle Ridge.

"Hey Theo," he greets me before throwing the car in drive and heading down the driveway.

"Hey Huey," I say before staring out the window. I'd thought I had done the hardest part by agreeing to go, but after a few seconds in the car, I am not sure. What the absolute fuck was I doing?

Huey must feel the anxiety because he doesn't try to force

any small talk in the car. We ride in amicable silence until we reach the Saddle Ridge city limits sign.

As soon as my eyes see the sign, my chest tightens. I try to breathe through it, but the harder I try, the more impossible it seems to be to take a deep breath. I feel Huey's eyes on me, but I try to focus straight ahead so that he doesn't ask too many questions. He drives for another minute as I continue to fight with my breathing. He pulls into a church parking lot, and says "We're here!"

As soon as he says the words, it feels like there's a hundred-pound weight sitting on my windpipe. I can't breathe at all. I fight for breath, much like I do in the dreams I keep having. I can feel my body trembling as the panic attack takes root in my body.

"Theo," Huey says, but he sounds like he's far away despite the fact that he's shaking my arm. "Theo, take a breath. Listen, you don't have to do this if you don't want to. But don't forget that asking for help doesn't make you weak. If you want to go in, don't let fear stop you. Think about what your family would have wanted. If you had died instead of Jake, would you want him to struggle with this the way you have?"

Just when I was convinced no one could say the right thing to me to pull me out of my panicked state, those words hit me like a lead weight. Thinking over them, I look at Huey and take a minute until I can breathe normally before saying, "Okay then, let's get this over with."

TWO HOURS LATER, Huey and I are walking back to the truck. After we had gotten inside, it hadn't been as bad as I expected. In fact, I have to admit I feel lighter than I had before. I'd been shocked at the turnout in the small town. The people had ranged from teenage girls to elderly men, and I had been comforted by the fact that almost everyone my age had talked about their spouses and children.

After the accident, I had become convinced that I could never deserve a life like that, but tonight had opened my eyes a bit. Maybe I could really make this thing with Caroline work.

But the other part of me tonight was sad for all of the people that were walking through similar tragedies as me. It reminded me that we are all truly one split second away from a moment that changes our entire lives.

I hadn't spoken tonight, preferring to just take everything in. Huey hadn't left my side and hadn't forced me to talk. We make the ride back to Spingside in complete silence. I think he's waiting for me to say something, but I am still processing everything I heard tonight.

He pulls up outside my house, and we both sit in silence. Finally, I say, "Same time next week?"

The older man nods at me and says, "Sure."

I go to get out of the car but after I open the door, I turn back and say, "And Huey?"

"Yeah?"

"Thank you," I say, feeling uncomfortable.

The wrinkled skin around his eyes crinkle as he smiles before saying, "Sure thing, son. See you at the game tomorrow night. Let's get us a win, okay?"

"Yes, sir."

CHAPTER THIRTY-TWO
CAROLINE

There is nothing better than the energy in a small town right before the first kick-off of the year.

My day has been a whirlwind of excitement, game day prep, and exhaustion. I didn't sleep much after my text to Theo went unanswered. I worried I had made him uncomfortable when he didn't respond right away, and that anxiety had grown all night. He texted me this morning apologizing and asking me to spend some time with him after the game tonight so I'm hoping everything was good, but I'm still anxious to see him later.

I work to refocus my brain on the field where the team just finished the spirit line. My girls make their way to the sidelines preparing to build up for kickoff while the boys and coaches huddle discussing last minute strategy.

Hannah knocks her leg against mine saying, "God, I love football season," before taking a big bite of a sausage dog she grabbed from the concession stand on the way into the stadium.

"Me too," I reply back, watching as the girls set for their extensions and load in.

The crowd stands to their feet as my squad leads us in a chant of "Gooooooooo Saints, Hey!" for kickoff. We are starting on defense, and the band starts playing "Swag Surfin" as one of the Springside players kicks the ball to our twenty-yard line. I smile as the cheerleaders dance in perfect unison in front of us.

As they are finishing their routine, Margaret walks up and sits in the seat next to me that we had saved for her. "Hey girlies!" she says as she reaches down and grabs a blue and white shaker out of her bag. "I couldn't find anything to wear! I need some gameday outfits for real. I haven't been to a high school game in almost ten years," she says with a laugh.

"I got you covered! Here," Hannah says, throwing her an extra Springside Varsity Cheer shirt. "I have a few more for you in my car, but Caroline and I thought we would help you out. If you want to throw that one on in the bathroom, I will throw your shirt in my bag."

Margaret looks ready to cry but she just hugs us and says, "Y'all are the best. I really never thought I would find friends like y'all. I will be right back."

Hannah and I hug her back and turn our attention back to the game. I try to keep my attention on my girls and the action on the field, but I can't help from sneaking glances at Theo too. He is wearing a powder blue polo with a cartoon Saint logo and khaki shorts. He seems completely absorbed in the game but during one of the timeouts I look down to feel his eyes on me as he listens to whatever Will is telling the boys.

The boys manage to keep the Saddle Ridge Wildcats from advancing past the fifty-yard line on the first drive, and the stadium is insane. Everyone is standing, cheering, and yelling as our team gets ready to receive the punt. Wesley Matthews catches it on our thirty-yard line, and takes off. He runs and twists out of the hold of several Wildcat players before sprinting towards the end zone. By the time he hits the Saddle Ridge twenty-yard line, the crowd is already celebrating our touchdown. There's no one to stop him as he sprints.

"Oh my God, look!" Hannah says, pointing to the sideline where Theo is sprinting alongside Wesley. The biggest smile I've ever seen crosses his face when Wesley finally scores and runs straight at him, jumping on him in celebration. I smile because as unwilling as Theo might have been to help with the team, it's clear he's damn good at this coaching thing.

The cheerleaders get set for the band to play "When The Saints Go Marching In" in celebration for the touchdown while Maggie grabs the large flag and runs it up and down the sidelines. The crowd smiles as the girls go through the tradition of dancing and kicking to the beat, and they yell along at the end with "Let's Go Saints!"

Hannah leans over and gushes, "I know I'm biased but the squad is looking so good tonight. I'm proud of you, Caroline. You have poured so much time and love into these girls, it really shows."

I smile as the girls build up into straight up libs and hold signs that say "Make Some Noise". The crowd engages with them as they call cheer after cheer and I know Hannah is right. "Couldn't do it without you, Han!" I say in response.

The game continues on, and it becomes clear the two teams seem to be pretty evenly matched. Both teams are expected to make it into the playoffs and I worry that this might not be the only time we find ourselves playing our rivals this season. Each time my eyes find Theo, he's completely focused on the game, and when he talks to his players it's clear they are hanging on every word he says.

Before we know it, it's halftime. Hannah and I leave our things with Margaret and walk onto the field. We sit with our cheerleaders as both bands perform before we take our place in front of the fifty-yard line as the squad runs out. They get set, while Hannah and I hold hands and sit in silence as we wait on the pressbox to press play on our music.

The opening lines of the "High Hopes" mix blast through the speakers and I squeeze her hand so hard I am worried I will hurt her. The triple toes are perfectly in sync, and the crowd that used to completely ignore this part of the game experience are already focusing on us. The girls dance and I let out a little cheer when they all nail the complicated ripple series we'd worked on for weeks this summer. They land their tumbling passes, and I squeeze Hannah even harder as the girls move to their stunts. This feeling never gets old, I think to myself as I pray the girls will keep all of the stunts in the air.

They nail the rippled heel stretches, the crowd cheers, and when they move to the pyramid formation, it feels as though every eye in the stadium is on my squad. The boys have even returned from the locker room, and Will has them stopped on the sideline to watch before the game resumes.

I refuse to breathe as the girls load Maggie into her stunt before they launch her into the air. One of the side groups braces her flip, and I hear the crowd suck in a collective breath as she flies around and shoots back up to her lib. The girls finish with a loud "Go Saints!" as everyone in the stadium cheers as if we just scored the winning touchdown. Hannah and I jump up and down screaming as the girls run to the sideline and all but tackle us.

"Great job ladies!" I say as we move out of the way of the players. I catch Theo's eye and he smirks at me before turning back to his players.

As far as I am concerned, this game can't end soon enough.

∼

BOTH TEAMS FIGHT HARD, and with less than thirty seconds on the clock, we are tied. It is our ball, and it's third and nine on the Saddle Ridge fourth-yard line. If we don't get the first down, we will either lose or be forced into overtime. The entire home section is on their feet chanting "Let's Go Springside" as the center snaps the ball to Blake. The quarterback starts to run, but sees that his options are limited.

Blake rears his arm back and throws the ball. At first, I think he must have decided to get rid of the ball instead of losing yards, but I am shocked when I see Wesley stretch out and catch the ball. He sprints towards the end zone as Hannah, Margaret, and I jump up and down and scream for him to run faster.

"Hell yes!" Hannah says as he crosses into the end zone.

We join in the chant of spelling out "Saints!" before screaming the last part of the cheer, "Black, Blue, White! Fight, Springside, Fight!"

I can't help the smile that breaks across my face as I see that Theo once again ran alongside Wesley and the two are celebrating on the sidelines while the kicker runs out for the extra point.

After he makes the kick, the girls and the band go straight back into "When The Saints Go Marching In."

After they finish, Saddle Ridge snaps the ball once, but they aren't able to complete the pass as the buzzer rings signaling the end of the game.

As the players and cheerleaders walk out to shake hands with the Saddle Ridge team, Hannah and I start our duties of cleaning up. After the handshake is finished, the team and squad come back and link arms facing the stands for the fight song. Once everyone is ready, the band plays, and we all sing along.

The song ends with thunderous applause and the crowd

starts to break off and the team heads towards the locker room. I feel my phone buzz and look down to see a text from Theo.

> Theo: Gotta finish up with the team. Meet me by my truck?

> Me: Sure thing. Good game, Coach

Tucking my phone back away, I start to pack up our run through sign, the emergency bucket, and coolers. Once Hannah, Margaret, and I make sure everything is put away, Hannah hugs me and says, "Go get 'em, Cowgirl," with a laugh.

I roll my eyes while Margaret wrinkles her nose at us. "Ugh, Hannah, you're the worst. You know that right?"

"I knew you were gonna take the nickname out of context," I tell them, while Hannah cackles away at her own antics.

"You know you love me. But for real. Go have fun. I want all the details tomorrow morning. Are we still on to pick pumpkins?" Hannah asks us both.

"Yep," I say. "Pumpkins in the morning, and the fair tomorrow night. I'll pick you both up around ten."

"Do y'all ever feel like you're living in a real life episode of Gilmore Girls?" Margaret asks with a laugh.

"Yep. But we don't have a Luke's Diner and our books are way smuttier," Hannah says.

"Yeah, it's too bad. I wouldn't mind having a hot Huntzburger to sweep me off my feet," Margaret says looking wistful.

"You're team Logan?!" Hannah and I scream in unison.

"Uhhh yeah," she says with wide eyes.

"No!" Hannah yells loud enough to gather the attention of a few fans making their way to their cars.

"What are y'all?" Margaret asks, narrowing her eyes at us.

"Team Jess," we say in unison while Margaret laughs.

"I should have known. You both may as well have 'broken

boys welcome' written across your forehead," she says, shaking her head at us and making us all fall into a fit of giggles.

"Well, Logan is fine. But it's a good thing you aren't Team Dean, or we would have to seriously reevaluate this friendship," I tell her, and we spend a few more minutes chatting before they both walk to their vehicles. I spot Theo's truck by the fence, and start to make my way over through the now empty parking lot.

I am halfway there when I see a boy coming towards me. Due to the poor lighting, it's hard to tell who it is, but I assume it's one of my students coming to speak to me. It isn't until he's standing right in front of me that I realize it's Michael.

"Oh, hi Michael," I say as he towers over me and looks at me with a look of disdain.

"You know, you really are such a bitch, Miss Caroline," the boy says with a sneer.

"Michael, I understand you're upset with me, but this isn't the way to handle it," I say, trying to make sure my voice doesn't shake as he takes another step towards me.

"You ruined my whole life because you couldn't just mind your damn business!" Michael explodes. "You know what happened? After that stupid shit in your class, it brought attention to me. Mr. Hale kept trying to call home, and when he couldn't get anyone he decided without a parent conference, I can't come back to school"

He looks at me and as he yells, I realize it isn't hatred I'm seeing in his eyes—it's pain.

Michael starts yelling again, "Because of your shitty journal entries, I won't graduate high school. Because guess what? I don't have a parent to come meet with Mr. Hale! I-"

"Son, I don't know who you are, but you better back the hell up," I hear a deep voice say as I make eye contact with Theo. His eyes blaze with anger, but I silently hold up a hand to him.

"Michael," I say while still looking at Theo. Recognition

flashes in his eyes at the name, and I keep talking before Theo can make the situation worse. "What do you mean you don't have parents? I've talked to your mom before. Did something happen?" I ask. Surely if there had been an accident, the school would have notified us.

"Yeah, something fucking happened!" Michael yells but must sense Theo moving closer because he lowers his voice a few octaves. "My mom left just like everyone else in my life does. She just decided she was tired of being a mom and ran off. She left me ten dollars on the counter with a note that said 'Good luck kid'.

"It wasn't enough that half the kids at school already hate me because she slept around with their dads. She couldn't be content with just stripping in Crestview, but she had to bring a different guy home every night. It wasn't enough that she said she was too damn drunk the night she got pregnant to remember who my dad was. But she couldn't hold on another year. I turn eighteen in eleven months, but she was so damn tired of taking care of me that she packed up and moved out while I was at school. It's pretty fucking ironic if you ask me because I've been taking care of us for years."

My heart breaks for the boy in front of me as he continues to rant. I don't try to stop him, and Theo makes eye contact with me as he listens to Michael go on.

"I started working when I was twelve. I found someone with chicken houses that didn't care how old I was. Worked from the time I got out of school until midnight every night. I was so proud when that farmer paid me the first time. Eighty dollars cash for the week. I was too stupid to realize the man was paying me about twelve dollars a day. I took it in the living room and showed it to her. I told her I'd gotten a job so that I could buy a used Xbox from Goodwill. She slapped me, took my money, and told me to stop being a brat. That went on for a few years, but I managed to hide it all."

"Michael," I say, wanting to comfort him, but he just keeps talking.

"By the time I turned fifteen, I had gotten bigger than her, so she quit trying to hit me. Instead, she just ignored me. I didn't really mind. I gave her most of the money I made doing odd jobs, but I hid enough back to pay for my cell phone and food. I told myself I just had to make it until I was eighteen, and then I would get out. But then she ran off. And that would have been fine because I've been taking care of myself for a long damn time. But then I was sitting in your class and you were talking about the American Dream. And I couldn't answer the question, because I don't have a damn clue what I want out of this life anymore. And then you started talking about calling a parent and I lost it. If I tell Mr. Hale why my mom can't come, I'll be placed in foster care. And it's all your fuc-"

"Enough," Theo says.

Michael blinks at him as if he forgot he was there while Theo continues. "Listen, Michael, I know you think no one in the world can understand what you're going through. But I swear, I do. You've been dealt a really fucking shitty hand. And we can talk about that. But you sure as hell aren't going to keep cussing and intimidating Miss Caroline."

"But, she-" Michael starts, but upon seeing the thunderous look on Theo's face, he stops.

"Michael, did Miss Caroline come to your house and tell your mother to slap you around?" Theo asks.

"No," Michael says quietly.

"Did she encourage her to run off on you or just be a shitty mother in general?" Theo continues.

"No," the teenager repeats.

"Did Miss Caroline ask to be screamed at in her own classroom or tell Mr. Hale she was requiring a parent conference as a term of condition to return to her class?"

"No," Michael says again, looking as if someone had kicked his puppy.

"So, did Miss Caroline do anything at all to earn all this hatred from you?" Theo asks finally.

"I don't guess so," Michael says, now looking at his feet.

"Apologize," Theo says, his voice leaving no room for argument.

"Miss Caroline, I am really sorry. You didn't deserve me being such a shit. I'm sorry," Michael says with tears in his eyes.

I wipe the tears that have gathered in my eyes as well, before I say, "I understand Michael. I am so sorry this happened to you. But I will help you figure all this out. And I hope you understand, but I will have to report this conversation."

"I know," Michael says, looking defeated.

"Michael," Theo says, "Listen, I know this isn't what you want to hear, but I think foster care could be really good for you. I was around your age when I went into the system, and while our stories are different, I think it will be a better situation than you've been in for years. I will help make sure the people they place you with are trustworthy. You don't have to do this alone if you can let us help you."

I feel a pang in my chest at the loss both the boys in front of me have been through. If you had told me a month ago that Theo would be this invested in a teenager from Springside, I would have never believed it, but I had to admit I was falling fast for the man who was always full of surprises.

We talk for a minute before we decide that I should text Mrs. Belle. She runs the local Department of Human Resources office, and since her daughter is on my cheer team, I have her cell number. After sending her a text, I tell Michael to plan for her to be in touch sometime tomorrow morning.

Theo gives Michael his cell number and tells him to call

when he talks to her. Michael thanks both of us before walking back into the darkness.

Theo turns towards me and holds out his arms for me. I run to him and he holds me for a moment, both of us trying to calm down after the surge of adrenaline we felt tonight. After a moment, he blows out a breath before saying, "Well what do you say Miss Tyler, you still up for a little date night?"

"Heck yes."

CHAPTER THIRTY-THREE
THEO

I can't say that the earlier events of tonight had been what I was expecting, but I had to admit, I liked being able to help.

When I first walked out to the dark parking lot to find a man yelling in Caroline's face, I was ready to lose it. But after I realized who it was, I mostly felt sorry for the kid. I may have lost my parents too, but I never doubted their love for me and that was more than could be said for Michael. I meant what I said about helping him, and I intend to check up on him as much as I can.

But now that things had calmed down, all I can think about is the fact that I'm finally alone with Caroline after one of the longest weeks of my life. I felt like total shit when I woke up this morning and realized I left her hanging with her flirty text, but I intend to make it up to her.

"What do you feel like doing? We could get something to eat or go to your apartment or-" I say but she cuts me off.

"I want to see your farm," she declares.

"Okay, well I don't have any animals yet, and Margaret is

probably consuming every inch of the kitchen and living room," Theo says.

"I'm not worried about either of those things," Caroline says as the sexiest smirk I've ever seen spreads across her face.

"Well, what do you want to do then?" I ask her, anxiously waiting to see what she'll say.

"Hmmm, let's just ride, Cowboy. I have some blankets in my trunk from baseball season, and when we find a spot we like, we can just get in the tailgate and talk," she says as her eyes sparkle with mischief.

If the look on her face is any indication, I have a feeling there won't be much talking, but you certainly won't hear me complaining. "Perfect, let's go."

Unable to stop myself, I grab her and kiss her deeply for a minute before jumping into motion. After she runs to her car and grabs the blankets, we jump into my truck, and I resist the urge to speed off towards the house, ignoring every stop sign and traffic law until I am between her legs with her lips on mine.

"So, Coach, I guess congratulations are in order," she says, winking at me from the passenger side as she leans over and reaches for my hand. "That was some game."

"Yeah, it was," I say with a small smile on my lips. "I thought when I gave up the sport in high school I would never know what it would be like to be on a team again. But tonight proved that wrong. And it feels pretty damn good."

"Theo, you're a natural. I know coaching wasn't in your original plans, but those boys have grown to really love you. You should be proud," Caroline says while she squeezes my hand.

"Thanks. The squad looked awesome tonight too. I've never seen someone flip like Maggie did in that pyramid."

"Thank you. She's so talented. I am really hoping that Hannah and I can help her get a cheerleading scholarship.

After everything she's been through, she really deserves it," she says.

We continue to make small talk while I drive until I pull into our long and winding driveway. One of the things that I love about the farm is the long driveway that hides the house from the street. I pull into the drive, stopping by the garage and grabbing us each a beer, before making our way to one of the pastures.

As I throw the truck into park, Caroline leans over. She brushes her hair back as it falls into her eyes and says, "I have a proposition for you, Mr. Johnson."

"Hmm, that sounds like it could be interesting. What is it, Miss Tyler?"

"You can have your way with me tonight. Anything you want. But first, you have to catch me," she whispers with a devilish grin. Before I can comprehend what she said, she is off—throwing the passenger door open and sprinting through the field.

My adrenaline from the game returns, and it feels like a bolt of lightning as it races through my veins. I let out a loud whoop and call out, "Sunshine, when I catch you, you better be ready to beg!"

The moon is almost nonexistent tonight, but the stars give off enough light to see a few feet in front of me. I start running in the direction she had headed off in, but I can't see any sign of her.

I race between my truck and the field, knowing she couldn't have made it far in the dark. After a few minutes, I finally see a flit of her figure before she ducks behind a hay bale that was left over from when Mr. Wilkerson lived here. I break into a sprint towards her, and she lets out a loud shriek before taking off again back towards the truck.

She laughs while she runs, and I race faster, closing in on her. I catch her wrist right as we pass my tailgate, and I haul her into my arms. "Hmm, looks like you're all mine now," I say as I clamp my arm tightly across her stomach, securing her to my side as she tries to wiggle free.

"Whatcha gonna do with me Cowboy?" she asks, sounding desperate to hear my response.

"Well, that depends."

"On what?"

"Are you gonna be a good girl for me tonight?" I ask and I hear her breath catch in her throat as she rubs her thighs together against me.

"Yes sir. Always," Caroline responds.

I sit her on the edge of the tailgate and grab the blankets she'd thrown in the backseat. After spreading a few out, I turn back to her. In the dim light, I can feel the desire rolling off of her body, and I am desperate to feel her close to me.

"Do you trust me?" I ask her while I wrap my arms around her.

"Clearly," she says, hugging me tightly to my body.

With that piece of encouragement out of the way, I reach for my belt. I unbuckle it and pull it through the loops of my jeans as Caroline tracks my every movement.

"Are you gonna spank me?" she asks with a wink.

"Nope, not tonight. Give me your hands," I tell her. My voice is barely above a whisper, and Caroline's eyes widen as she places her hands in mine. Watching her closely, I slowly wrap my belt around both of her wrists and secure the leather-to-bed hooks inside the tailgate. In that moment, the electricity between us feels like it is going to burn me alive, and damn if I won't let it.

"Is that too tight?" I ask as I lean in and brush a stray hair away from her eyes. She shakes her head at me as I whisper, "Let me know if I need to loosen them later. You said any way I want right?"

"That's right," she says, all traces of her previous teasing gone from her tone.

"Good, because darlin', I haven't been able to think about anything other than your perfect pussy since last weekend. I can't wait to taste you again," I growl at her as I tease her sides with my hands.

In her new position with her hands bound above her head, I shove her shirt up and immediately reach for her breast. She arches her back to get closer to my touch, and after a minute of teasing her nipples through her lacy, black bra, I lean in and run my teeth against the rough fabric. She cries out and wraps her legs around my hips as she tries to pull me closer.

"Theo, please," she whimpers.

"Please what? What do you want?" I whisper as I kiss and lick up and down her neck, enjoying the noises she makes each time I make contact with her perfect skin.

"You, Cowboy. Whatever you'll give me. I'm yours," she says, and I see the trust and sincerity in her eyes.

I run my fingers up her jean-clad thigh until I reach the button. Making quick work of it and the zipper, I yank her pants off and see a skimpy black thong that matches her bra.

"Did you wear these for me, baby?" I ask as I skim my fingers across her center.

"Yes sir," she whispers as she withers under me.

"Such a good girl," I mutter as I tease her with my hand. After a minute of grazing my finger over the wet lace, I grab her thong and tear it off her body so that she's completely bare for me. I look up at her and through the moonlit darkness, I see her eyes are hazy with desire as I move closer and tease her quickly with my tongue before pulling back again.

"Scream as loud as you want to, Sunshine. There's no one out here to hear you except me and the critters. By the time we're done tonight even the coyotes are gonna know who owns your body," I say before bending back over to suck her clit into my mouth.

Damn, she tastes so good. I take my time licking and biting as she moans and cries under me. She wraps her legs around my hips again, and as she rocks against me, I have to remind myself that we agreed to take this slow. I want nothing more than to push into her wet cunt, but I'm determined to prove to Caroline that I can be the man she deserves. So instead, I settle for slipping two fingers inside her as I tongue her clit. Her legs shake as she screams my name, and I slip a third finger inside her as she comes on my tongue and fingers. I keep going, not stopping until her body is entirely spent before I pull back and lick her climax off my fingers.

"Damn. Is that all you've got?" she asks, and through the moonlight, I see the familiar look of mischief is back in her eyes.

"Oh I'm just getting started. But first, I need to feel your mouth on my cock," I tell her, and I don't miss the desire that floods her face.

I lean up and untie her hands so that she can touch me. She immediately grabs for my pants, unbuttoning and ripping them and my boxers off at one time. I wrap my hand around her throat and drag her lips to mine before she can get any further. I know she can taste herself on my lips and that seems to make her more frantic as we kiss.

I tighten my hand around her throat just enough that she lets out a small moan before she reaches her hand down to my hard cock. She wraps her small hand around my length and begins pumping her hand up and down causing me to curse.

"Fuck, darlin'," I growl at her as she pushes me onto my back. She crawls over me before sinking her hot mouth onto my hard cock as she continues to work me with her hand.

"You keep that up, and I won't last much longer," I warn her but she continues licking me like a damn lollipop. After a minute of fighting it, I start to pump my hips in time with her hand, and before long, I know I am about to come. "You— feel — so— damn— good," I whisper right before I let go and start to come. I keep working my hips in time with her hand as she sucks.

I go still, and I feel her pull back to smile at me before she asks, "Does this mean it's my turn again?"

Damn, if this woman isn't perfect.

CHAPTER THIRTY-FOUR
CAROLINE

As I make my way to grab Hannah and Margaret Saturday morning, I can't wipe the smile off my face. The effects of our time together in the pasture has given me a major burst of endorphins, and I wasn't sad about it. After I tasted him, Theo managed to make me come three more times before dropping me back off at my car around two this morning.

I pull up in front of Margaret and Theo's house, shooting Margaret a text that I'm outside. As I press send, I see a notification from Theo.

> Theo: You just can't stay away can you, Sunshine?

> Me: Nope. But if I could, I bet you would still chase after me.

> Theo: Damn right.

I am still smiling at my phone when Margaret launches

herself into my car. "Good morning Caroline. I am gonna pretend like it's not my brother we're talking about for the next five seconds and ask—did you have a good night?"

"Good morning, Margaret. And yes, the best night actually," I respond as Margaret makes a face that is somewhere between a smile and a grimace.

"Oh my gosh, I am so excited about the pumpkins today! I am truly so ready for fall! All the cinnamon, apples, and pumpkin spice a girl could want!" Margaret says as she looks wistfully out the window.

"Of course you're excited about the baking," I say with a laugh. We chatter on about Margaret's idea for creating a pumpkin pecan cinnamon roll with spiced cream cheese icing, and by the time we pull up to Hannah's long driveway, my stomach is growling. I pull in front of the farmhouse and honk the horn. As we wait, I see a flash of pink come across the front porch.

Margaret and I look at each other before letting out a groan. "Leroy," we mutter in unison before opening our doors and sprinting towards the porch.

As we get closer, I notice that Leroy is content on the porch munching on a pizza crust he found on the table nearby. He looks at us and wags his short, curly tail before rolling over for us to rub his large stomach. He puts his hooves in the air like he is trying to hold the crust in place while he wiggles and grunts at us for attention.

"This baby really thinks he's a dog huh?" Margaret asks with a laugh.

"One million percent," I say, shaking my head. I bend down to play with Leroy before yelling, "Hannah, you good?"

I hear footsteps coming from down the hall inside the house, and Hannah sticks her head out the door. "Yep, I'm coming! Wait, what's Leroy doing?"

"Looks like he managed to escape again. We found him on the porch eating pizza when we pulled up," Margaret explains.

"Damn little booger. I swear I can't do anything with him," Hannah says as she puts her hand over her face in a look of defeat. "Last night was a freaking disaster! I picked up pizza on the way home because I was starving. I was sitting out here eating and looking out at the farm when I realized there was another break in the fence, right where that light from the barn shines."

"Oh no! Why didn't you call us?!" I ask, already knowing the answer before it's out of my mouth.

"I knew you were otherwise occupied," Hannah says with an eye roll. "So anyway I ran out there and grabbed the stuff to patch the hole the best I could before the cows could realize it was down. I figured I would feed them to keep them distracted, but when I went to scoop it, I realized somehow water had leaked in and ruined all the feed. Apparently, the storm we had this weekend had knocked the tin roof loose and I didn't notice until last night. I was out here until after 1 AM trying to fix the fence, and then was at the Co-Op this morning when they opened at seven to replace the feed. I spent the last two hours out here making sure they were taken care of before I grabbed a quick shower."

"Hannah!" Margaret exclaimed. "I swear you are too freaking hard-headed for your own good sometimes!"

Hannah lets out a laugh and turns to Leroy. "And just what do you think you are doing sir?"

Leroy lets out another grunt and gives Hannah a look that is a mix of pure devotion and mischief as he continues to gnaw on the crust from Hannah's forgotten dinner. Hannah leans down and leads him back to his pen where it appears that Leroy shimmied open the door earlier this morning. Hannah, Margaret, and I work together to get the pig inside before closing him in and stacking a few pieces of wood in front of the door to prevent him from escaping again while we're gone.

Blowing out a breath and ignoring Leroy's sounds of displeasure at being back in his cage, Hannah turns to us and says, "Alright ladies, let's get our girl's day started."

WE PULL up to the local farm where the pumpkin patch is hosted each year, and I am not surprised to see that the lot is filled with people, despite the fact that the high for today is still over eighty degrees. Today may be full of fall activities, but as usual, the Alabama heat hasn't gotten the memo that summer is over.

As we make our way to the entrance, we take turns chatting about the upcoming holiday season. The late September air holds the promise of new traditions, and I feel a bubble of excitement in my chest over all the possibilities.

After grabbing a wagon, Hannah, Margaret, and I begin walking down the aisles of the field looking for the right colors and sizes to match the Pinterest photos we saved earlier in the week. I am leaning down to grab a smaller white pumpkin, when I hear a chorus of, "Hey, Miss Caroline! Hey, Miss Hannah!"

I look up to see Maggie and a couple of the other girls on our cheer squad running over to us. They are all wearing big smiles, and a few of them are pulling wagons so full of pumpkins, I am surprised they can roll them.

"Hey, girls!" Hannah and I shout. "Y'all having a fun morning?"

"Yes ma'am," the girls chorus.

"Miss Caroline, I heard you were kissing a boy last night," one of the cheerleaders named Heather sing-songs.

I must have looked surprised because the girls break into a

chorus of giggles as Maggie explains, "A couple of us were riding around last night after the game and we saw you kiss Coach Johnson in the parking lot. It was dark, but we saw your vehicles and put it together. Pretty sure everyone knows since Willy was in the car. You know he can't keep his mouth shut about anything."

I roll my eyes before responding, "Small-town life, I guess it was bound to happen eventually. Anyway, you girls have fun, and we will see you on Monday."

"Yes ma'am," the girls chorus back at us before making their way towards the entrance of the patch.

As they walk away, I turn back to Margaret and Hannah before saying, "Great. I'll bet you both anything that I know what the headline of the STS was this morning."

Hannah and Margaret break into a fit of laughter before Hannah says, "Hmm, probably something along the lines of 'Hot School Teacher Falls Victim to Asshole Fire Chief—Prayer Circle Today at Noon'."

"This won't cause any problems for you will it?" Margaret asks, looking concerned.

I shake my head before responding, "No. Theo isn't a true employee for the school system, so we're good there. It's not like we were trying to hide our relationship anyway. We'll just have to be prepared for a few days of gossip."

Hannah makes a noise in her throat before saying, "Bestie, I love you but I think you're forgetting what this town is like. I would plan for the next year to be full of the older ladies asking when the wedding will be. And Mrs. Sally is going to have a field day. But don't worry, we have your back."

"Well, I never doubted that. Enough about me, let's get these pumpkins!" I say before bending back over to grab the white one I'd been eyeing.

An hour later, our wagon is full of white, pink, green, and orange pumpkins, and we are all starving. We make our way to the entrance of the field where there is a small counter set up for us to check out along with a small mobile flower booth and a stand for iced pumpkin coffees. Mrs. Leah, the owner of the patch, checks us out and we all grab coffees and flowers before we head to the car to load our purchases.

As we get into the car, Hannah says, "I could really go for some tacos and a beer. Do y'all want to grab lunch at Maracas?" Margaret and I nod in agreement, and I take a sip of my coffee before I pull out of the parking lot heading that way. Hannah connects her phone to the Bluetooth, and I smile as "Hole in the Bottle" by Kelsea Ballerini blasts through the speakers.

We take turns singing loudly down the back country roads until I am turning onto Main Street and hear Margaret's phone ping. She pulls it out and says, "Ladies, we may have a change of plans."

"Is something wrong?" I ask quickly, my mind immediately going to Theo.

"No, I don't think so. But Theo just texted and said the animals have arrived. I know he thinks he's Superman, but I would feel better if he wasn't alone. Would y'all want to pick up a chicken sandwich from the gas station and head over?"

"Sure," Hannah and I both say, and I wheel into the Chevron station that houses Mama Roo's inside.

"If you had told me this time last month I would be eating fried chicken from a gas station and heading to work on a farm, I would have told you that you were crazy," Margaret says with a laugh.

"Don't hate on Mamma Roo's. Her chicken sandwich will put anyone else's to shame," Hannah says as we make our way inside the rustic station.

After ordering our sandwiches and sweet teas to go, we hop back in my car and we make the short drive over to Theo's farm.

I didn't know what to expect, but nothing could have prepared me for the chaos that greeted us when I pulled up to the farmhouse. Looking around with wide eyes, Hannah and I make eye contact before reaching quickly for our cell phones.

"Oh my gosh, what are we gonna do?" Margaret asks, taking in the array of animals running around us.

"Call in reinforcements," Hannah and I say together.

CHAPTER THIRTY-FIVE
THEO

How hard could this whole farm thing be?

That had been my attitude this morning as I prepared for Mr. Willy to drop off my animals.

But after an hour with the animals, it turns out the answer to that question was pretty fucking hard.

Things had gone smoothly for the first few minutes while Willy and I had chatted and unloaded. But as soon as his truck had disappeared down the driveway it was like the animals decided to stage a revolt. The small donkey named Petunia, that Willy had convinced me I needed to help with coyote protection, kicked all of the gates open and led the horses and cows out of their fields.

I knew I'd hooked the chain on the gate before I turned my back to grab some water from inside, but it's clear the chain was no match for a pissed off Petunia as she led the charge into my driveway.

I let out a small breath, trying to plan the best course of attack in order to get all of the animals back where they need to go when I see Caroline's car pull up in my driveway.

I grab my hat off the porch and walk into the September

sun yelling for the animals as the girls get out of the car and make their way toward me.

"What the heck happened, Theo?" my sister calls out, not taking her eyes off the nearest calf about a hundred feet from her.

"It looks like even the animals have heard about the whole asshole fire chief thing, and they don't want to be around you either," Hannah teases before letting out a loud laugh.

I roll my eyes at the joke as Caroline and Margaret giggle, before asking, "Are y'all here to laugh at me or do you plan on helping?"

Caroline holds out a wrinkled brown paper sack in my direction and says, "We come in peace, Theo, I promise. Here. Eat this sandwich from Mamma Roo's while we look for some empty feed buckets. I'm sure there's some around here somewhere."

I nod at her before taking the bag and pulling out the sandwich. I point in the direction to the old barn about a half mile away where I had seen a pile of old farm stuff earlier in the week. "There's a couple bags of feed on my tailgate. I'll come help you."

"Listen, someone has to stay here with the escape artists. If anyone is gonna have to go chasing after a jackass today, it's you. Eat, and we'll be right back," Caroline says before leaning over and dropping a quick kiss on my mouth and leading the girls across the lot to my truck. "Oh, and we called in some help too. Will and Seth are on their way," she says over her shoulder. "Looks like everyone doesn't hate the Fire Chief as much as you thought."

I shake my head at her while unwrapping the sandwich the girls brought me and glaring at Petunia. The donkey makes eye contact with me before walking over to one of the shrubs I had just planted. Letting out a loud snort, Petunia grabs the bush with her teeth and tugs hard enough that the entire plant comes out of the ground. I start to walk towards her, but she starts kicking out her back legs and turning in violent circles. Why the hell did I let Willy talk me into a donkey? I didn't know shit about the animal and it has become increasingly clear that Petunia isn't the most amicable creature I've ever met.

I scarf down the sandwich and decide to try my luck with the horses first. I've always loved horses. I can do this. After my mental pep talk, I walk towards one with my hand out, trying to show the creature that I am not going to cause it any harm. I have just gotten close enough to pet his snoot when Will's truck comes flying into my driveway causing all the animals in the vicinity to panic.

"Holy shit man, this is a mess!" Seth calls out as he jumps out of the truck.

"Yeah, I'd say so," I say, not taking my eyes off the spooked horse as he jumps in place and bucks from left to right.

About that time, the girls pull back up to the front of the house with the buckets. I move slowly over to my tailgate in an effort to prevent them from startling the animals any further.

"Here you go," Caroline says, holding out the bucket, and I open the feed bag and pour some of the cow's pellets into the bucket. After it's about half full, I take the bucket from Caroline's hand and shake it hard.

"Come on," I holler while making as much noise with the feed as possible. "Come on!"

The cattle finally look up from their grazing on the grass beside my front door and slowly start to make their way towards the gate that Petunia had broken them out of. It takes about twenty minutes, but with everyone's help, we manage to get all ten cows inside the fence. When I go to close it, I realize that Petunia's kick damaged the post that held the gate in place and I let out a low groan of frustration.

"What's wrong?" Will asks as he looks over my shoulder at the fence.

"Damn jackass knocked the post loose. If I try to close the gate, we'll be back rounding them up before dinner. I swear, I've done cows and horses before but this donkey shit is for the birds," I reply.

Everyone laughs as Huey pulls up in the drive and jumps out of his Ford pickup before declaring, "Sorry kid, I got stuck helping Mrs. Mabel move some furniture around this afternoon, but I came as quick as I could after Will texted me."

Huey looks around, quickly assessing the situation before letting out a loud laugh, "Damn son, don't tell me Willy convinced you to take Petunia!"

"What do you mean? He said she would help keep the coyotes away from the pasture," I respond defensively.

At this point, Huey is almost doubled over in laughter as the rest of us watch, all of us with obvious looks of confusion on our faces. "He- You- He-" Huey wheezes as he tries to explain through his fit. "No wonder you had to send out an SOS. That thing right there is the meanest little bitch I ever did meet. Willy's been trying to get someone to take her off his hands for at least a year."

"And you didn't think that was something you should warn me about?!" I ask, throwing my hands up in the air.

"Well, no. I thought the whole 'jackass' name kinda stood for itself when it came to these animals," Huey says, causing the rest of the crew to titter with laughter. "Come on, let's get the horses sorted and then we'll figure out what to do with ole' Petty Petunia."

The girls and Huey work together for the next hour, slowly winning the trust of the horses together and leading them back to their pen while Will, Seth, and I mix up a sack of concrete to pack around the posts Petunia had knocked loose. While we wait for it to set, Margaret goes inside and comes back out with glasses of fresh lemonade a bit later.

Finally, once the other animals are settled, the men help me install a sturdier lock on the gate, and we all team up to lead Petunia back into her newly reinforced pasture.

"Thanks, y'all. I appreciate your help," I said to the friends standing around us.

"That's what we're here for," Caroline says as Will responds with, "No problem, man."

"Do y'all want to come inside? It's almost two-thirty so the Alabama game is about to kick off and I can throw some snacks together."

The group lets out a chorus of agreement before Huey says, "Well, I am gonna leave you young folks to it. See you all later!"

Huey drives off as Margaret leads the way back into the house. We all collapse on the couch as Will grabs the remote and quickly locates CBS where the Tide is about to kick off against Arkansas.

I feel a quick pang in my chest remembering the game my brother had played against this team. His eighty-yard catch in 2008 had garnered him more attention than he ever could have dreamed of, and I take a breath expecting to feel the panic clawing its way up my throat until I can't breathe. But instead, Caroline reaches over, squeezes my hand, and throws herself across my lap.

"Let's watch some football," she suggests with a wink, and just like that, the panic I expected to feel is nonexistent. "By the way, Chief Johnson, if I didn't know any better, I'd say it looks like you might not be enemy number one around here anymore."

Blowing out a breath, I turn to look at everyone who had dropped everything and came running for my sister and me. Hannah and Will are arguing over the difference between crimson and cardinal as the teams take the field. Seth returns from outside carrying a small case of beer he'd had in the cooler on the back of his truck before handing one to each of us. Margaret scurries around the kitchen cutting up crescent rolls to throw together some pigs in a blanket while the mixer beats together cookie dough. And Caroline leans forward to drop a kiss to my mouth again before turning her attention back to the screen.

I have to admit, Caroline is right. Springside might not be perfect, but I can't deny that after the last month it is starting to feel like home.

CHAPTER THIRTY-SIX
CAROLINE

After watching the Tide defeat the Razorbacks, Hannah and I run to my apartment to get ready for the night at the fair. After years of last minute events, Hannah has a drawer in my dresser stashed with extra clothes and makeup, to keep from driving the extra twenty minutes out to her house.

We haven't been in the car for more than a minute before I feel her eyes on me. "Go ahead and spit it out," I say with a laugh. "It's not like you to keep your opinions to yourself."

My best friend smiles at me before she says, "You look happy,"

"I am happy, Han. I know it sounds crazy, but I have no doubt he's it for me," I say, keeping my eyes on the road and ignoring the way my nerves have gone haywire at my declaration.

"Wow. Okay. So y'all are really that serious already?" Hannah asks, and I try to ignore the surprise in her voice.

"I don't know. I know he's got some things to work through, but I'm in. Honestly, it scares the shit out of me, but I want him. He came out of nowhere and completely took over my heart."

"Shit. Okay. Well, I'm happy for you, Caroline. And I'm here for whatever you need. I just want you to be happy," Hannah says, and I hear the sincerity in her voice. "So, it looks like you found yourself a cowboy after all, huh?"

"Yeah. I just hope I get to keep him," I say as I pull into my apartment.

We run upstairs and make quick work of changing clothes and touching up our makeup. I grab a light pink v-neck and jean shorts while Hannah throws on a pair of black shorts and a cropped gray shirt. Feeling slightly more presentable, I grab my lipgloss and smear it on before walking back to the door.

By the time we return to Theo and Margaret's house, night has fallen and everyone is ready to go. We'd invited the boys to go with us to the annual fair while we watched the game. Hannah and I had made it a tradition while we were still in high school, and we hadn't missed a year since. The rides were a complete safety hazard, and the food contained at least a couple of days' worth of calories, but we didn't care. Margaret had already been looking forward to going with us, so we'd decided to turn it into a group event after the great escape.

"Y'all ready?" the boys call out from the porch before we are even completely out of the car. "We're starving!"

"We literally just ate," I argue back, teasingly.

The boys just roll their eyes at me as we pile into Will's truck. He blares the latest Luke Combs album as we drive, We haven't even made it to the end of the driveway before he and Hannah are bickering over which song on the album is best. Margaret and I share a look before dissolving into a fit of giggles. I know we are both thinking about the fact that Hannah and Will are like an old married couple, but neither of us are brave enough to say it out loud.

Theo wraps his arm around my shoulder and tugs me into his side. He drops a kiss to the temple of my forehead, and I let out a contented sigh as we ride in companionable silence. After a few minutes, I see the lights of the fairground coming closer while Hannah and Will continue to throw verbal jabs at each other.

By the time we pull in and find a parking spot, they are almost screaming at each other over whether Reba McEntire or Shania Twain has the better voice. Finally, Seth is brave enough to step in and diffuse the situation and we make our way inside.

As we walk up to the ticket booth, I reach for the small wallet I had tucked into my shorts. Theo tracks my movements before saying, "What are you doing?"

"Uh, getting my ticket. Is that okay?" I ask, not understanding what he's saying.

"Baby, I can practically still taste your sweet pussy on my tongue. I'm buying your damn ticket," he growls low enough that no one else can hear him.

My shocked expression must be all the affirmation he needs because he steps in front of me and pays for both of our wristbands to get inside. Once Mrs. Darleen, the woman working the ticket booth for the Kiwanis club, hands him the pink plastic bands, Theo turns back to me and grabs my hand to pull me out of the way. When we are no longer blocking the line, he wraps his hand around my wrist. My mouth goes dry as I remember what he did last night, and I feel my face blush with desire.

We step inside the entrance as we wait for the rest of the crew to make their way inside. As we stand there, Theo reaches out and wraps his large hand around mine, pulling me into him. He drops a kiss on my forehead, and I bite back a smile at his show of affection. Hannah catches my eye as she walks through the entrance and I don't miss the look of approval on her face as she takes in our proximity.

After we've all made our way inside, Seth says, "I'm grabbing a funnel cake. I'm freaking starving. Anyone coming with me?"

We all nod in agreement, and Theo wraps his arm around my shoulders as we follow our friends over to the food cart. The late-September evening is comfortable, and I love feeling his large body close to mine as we walk. I can feel the eyes of several parents and students on us as we stand in line, but I can't find it in me to care what anyone thinks.

"So, Chief, how's Springside treating you?" Seth asks as we stand in line.

"Well, I have to admit, I have found some things I like a lot more than I planned," Theo says, squeezing my shoulder, making me smile.

Seth grins at us before saying, "Hmm, I see. Funny how that happens, isn't it?"

After waiting in line for another minute, we make it to the front and the boys order their funnel cake. Once the employee hands them the plate full of fried dough, Theo tears off a piece and feeds it to me. My lips wrap around his fingers, licking the sugar off him before he withdraws his hand, and I chew the sugary goodness. After a moment, he leans in close to me and whispers, "You have sugar on your lip. If you don't get it, I will, but you better be ready to give our friends a show."

"Hmm, is that right, Cowboy? You know, I've always loved a challenge," I whisper back with a smirk.

"Just remember, you asked for this," he growls before gently pushing me against the picnic table beside us and kissing me hard.

I lose myself in kissing him back for a moment, loving the way his arms cage me in and his mouth makes good on his promise by claiming mine, before I remember where we are. As I pull back, I realize Hannah and the rest of our friends are cheering and catcalling loudly enough to gain the attention of several other people in the vicinity. It seems like everyone is staring at us, except for Margaret who has resorted to scrolling on her phone. I worry we've made her uncomfortable, but a moment later she looks up and gives me a small wink letting me know we're good.

"Sorry, y'all. Uhh, so y'all ready for some rides? That Ferris wheel is calling my name," I say with a shy laugh.

With that, we all split up with Hannah and Will heading toward the carnival games. Will challenged Hannah in the car to the balloon dart game, and I wouldn't be surprised if they are still there battling it out when we are ready to leave. Margaret and Seth bonded earlier today when they realized they were both obsessed with the swings that spin you out over the fairground. So, that left Theo and I to entertain ourselves.

No complaints here.

"Come on," I say, grabbing his hand and pulling him toward the large Ferris wheel in the center of the fairgrounds. There is no one in line, so we walk straight to the front while the employee checks our wristbands before pointing to the mostly enclosed passenger car. I walk in and take a seat while Theo says something to the employee before making his way towards me.

He sits beside me and pulls the door closed before nodding at the employee he just spoke with. The Ferris wheel begins its slow ascent, and I lean against Theo without taking my eyes off the view. From this vantage point, it feels like I can see all of Springside. After a minute, I look over at Theo, expecting him to be admiring the view the same way I am. But instead, he's staring at me with a look of unrestrained passion in his eyes. At the same time, the Ferris wheel creaks to a slow stop. My eyes widen as I start to panic.

"Oh my God, are we stuck?" I ask, but before I can get another word out, Theo lets out a low laugh.

"No, Sunshine," he murmurs. "I paid the guy to give us five minutes up here alone. Any suggestions as to what we should do?"

My breath catches in my throat as he teases his hand up my

leg. "Nope, but I'm guessing you have something in mind, Chief Johnson."

"Hmm yeah, I have a few ideas. But the windows are open so unless you want everyone to hear, you're gonna have to be quiet," Theo says, his voice dropping to a whisper.

"Yes sir," I say without thought just before Theo pulls me into his lap and wraps his hand around my throat. He kisses me hard, and I let out a low moan as I grind against him.

"Damn, baby," he groans as he pulls back to kiss and suck down my neck.

I am lost in desire when suddenly I feel his hand trace up the inside of my thigh. He slides inside my shorts and I bite back a moan as he slips one finger tip inside my panties. He teases me for a moment before pushing the rest of his finger inside me as I let out a whimper.

"Quiet, Miss Tyler. You don't want anyone else to hear how good I make you feel do you?" he mutters and I feel myself tighten at the reminder that we aren't really alone.

"Ride my hand, Sunshine. I want you to come for me," he whispers, before nipping at the sensitive skin on my neck. My movements become frantic as I chase my orgasm, rocking my hips hard against his hand.

I feel the pleasure building as I whisper, "So damn good, Theo," and with that, I come hard on his fingers.

"Oh my God!" I groan as I grind against him, riding out my orgasm.

Effectively satisfied, I pull back and drop a kiss on his cheek before reaching for him.

I run my hand over his hard cock through his jeans teasing him. I reach for the button on his jeans, but Theo shakes his head at me, "No, baby. Tonight was about you. You can make it up to me tomorrow. Now come here and let me hold you."

I reclaim my seat beside him, and he wraps his arm around me pulling me close.

I brush a hand through my tousled hair, trying to gather myself as the Ferris wheel starts to move again. "Do I look okay?" I ask, worried my appearance is going to tip everyone off as to what we were just doing.

"You look perfect, Sunshine, because you look like you're mine."

CHAPTER THIRTY-SEVEN
THEO

Sunday morning comes and I can barely keep myself from grinning as I think about Caroline's face of shock when I teased her on the Ferris wheel. I have a few hours until she comes over to help me around the farm, and I am having a hard time focusing on anything else.

I throw on my hat and grab my gloves, heading to examine the fenceline at the back of the pasture before she gets here. As soon as I open the gate, several of the horses come running towards me. I scratch each of their heads and look out to the open grass where Petunia is glaring at me. I tried to pet her yesterday, thinking if I brought her enough treats we could be friends. Instead, she almost bit my hand off taking the treat and then tried to charge at me in retaliation for daring to enter her pasture. Clearly, she still isn't over it. And to think, this time last week I thought Hannah had it rough with Leroy.

Ignoring my jackass's attitude, I continue toward the back of the pasture. Checking my phone, I decide to call Michael and check on him as I walk. We talked briefly yesterday morning before the animals arrived, but I wanted to make sure he didn't feel like he was on his own in all this shit.

I dial the number and wait for him to pick up. After a few rings, I hear the sound of the call connecting before he says, "Hey, Chief. How are you?"

"Pretty good, kid. You holding up okay?" I ask, using my shoulder to keep my phone pressed to my ear so that I can open the gate.

"Yeah, the Chambers are really nice. Mr. Blake and Mrs. Kelsey took me to get some new clothes yesterday. From a real store. I haven't ever had anything that didn't come from Goodwill or one of the church care closets. I tried to tell them I didn't need it, but they did it anyway," he says, and it's hard to believe that the boy on the phone is the same kid that wreaked havoc in Caroline's classroom last week.

"That's cool. Did they get everything worked out with the school?" I ask as I put on my work gloves.

"Yeah. Even though it's the weekend Mrs. Belle called Mr. Hale and explained everything. He said we would handle the logistics on Monday, and while I'll still have some consequences, I can return to school. I know I screwed the whole thing up, so I'm just glad they're letting me come back. I just hope Miss Caroline can forgive me," Michael explains, sounding embarrassed about his actions.

"Well, I can't speak for her, Michael, but as someone who has also treated Miss Caroline unfairly, I'll just say, treat her the way she deserves. And don't ever let me catch you trying to intimidate her again, got it?" I say sternly.

"Yes sir, I won't," Michael replies, sounding effectively intimidated.

"Good, well you have my number if you need it. I'll check in with you soon, okay?" I say as I tug on the barbed wire fence, making sure it doesn't give when I push on it.

"Sounds good. Enjoy your weekend, Chief."

"You too, Michael," I say before disconnecting the call and tucking my phone back into my pocket. I move along the fence, and spend the next hour checking the line of barbed wire and reattaching the pieces that have worn loose.

When I'm satisfied with my progress, I take off my gloves and begin the trek back to the house. I pull my phone out and send Caroline a text.

> Me: I can't stop thinking about you. What time are you heading this way?

> Caroline: Getting dressed now. See you in thirty?

> Me: Sounds good. I am going to jump in the shower. And darlin'?

> Caroline: Yes?

> Me: Don't bother wearing any panties.

> Caroline: Yes sir. ;)

Yep, it's going to be a good afternoon.

I BARELY HAVE time to throw on some old jeans and a black T-shirt when I step out of the shower before I hear Bear let out a bark announcing Caroline's arrival.

I walk down the hall barefoot to let her in, grabbing my hat as I pass where I left it sitting on the counter.

I open the door and smirk at Caroline's ripped jean shorts and a solid black T-shirt. She has her dark brown hair piled on top of her head, and I swear I have never seen someone as beautiful as she is right now.

"Come on in," I say politely, like I wasn't just picturing her naked a moment ago. "I'm gonna grab my stuff before we check on the property."

"Sounds good. What all are we working on today?" Caroline asks while I try to think about any of the tasks I planned for us to start today. If I don't focus, I'm going to have her in my bed while I tease her, and as much as I love that idea, I really could use her help on the farm today.

"Well, there's a few things in the barn I could use a hand with. Do you mind?" I respond, looking for my work gloves that I used right before I got in the shower.

"Sure. I told you I would help you with anything you need. And I did mean anything." Caroline flirts with a wink.

Damn it, I'm so screwed.

I pin Caroline against the counter and steal a long kiss. We're both breathless when I finally pull back and say, "Let's go, baby."

We walk outside hand in hand, and I lead Caroline up the walkway into the large barn. "So I was thinking we could work on getting some of this old junk cleaned out," I suggest, gesturing to the plethora of stuff left on one side of the barn.

Caroline takes in the large hay barn and walks over to the opposite side where I'd stacked several rolls of hay I purchased this week. "Hmmm, we could do that..." she says with a grin.

"Or we could pick up where we left off last night, and I could beg you to fuck me against the haybale..." she finishes, and my breath catches in my throat.

"I would love that, but I don't have a condom with me," I tell her, and I know she doesn't miss the disappointment in my voice.

"I'm clean, Cowboy, and I have an IUD," she says shyly. "I just want to feel you bare."

I stalk toward her as she smirks at me. "Well, Miss Tyler, you know how I like it when you beg." With that, I push her against the closest round bale and wrap her legs around my hips.

She lets out a low moan as she grinds her hips against me. I lean in and whisper, "But if we start this, we aren't leaving this barn until you're dripping with my cum."

Her eyes darken, and she gives me a small nod letting me know she wants this as desperately as I do.

With that, my hands grip the hem of her shirt and I tear it off of her before attacking her mouth. My hands are everywhere as I try to touch every part of her all at once. She kisses me back, her tongue tangling with mine as she reaches for my shirt and pulls until I help her take it off me.

I swear I will never get enough of this woman.

I grip her ass to secure her to my front and carry her across the barn to where I stacked some smaller square bales. I strip her jeans off her legs and sit her down, before pulling back to unbuckle my jeans. Dropping them to the floor, I wrap my hand around her neck again and tighten it a bit, watching her eyes blaze with desire. "You like that, baby?"

She nods before whispering, "Please, Theo. More."

With that, I tighten my hand around her neck and move her so that she's bent over the bales with her ass in the air. I run my hand against her ass, and give it a light smack before I line myself up with her entrance.

I pause to admire her perfect curves laid out across the hay bales before slowly pushing my cock into her leaking core.

"God, you feel so good, baby. You're so wet for me," I mutter as soon as I am fully inside her, pausing to let her adjust to my size.

"Oh my God, Theo, please fuck me," she moans bucking her hips against me.

"Well darlin', only because you said please," I growl, grabbing her hips and thrusting hard in and out of her tight pussy.

It doesn't take long before I feel her walls tighten against my cock as her breathing becomes shallow.

"Scream for me when you come," I whisper as I pound harder into her before I move my hand between her legs and stroke her clit. She screams and her pussy clenches so hard I can barely move.

"That's my girl. Come for me baby," I say as she rides out her climax. When I am sure she's satisfied, I finally allow myself to lose control coming with a roar.

I bend over the hay bale where Caroline is still sprawled out and pull her close with my cock still buried deep inside her.

"I swear, Sunshine," I say with a satisfied chuckle, "you are always full of surprises."

CHAPTER THIRTY-EIGHT

CAROLINE

"Let's run it again girls!" I shout to the squad as they finish grabbing water after running the new routine for the week. We'd pulled out a few elements of their competition routine for later in the season and added in a few new dance counts to ensure we are getting the practice in without boring the crowd.

Maggie and the other seniors decided to go with the country theme, and the line dances need a bit of cleaning up, but overall I am pleased with their performance for a Tuesday. "One more time and if you're sharp I'll let you go home early!" I tell the girls, and I'm met with a chorus of excitement.

As the girls get set, I grab my phone to check my messages and see I have a text from Theo.

Theo: Hey, Sunshine. How's your day?

Me: Good! Michael was back at school today, and he had a really good day. How about yours?

Theo: Yeah, he called me a few minutes ago. Today's been pretty good. Derrik convinced me to try learning some TikTok dance this morning because he's bored with Zach gone. I was trying to be a good sport, but I bet you can imagine how that went.

Me: Oh, God. Please tell me there's video evidence…

Theo: Not a chance, Miss Tyler. You at practice now?

Me: Yeah, we're wrapping it up.

Theo: Us too. You want to come for a ride tonight?

Me: That depends: you or the horses?

Theo: Why not both?

Me: You're on, Cowboy.

I glance up from my phone and see the girls are ready. I turn their music on, and as they dance, I have to admit they look much sharper than they had the time before.

"Good! Yes!" I exclaim to one of the girls who has been struggling with the motions as she hits each one this time.

When the music ends, Hannah and I make eye contact, silently ensuring we're on the same page.

"Great job! Y'all get out of here!" I yell so that they can hear me over the music.

The girls scatter, and I turn back to Hannah, "That wasn't bad! Ready to get out of here?"

"Hell yeah! Let's go," she says, standing from the bleachers and grabbing her bag.

After making sure everything is turned off in the gym, we make our way across campus to the faculty parking lot. "You have plans for tonight?" Hannah asks as we walk.

"Yeah, I think so. Theo asked if I wanted to come ride horses with him," I say with a small smile while Hannah giggles.

"Damn right, he did. Long live cowgirls, you know?" she says with a laugh.

I roll my eyes at her teasing and wink at her as I open the door to my car, "You know what they say– save a horse..."

Hannah cackles and flips me off as I drive off to change clothes before meeting Theo.

I speed home, anxious to see Theo again. I am halfway up the stairs when I meet Seth leaving his apartment. He stops on the stairs when he sees me before saying, "Hey, Caroline. How was your day?"

"Not bad. I never see you now that your workshop is on the other side of campus. How was yours?" I ask as he runs his hand through his shaggy brown hair.

"Oh, it was good. I've gotta go meet Margaret at her new bakery. I promised I would help her figure out how to tackle all the repairs. Can you believe Springside is getting a coffee shop?"

"That's so sweet of you. I can't wait. Everything she makes is so damn good," I say, wishing I had one of her cookies right now.

"Yeah. Anyway, I gotta go. Tell Theo I said hey," he says, continuing down the stairs.

I look at him in confusion before asking, "How'd you know I'm going to see Theo?"

Seth lets out a laugh, "Come on, Caroline. You know there are no secrets in Springside. Enjoy your date."

I shake my head and giggle at how fast news travels in this damn town. Making it to my door, I unlock it and hurry to change clothes.

The October evening is still warm, but I know I will want to be covered depending on how long we plan to ride, so I throw on a pair of jeans and a thin flannel before grabbing my cowboy boots and braiding my hair out of my face. When I'm sure I have everything I need, I grab my keys and rush down the stairs while texting Theo that I am on the way.

As I drive, I blast "Strawberry Wine" and sing at the top of my lungs. I pull up to Theo's farmhouse, looking out toward the pasture, and see him saddling up two of his new American Quarter horses in preparation for our ride. I park my car and call out, "Hey!" causing him to raise his arm and tip his cowboy hat in greeting.

I am about to make my way over to him when I hear a loud bark and look at the house to see an excited Bear barreling toward me, wagging his tail and howling in excitement. When the lab reaches me, he jumps up and places his large paws on my shoulders before giving me a wet kiss on the cheek. "Hey, buddy. Who's a good boy? You want some tummy rubs?" I ask as I sit on the gravel and scratch the dog's stomach. After petting the pup until he is almost asleep, I stand and make my way over to Theo.

He looks up at me, and his face breaks into a wide grin. "Damn, Sunshine. You look so damn good."

I stop in front of him and lean in for a kiss. He slides his large calloused hands into the back pocket of my jeans and drags me closer to him as he sucks on my bottom lip. "God, I missed you baby."

"I missed you too. Yesterday felt so long even with margarita Monday to look forward to," I say with a laugh as Theo leans back but keeps his hands on me.

"Agreed. I see Bear and I are apparently going to have to compete for your time, huh? He's such a little asshole" he asks and I roll my eyes at him.

"No need to be jealous, Chief Johnson." I tease before leaning back in for another kiss.

"So, you ready to ride? I have something I want to show you after." Theo states, and I don't miss the glimmer of mischief in his eyes with that statement.

"Yep, let's go. Have you decided on names for these babies yet?" I ask, gesturing toward the horses.

"I was going to ask if you had any suggestions?" he says, looking at me expectantly.

"Hmmm..." I say, taking a minute to consider our options. "Since all four horses are females, what if you named each of them after a classic female country music singer? So something like Dolly, Shania, Martina, and Trisha?"

"Sounds good to me," he says, smiling at my suggestion before asking. "You ready?"

"Let's do it," I say, leaning out to let the chestnut horse get accustomed to my scent before taking her reins from Theo. "Come on, Trisha, let's ride."

I slip my boot into one of the stirrups and hoist myself up onto the large horse's back before turning back to Theo. He double checks his saddle before mounting the red dun horse I have already decided is going to be named Dolly. Once he's sure she's comfortable, he nods to me and says, "Keep up."

With that, he and Dolly take off, and I do nothing but sit there and admire the view for a moment. What is it about a cowboy that's so damn sexy?

Shaking my head, I signal for Trisha to follow, and she breaks off into a canter after Theo. He leads us in the opposite direction of the barn, and we spend the next thirty minutes riding in comfortable silence before he loops us back to the barn. After dismounting and caring for the horses, he turns to me and asks, "You up for another adventure?"

"Always. Whatcha wanna do?" I question, already following him to the truck parked outside the barn.

"Just come on," he says, and I roll my eyes at his secrecy.

We ride out to a part of his property that I haven't visited yet, and he parks at the edge of a clearing on the edge of the forest.

"What are we doing?" I ask as I follow him through the trees.

Instead of responding, he motions ahead where I see a small creek surrounded by the trees.

"What do you say to a little evening skinny dip?"

"Oh, I'm so in," I say with a laugh, already running to the water and stripping off my shirt.

Theo chases after me with a whoop. We each rush to strip off our clothes and, by the time we hit the water, there is a trail of clothes marking our path and we are both completely naked.

I sink under the cool water for a moment before Theo's hand reaches in and pulls me to him, leaning forward and kissing me hard.

I reach my hands up to circle his neck and wrap my legs around his waist, needing to feel his bare skin everywhere.

"Well, Theo, what now?" I ask, teasing, before leaning in and dropping a kiss on his exposed collarbone.

"Now I taste and tease you until you're dripping for me," he says, holding me up and walking us out of the water until he drops me to my feet and presses me against one of the trees in the clearing. The rough bark against my back paired with the October breeze overwhelms my senses and leaves me desperate for his touch.

Theo kisses me hard while wrapping his hand around my throat holding me captive against the tree before kissing down my neck and taking my nipple in his mouth. I moan loudly as I arch my back to get closer to his touch. Using his other hand, he slides between my legs and teases my clit just enough to drive me insane.

I rock my hips against him before groaning, "Theo, please."

"God, you're so fucking beautiful when you beg," he growls before falling to his knees in front of me. He lifts one of my legs and places it around his shoulder before attacking my dripping core with his mouth. He takes turns lapping at my center and nipping at my clit hard enough to make me scream.

"Theo, I swear to God," I groan, completely lost in how good his mouth feels on me.

He lets out a low laugh, and my pussy contracts as his beard rubs against me.

"Baby, you taste so damn good," he mutters as he continues tasting me before running his hand up my bare leg. He lazily inches his hand up my leg until he thrusts two fingers inside my leaking core.

"Cowboy, I need you to fuck me... Now," I whimper as my legs shake and seek to pull him closer.

"Well Miss Tyler, since you asked so nice..." he says, dropping my leg and taking my hand to pull me from the tree.

He leans in, kissing me again, and I go feral from tasting myself on his lips. "So damn perfect," he whispers in my ear before helping me lower myself down to all fours and leaning down to kneel behind me. I lean up to press against him and claim another kiss before resuming my position on all fours facing the creek.

Theo leans down and kisses my shoulder blade before grabbing my braids and lightly tugging on them. My back arches as he pulls my hair, and he slides one finger inside me moaning, "Shit baby, you're fucking drenched for me."

As he lines his cock up with my entrance, he smacks my ass hard making me cry out. "Is this what you want, Caroline?" he asks as he teases his cock against my entrance.

"Theo... fuck.... me... now... please..." I moan as I buck my hips wildly, desperate to feel his cock slide inside me.

"You know I love it when you're a good girl and say please," he growls before slamming into me wildly. "Damn, baby. You're so damn tight. Fuck yourself on my cock because there's no way I am gonna last with the way your pussy's leaking for me."

Taking his advice, I grind my hips up and down as he continues to tug gently on my hair and lightly spank my ass in time with his thrusts. I feel my orgasm building and continue to work my hips against him until I am screaming and coming harder than I ever have in my life. Theo growls, and I feel his cock twitch inside me as he pounds into me before he stills.

After a moment, he slides out of me and helps me stand before pulling me tightly to him and kissing my forehead. I look up at him and can't help but grin at the satisfied smile on his face. He leans in and brushes a piece of hair that came loose from my braid behind my ear, before dropping a kiss on my lips and whispering, "So damn perfect, Sunshine. So damn perfect."

CHAPTER THIRTY-NINE
THEO

As I am walking out of the stadium Thursday afternoon after practice, I hear my phone ping. Pulling it out of my pocket I check my alerts and see a text from Huey.

> Huey: Are we still on for tonight?

> Me: Yep, see you in an hour.

After responding to Huey, I jump in the truck and head home. After pulling into the driveway, I make my rounds to check on the animals before heading inside. The cows are content, and the horses are running happily through their pasture. I ignore Petunia as she makes noises at me and makes another attempt to kick down the reinforced fence posts, not having time for her antics today. By the time I make it inside, grab a shower, and fix a sandwich, it's already time for Huey to pull up.

Margaret isn't home so I figure she must be with the girls

this evening. I feel a tad bit guilty that I'm grateful I don't have to explain to her where I am going, but I am just not ready for the pity I might see on her face if I tell her. I know she and Caroline would both be supportive, but I am desperate to put that conversation off for as long as possible.

I'm walking outside as I see Huey making his way down the driveway, and I lock up quickly before jumping into his passenger seat.

"Ready, kid?" he asks, and I just nod at him. We ride to Saddle Ridge in silence again this week, and I attempt to ignore the twinge of panic I feel in my chest once again at the knowledge that I am going to have to face my past again tonight,

By the time we pull up in the parking lot, I am a ball of nervous energy. Sensing my mood, Huey looks at me as he puts the car in park and says, "Theo, it's gonna be okay."

"Yeah," I respond, unsure of what to say. "Let's go."

Huey just nods at me and we both get out of the car, walking in silence into the old church fellowship hall where the meetings are held. I take a seat in the circle of chairs, and Huey sits beside me. I see a few faces from last week along with the therapist who facilitates the meetings, Mr. Bill. Bill is a middle-aged man who explained last week that he became passionate about helping survivors of PTSD after he returned from Afghanistan in the early 2000s. He decided to leave the military and go back to school for his degree so that he could help other people like him cope.

The meeting starts at seven, and I listen as five or six people close to my age share about their struggles with PTSD. Like last week, I can't believe how freely they share about their past. But the more I listen to them talk, the more I realize their stories are similar to mine. By the time we get to the end of the meeting, almost everyone else has shared some part of their story, and Bill turns to me. "Theo, do you want to share anything tonight? Obviously, there's no pressure."

I open my mouth to decline, but instead hear myself saying, "Yeah, actually I would."

Huey tries to hide the shock on his face at my declaration, but I catch it before I turn my attention back to Bill. "Well, uh, my name is Theo, and I was diagnosed with PTSD at sixteen after I lost my parents and brother in a house fire. It took less than four minutes for my life to fall apart that night, and I've spent the last fourteen years trying to put it back together."

The group looks at me, and Bill silently nods his encouragement to keep going. "I've done everything I can to try to keep from feeling like I felt that night. I've shut people out, worked myself like crazy, and convinced myself there's no way anyone could ever love someone as broken as me. But I'm so damn tired. And recently, I met this woman who deserves the whole damn universe, and I want to give it to her."

Huey gives me an encouraging smile, and I finish by saying, "I know I am gonna have to work through some shit to be worthy of her, and honestly, it scares the hell out of me. But I have to try."

I sit and it takes me a minute to realize my hands are shaking while my heart feels like it's going to beat out of my chest. I breathe through the knot of panic as Bill wraps up the meeting, then Huey and I return to his truck.

We both sit in the truck silently for a few minutes before I look at him and ask, "You have anywhere to be tonight, Huey?"

He shakes his head at me, and I blow out a long sigh. "There's something I need to do. Can you take me to Clairville?"

Huey doesn't say anything. He just puts the truck into drive and slowly makes his way out of the parking lot. I try not to focus too hard on where we're headed, but as we drive, I can feel the familiar grip of anxiety fighting its way up my throat. I breathe as we ride in comfortable silence, Huey seeming to know I am struggling to hold it together.

After thirty minutes, I recognize the familiar "Welcome to Clairville" sign and gulp in another gasp of air. I have avoided the town where I grew up since I moved away years ago, but like most small southern towns, it doesn't look as if much has changed in my absence. I give Huey one-word directions, telling him to take a right or left until I see it.

Clairville Community Cemetery.

He pulls in and parks where we, once again, sit in silence for what feels like hours. It's dark outside, and while the area is well lit, it's also deserted.

"Kid, you don't have to do this tonight if you don't want to. We can—" he starts, but I cut him off.

"I haven't been here since the day we put them in the ground. I need to do this," I say fiercely, pretending that the thought of stepping foot out of the truck doesn't make my heart want to beat a million miles a minute.

Huey must see the determination on my face because he just nods at me before saying, "I'm here if you need me, Theo."

I nod back at him and take a large gulp of air before I open the door and step out. My legs feel like they could collapse under me at any moment, but I continue to take slow steps toward the area where my parents and brother are buried. When I arrive at their tombstones, I fall to my knees on the grass and cry.

I haven't cried since the last time I was here fourteen years ago. I convinced myself at sixteen that if I put on a good enough act that I could pretend this didn't happen. I thought if I could block out every emotion I felt, I couldn't get hurt again. I realize now how wrong I had been, and once I feel the first tear hit my cheek, I can't stop.

I cry for the teenage boy who thought he had to carry the weight of the world on his shoulders. I cry for my parents who would have been devastated by the way I chose to live my life, shutting everything and everyone out. I cry for my brother who should be changing lives as a high school coach, helping boys just like the ones I work with discover their potential. I cry for the future I should have had before a tragic accident changed the course of my life. I cry for my sister who had to grow up without the comfort of her mother.

After I have cried and screamed and hollered enough to make my throat hurt, I look at the headstones in front of me and blow out a breath. "Mom. Dad. Jake. I'm sorry. I'm so damn sorry. I'm sorry I couldn't save you. I'm sorry I quit living when you died. I'm sorry you aren't here to kick my ass. And I love you. I love you so damn much it hurts. But I can't live in the past any longer.

"I met this girl. She's funny and sweet and way too damn good for me. But, by some miracle, I think she might love me. She looks at me and sees more than the broken man I've seen every time I've looked in the mirror. She looks at me and sees someone worth loving, And I know if you were here like you should be, you'd love her as much as I do."

I feel a light breeze hit my face in the dark night as the lights of the cemetery shut off. Taking that as my cue to leave, I stand and say, "I'll always miss you. But I'm gonna do my best to live for you instead of wishing I'd died with you."

Shuffling toward the truck, I walk slowly, since it's pitch black outside without the overhead lights. After a moment, I turn back for one last look at the grave and stop dead in my tracks. As I had walked, a swarm of fireflies had descended, and through the darkness, they take turns lighting up the black night as their lights flicker. I wipe a stray tear as it slips down my cheek at the view and shake my head.

The weight of shame I have been carrying for years lightens, and I feel like I can take a deep breath. I know I still have a long way to go, but tonight feels like a good step in the right direction.

When I first met Caroline, I remember being afraid that the

darkness inside of me would one day overshadow her light. But tonight is a reminder that even the darkest night can't overtake a glimmer of light. And Caroline Tyler is so much more than a damn glimmer.

CHAPTER FORTY
CAROLINE

By the time Friday afternoon arrives, the school is abuzz with excitement about the game and pep rally. I had given up trying to hold the attention of my afternoon students, and I felt like I had run three miles around the campus by the time students started entering the gym for the pep rally.

I nervously pace the gym and straighten the mats for the hundredth time as the girls make their way out of the locker room and begin to stretch. They begin warming up their stunts, while Hannah and I take turns making sure the signs, flags, and spirit sticks are all where they are supposed to be. After checking everything for what feels like the millionth time, I lean over to Hannah and whisper, "I am running to the bathroom before everyone gets here. That one is packed with the band getting changed. I'll be right back."

She nods at me as I make my way out of the gym and head towards the restroom. As I leave the small staff bathroom, I think about the changes we need to make to our routine for next week until I hear a voice say, "Hey, Sunshine."

I turn to see Theo leaning against one of the lockers outside of Will's room. He gives me a smile that makes my heart stop before I respond, "Hey. What are you doing here?"

"Well, I know this may come as a shock, but every once in a while, we have a super slow day at the station. I'm so damn bored. We've had exactly three calls in the last month, and not one of them has been an actual emergency. I was going stir-crazy, so I figured I would come watch the pep rally. I'm just waiting on Will and the other coaches," he says before reaching out and grabbing my hand.

"Well, aren't you just Mr. Springside, Chief Johnson?" I tease, and he lets out a laugh. "Wow, you're in a good mood."

"Yeah, I guess I am," he says.

"Hmm, I like it. How was yesterday? I texted you but I never heard back, so I wasn't sure if something was wrong," I ask, not wanting to sound insecure.

"Oh sorry babe. I didn't mean to ignore you. I just got busy. Forgive me?" Theo asks, rubbing his thumb up and down my hand like he is trying to settle his nerves.

"Of course."

He smiles at me before he pulls me to him and kisses me. I kiss him back for a moment before I remember that we are in the hallway at the high school.

"Okay, calm it down. We don't need to do this here. My girls are waiting on me. I need to get back," I tell him, the disap-pointment in my voice obvious.

"Okay, go ahead. Just know after the game tonight, you're all mine," he growls before dropping a final quick kiss on my lips.

"I told you I'm always all yours, Cowboy," I say with a wink just as the classes in this hallway are dismissed to the pep rally and the students flood the hall. "I'll see you in there?"

"Yep! Go Saints," Theo says with a smirk.

I shake my head as I hurry back towards the gym. I don't know what's gotten into Theo today, but whatever it is, I have no complaints. He seems happier than normal, and I can't help but smile at that thought.

As I walk back into the gym, I see the girls already huddled up in the corner with Hannah. I hurry over to them and say, "Y'all have fun out there ladies. Remember the counts for your baskets, and make sure you hit your ripples hard. Y'all got this!"

A few of the girls on the squad smile and nod at me before Maggie calls out our pre-performance chant. "1-2-3. Saint's on me! 1-2-3..." The girls and I yell back "Saints" before Hannah and I walk back to the bleachers to take our seats on the first row.

"Why am I always so damn nervous?" I whisper to her as the girls get into their stunt groups for the football players to walk through.

Hannah just grabs my hand, and we take turns holding our breath as the girls flip and fly through the air. Theo and the rest of the coaches walk in with the team as our girls show spirit, working to get the crowd on their feet and cheering. Once the team is seated, the girls move into their position on the mats and fold their heads down, waiting on the music to start.

Hannah and I cheer loudly as the volunteer running sound presses play. The girls dance and tumble in perfect synchronization. By the time they hit their last stunt sequence, I am surprised I still have a voice. I resist the urge to jump up and down over the progress these girls have made, and I catch Theo's glance from across the gym. He gives me a thumbs-up, and I smile widely at him.

God, I think I love this man.

CHAPTER FORTY-ONE
THEO

The locker room is charged with an energy like none other as Will stands and begins his pregame speech. "Big game tonight, guys. Y'all can do this! Our path to state depends on us winning this game!"

The boys sit silently, listening as Will goes on reviewing the things we've worked on in practice. I swear there is so much adrenaline in the room already, I can almost taste it. The team is ready, and despite the situations that may have surrounded me working with the team, I am pretty damn happy to be a part of this family. After Will finishes his talk, we break into our departments, and I look at the six wide receivers standing in front of me. "Boys, I'm already proud. Y'all have worked your asses off, and it's time to reap the rewards. Let's get that win!"

Wesley leans over and claps me on the shoulder before he says, "Coach Johnson, I know it was a mess when you started here, but we're really glad you're coaching us. We didn't expect the asshole fire chief to actually know what he was talking about, but you proved us wrong." The other boys and I laugh at his statement, and I am about to reply when I hear my phone ring. I grab it out of my pocket to put it on silent, but freeze when I see the number. Why is 911 dispatch calling me?

"Sorry boys, I have to take this," I mutter before I step into one of the offices in the field house and hit accept. I press my phone to my ear, and I only hear the first few words before my world stops. I sprint out of the office and continue running out the back of the stadium until I reach my truck. I only got a few words, but they were enough to tilt my world on its axis: house fire, emergency, and possible fatalities. I hear her say that the on-call unit has been called in and will be there momentarily, but I know that I am closer than they are.

My truck hits at least ninety-miles-an-hour as I race through the deserted streets to the address of the small duplex that was called in, trying to stay calm. It's all going to be okay.

My mental pep talk is thrown out the window as soon as I see the smoke billowing into the air while I am still a few blocks away. When I finally make it, I throw my truck into park in the street and jump out. A small crowd stands across the street, and I run over yelling, "I'm Chief Johnson, what happened? Do you live here? Do you know if anyone is inside?"

An elderly woman speaks first and says, "It happened so fast, and yes I think so. I just can't believe it. I didn't think—"

"Is anyone inside?" I snap, not having time to comfort her right now.

"We thought so. Mrs. Rachel lives on that side. Her daughter is thirteen, and she usually stays home by herself until her Mom gets off. That's what I told the other firefighter. But I finally got Mrs. Rachel to answer the phone. She said her daughter went to the football game tonight so no one's here. But by the time we figured that out, he was already inside."

I look around to make sure I didn't miss the arrival of the fire truck, confirming there's no one else from the station here. "Ma'am, what firefighter? The on-call unit isn't here yet."

"No, no," she says frantically. "There's this young firefighter that lives down the street. His sister's in a wheelchair, I think. He saw the smoke and ran over. He went in to look for Rachel's daughter."

My vision clouds and my heart stops. No. No. This can't be happening.

And in the next breath, I look over to see the back part of the duplex collapse.

"ZACH!" I yell as I take a step to run towards the collapsing building, but before I can cross the street, the fire engine pulls between me and the fire.

A couple of men jump out and yell to be heard over the sound of the fire, "Chief Johnson, what are we dealing with?"

"Zach's inside," I say, barely able to get the words out. The other firefighters' eyes widen before settling their expression and turning back toward the fire.

"Well, let's go get him," one of the men standing in front of me says. I give him a quick nod, and we start walking toward the building.

The smoke is so thick I have no clue how we are going to find Zach. I struggle to settle my nerves, running back through protocol in my head before sending up a silent prayer for a miracle. We are less than ten feet from the door when I see a figure come sprinting toward us, yelling over the roar of the flames, "GET BACK!"

It feels like he's running in slow motion as I look up to see the roof starting to cave in. Zach has just made it to the door when a fiery beam comes loose and knocks him down. He scrambles to clear the porch as the fabric of his shirt smolders, and his shoulder blazes with a small flame. He is covered in soot and ash and it's clear he's struggling to breathe due to the smoke he's inhaled. He dives into the grass just as the rest of the building comes down, and as I run to him, all I can focus on is the fact that he isn't moving.

I run forward without thinking and do my best to put out

the flames on his back without moving him. I manage to avoid getting burned but as I rip his burned shirt to get an idea of his injuries, I feel the ash covering my hands and I get hit with a flashback of the same sight from the night my life changed. Fighting to stay in the present, I focus on Zach. He is not going to end up like my parents and brother. I refuse to accept it.

I hear the ambulance sirens blaring ominously as the on-call unit rushes to connect the fire hose and extinguish the fire. As the ambulance arrives, I don't miss the fact that Zach has yet to gain consciousness, but I can tell he's breathing. I briefly report Zach's status to the paramedics, who rush to check his vitals. "Breathing is shallow, but his pulse is present and strong," the one closest to me says. They assume care, making quick work of assessing and loading him onto the stretcher for his transport to the hospital.

I look at my men who have almost finished putting out the fire, and struggle with a moment of indecision. I hate the idea of Zach being alone, but I can't risk anyone else getting hurt. Derrick sees me and must immediately read the emotions on my face because he says, "Chief, we've got this. Go check on him."

I stand there for another moment before nodding at him and sprinting off to my truck and speeding in the direction of the hospital.

He has to be okay. I can't do this again.

I MAKE the eight-minute drive to the hospital in less than three, and after wheeling into a parking spot, I sprint inside the emergency room entrance. Stopping at the front desk, I exclaim, "One of my firemen was just brought in. I'm the new Fire Chief. Is he okay?" The nurses at the front desk take one look at my soot-covered hands and point me to a small waiting room on the opposite side of the hall. "The doctor's checking him now, then he'll be with you, hun," one of the older nurses says with a weak smile.

I nod at her and make my way into the private waiting room. I sit for a second, but I feel like I am going to lose my mind since I am unable to help. I stand and pace for what feels like hours until an older doctor enters the room. "Chief Johnson," he asks, and I give him a quick nod, waiting to hear the prognosis.

"He's got a bit of a recovery ahead of him, but he's awake and from what I can tell, he's going to be okay. He dislocated his shoulder, and we reset it already. He's on a hefty dose of morphine right now, but he'll just need rest and some PT for that. As for his other injuries, he inhaled a whole lot of smoke and he has a bunch of second-degree burns on the backside of his body—roughly twenty percent."

I visibly wince, knowing from my first aid training that his burns are some of the most painful due to the layers of skin they affect. My grimace eases only slightly with the knowledge that they've already given him some strong IV pain meds, so hopefully he's not too miserable. Poor kid won't be running marathons anytime soon, that's for damn sure.

Interrupting my thoughts, the doctor continues, "They're hooking him up to IV fluids and have already started him on some high flow oxygen therapy for the smoke inhalation. Once he's stable, we will transfer him to the ICU where, with the help of a great team of doctors, we can monitor his airway and wounds for complications.

"Also, he was pretty out of it when he came in, but he kept trying to ask about his sister. I talked to one of the other doctors who recognized him from the night of his family's accident. He's one of the leads on his sister's case, and his wife has helped Zach with Bethany in the past. She went to get her, and they're gonna make sure she's taken care of while Zach is out of commission. I don't know many people who would have run into that building the way that he did, but I have to say, he's damn brave. It'll be a while before he's allowed to have visitors, but if you'll leave your information with the nurse, I will call if anything changes."

I nod, frustrated I can't see him but thankful he's getting the care he needs. I thank the doctor before making my way out and giving my information to the front desk. I stand there for a moment taking in the scent of antiseptic and smoke before darting out to my truck. For the second time in twenty-four hours, I am overcome with a myriad of emotions, and I drive toward the only place that I think can calm the chaos raging inside me.

CHAPTER FORTY-TWO
CAROLINE

The team runs out, and I shake my powder blue and white shaker in the air as the cheerleaders lead the crowd through some chants. I look through the mass of players and coaches on the sideline, trying to find Theo. I search through the faces twice before I realize he isn't here.

Weird. Maybe he's dealing with something in the locker room.

Margaret sits beside me, wearing another one of the Springside shirts we gave her last week. She leans over and bumps my shoulder. "Hmm, is Theo not here?"

I shrug at her. "He was. I was talking to him on the phone when he said he was pulling up to the stadium for pregame warmups. Maybe there's something with one of his players that he needed to handle. He could be in the locker room."

"Yeah, that's probably it," Margaret says, but I can tell she's as unsettled by his absence as I am.

We all stand as the band plays the national anthem, and Hannah hip-checks me as the boys run out to the fifty-yard line for the kickoff. "Hey, it's gonna be okay. He'll be here soon. He's grown to love these boys. No way he would miss this."

I nod at her, trying to hide the fact that her words have made me more anxious. She's right. Whether he's willing to acknowledge it or not, Theo has fallen in love with this team. He wouldn't miss this game for anything. I ignore the knot in my stomach and settle in to watch the game.

The boys play hard while the girls cheer loudly, as I fight to focus on the game. We score twice in the first quarter, and I shake my pom along with the beat to "When the Saints Come Marching In". Hannah and Margaret squeeze my hand every once in a while, and as I smile at them, I can see their concern is growing alongside mine.

As halftime rolls around, I fight the urge to scream. Theo has been missing from the sidelines all game and no one seems to have any clue where he disappeared to. I have sent him at least ten panicked text messages, but they have all gone unanswered.

Beside me, Margaret twists her hands nervously. "I just don't understand. He wouldn't miss this game. Where the hell is he?"

"I don't know. Have you tried calling?" I ask as I try to focus my attention on my squad taking the field. Tonight, there's no excitement in me for their performance because every part of my soul is focused on finding Theo. I try to put a pleasant smile on my face as the girls get into their formation, but even I can tell it looks forced.

"Let's do it, girls!" I shout right before their music starts to boom loudly through the stadium.

The girls execute a complicated jump sequence as the music plays, and normally I would be bouncing right along with them. Tonight, I feel as though I barely have the energy to stand on the sideline as they begin the dance portion with a ripple. They call out "S-A-I-N-T-S" as they dance, and the crowd cheers along with them. They move to the stunt sequence as Maggie runs through the formation and completes her tumbling pass. She lands her full, and I know I should be screaming at the top of my lungs for her.

Instead, I just stare blankly at the sidelines as the girls throw the basket tosses in time to the beat of the music. Beside me, Hannah is going absolutely insane, jumping and screaming, until she reaches over for my hand and realizes that I haven't moved since the routine started. She looks at me and wraps her arm around me before turning her attention back to the squad who is moving to their final formation. The bracing groups build up and wait for Maggie to load in before grabbing her arms and flipping her around one way and then back the other. From there she shoots up to her perfectly executed liberty while they scream, "Springside Saints" as the crowd screams in excitement.

I manage to clap my hands and give the girls another small smile before I turn back to the bleachers and take my seat. As soon as I sit, several fans come to tell me how impressed they were with the routine, and I do my best to be polite despite the fact that I am completely unfocused.

As the team runs back out onto the field to start the second half, I notice Huey coming my way. He stops in front of me and says, "Caroline, come on. We need to go."

My heart stops. "What's going on? Do you know where Theo is? Is he okay? I can't leave the girls. The game isn't over. Huey, what-"

"Caroline, breathe. I need you to come with me. Theo is safe, but he needs you," the older man says, and I feel his anxiety as he tries to explain.

I open my mouth to ask another series of questions, but Hannah stops me. "Caroline, go! I have the girls. Keep us updated."

I look over to Margaret who seems to be having a silent conversation with Huey. "Are you coming with us, Margaret?" I ask.

"I don't think it's me that he needs right now," Margaret says with a worried smile. "Go figure out what's going on. If there's something major, text me, and I will come running."

"Okay," I say as I scramble to gather my things. Maggie looks up at me with worry in her eyes, and I give her a small smile. "It's okay," I mouth to her over the noise. "Y'all listen to Miss Hannah."

She nods, and Huey and I run to the exit. When we finally make it to his truck, we both throw open the doors and I blow out a breath. "Huey, you've got to explain. What's going on?"

Huey looks conflicted about how much to tell me before he says, "There was a huge fire tonight. Theo is okay, but one of his guys isn't. I just got a call that Zach's gonna pull through, but as soon as Theo heard he was okay, he tore out of the emergency room like a bat out of hell. I don't know how much you know about his past, but-"

"Just like his parents," I whisper, cutting Huey off.

He gives me a sad grimace and nods. "But Zach's okay. And I know Theo hasn't told you because he thinks it makes him unworthy of your love or some bullshit, but he's been fighting like hell trying to convince himself he's worthy of having your love. I've been taking him to a support group for PTSD survivors, and he had a real breakthrough last night. But today, he needs you to remind him that he's not broken."

I feel a wet drop hit my arm and wipe my face before I realize I am crying. "Do you know where he would go? You said he ran off. How are we going to find him? He isn't answering the phone."

"I have an idea. If I'm wrong we will reassess, but I don't think I am," Huey says as he turns off towards Clairville. "It's about a forty-five-minute drive, but I think we can make it in thirty."

I nod, and we ride in silence. While Huey drives, I think about the way Theo has silently battled his demons for years.

For fourteen years, he has shouldered the blame for an acci-dent when his only downfall was that he survived when his family didn't. As we ride, I decide it ends today. I decide I am going to find a way to make him see himself the way I see him, and if he doesn't like it then it's too damn bad.

I'm coming, Cowboy.

CHAPTER FORTY-THREE
THEO

I sit in front of my parent's grave in the dark cemetery for the second time in the last twenty-four hours, and I fight the lump in my throat as I try to understand why this keeps happening to me.

It isn't fair. Zach isn't supposed to be in the hospital. My parents aren't supposed to be in the goddamn ground. My brother isn't supposed to be gone. He was supposed to be the one coaching, not me. What the hell have I been thinking?

And Caroline. What if something happens to her? I'd barely survived the other tragedies with my sanity intact. If something happens to her, I'd-

My thoughts are interrupted by a truck flying into the cemetery. I look at the white Ford and recognize it immediately —Huey.

I blow out a breath knowing I should have figured that he would find me. I am grateful for his concern, but I am not ready for him to tell me it's okay.

I open my mouth to tell him to leave me alone, but before I can get the words out, his passenger door opens. A flash of brunette hair in the headlights is all I see before Caroline jumps into my arms, almost taking me down with the force of her hug.

"What are you doing here?" she asks, and I can see the absolute terror my disappearance caused her. I ignore the twinge of guilt in my gut and brush a stray piece of hair out of her face.

"You should be at the game," I tell her, ignoring her question.

"I could say the same thing to you, Theo," she says as her eyes blaze.

"There was an accident, and I-" I start but she interrupts me.

"I know what happened to Zach. But what happened to you?" she asks. I feel my chest tighten, as I try to figure out how to answer her question.

"Look, Theo, I'm gonna talk for a minute and you're going to listen. Clear?" she says. It was phrased as a question, but her tone left no room for argument. Instead, I just nod at her and try to focus on my breathing.

"I know you think you can control the whole world and everyone in it, but Theo, you aren't Superman. And what happened tonight is no more your fault than your parent's death. Did you start that fire at that house tonight?" she asks as her eyes blaze with ferocity.

"Did you tell Zach he had to work tonight? Did you ask for him to get hurt? Better yet, did you ask to lose your parents?" she continues, and all I can do is shake my head at her.

"Right, of course, you didn't. And I'm so sorry all of those things happened, but they aren't your fault. Sometimes the perfect life you envisioned for yourself is just an illusion. Sometimes our life really is pretty close to perfect but fires come and we can't stop them. When it all burns down, all that matters are the ones standing beside us helping us rebuild. I don't know much, but Theo, I know this— when it all burns down, there's no one else in the world I want beside me."

I look at her and struggle to breathe. My heart attempts to slow down to a more normal pace, and I reach for her, needing to feel her close to me.

"Caroline, I don't deserve you. I'll be damned if I ever let you go, but if I was a better man I would. I came here last night and promised my parents I wouldn't ever let fear keep me from living, but damn if I didn't end up right back here less than twenty-four hours later," I tell her.

"Theo, there's nothing wrong with being afraid—it just means you care. We aren't afraid to lose things we don't value. It's how we handle that fear that matters."

I think about her words and realize she's right. She must see it on my face because she moves closer and wraps her arms around me. "I'm here Theo. If you want this, just don't shut me out. I love you." My heart stops, and once again, I find myself struggling to breathe. She must recognize the shock on my face because she starts to ramble, "You don't have to say it back. I just wanted you—"

"I love you too," I whisper, cutting her off as I hold her face in my hand.

She smiles at me and leans in to kiss me quickly. "Well, now that that's settled you should know, you aren't getting rid of me, Cowboy. I don't care how noble your intentions might be, if you want me gone, you're gonna have to force me to leave."

"Sunshine, you came into my life, and damn if you didn't light me on fire. In one of the darkest times of my life, you burst in like a goddamn sunrise and made me realize how dark everything had become. There's no way you're going anywhere."

"Is that a threat or promise, Chief Johnson?" she asks with a wink, and in that moment, I know it's all going to be okay.

CHAPTER FORTY-FOUR
CAROLINE

I feel like I am floating by the time Theo drops me off at Maracas Monday night. I enter the restaurant, and sink into our usual booth. I can't believe how much my life has changed since last week when we were here.

After the events of Friday night, Theo and I spent most of the weekend together in bed. Margaret stayed the weekend with Hannah, and I was grateful she was spared from our weekend shenanigans, considering we only got dressed to check the cows and ride the fence lines.

After ordering a drink, I momentarily lose myself in the memory of Theo asking me to move in.

We were tangled up in the sheets and I was enjoying my post-orgasm haze when Theo leaned over and wrapped his arms around me before whispering, "I know this may be a little fast, so you can tell me no, but what do you think about moving in with me?"

I blinked up at him to make sure I heard him correctly, but the sincerity and insecurity in his voice was impossible to miss.

"You want me to live with you?" I asked, trying to keep the shock out of my voice.

"Well yeah, but only if you want to."

"How will Margaret feel about that?" I questioned.

"Well she's mentioned looking for a place closer to town since she's getting ready to start work on the bakery," Theo explained.

"Oh, that makes sense. Do you think she would be interested in moving into my apartment? I don't want her to feel like we're forcing her out, but we could just swap," I said, cuddling closer into his chest.

"Let's talk to Margaret and see what she thinks. The last thing I want is to hurt her. Honestly I just want to be wherever you are. But if it's too fast—" Theo started to ramble, and I cut him off.

"Theo, I want to be wherever you are too," I told him honestly. "But also just remember, I'm not going anywhere."

"Good, because I'm never letting you go, Sunshine," he whispered, brushing my hair out of my face and leaning over to kiss me. The kissing eventually led to more as he teased me with his fingers and tongue. By the time he slid his cock back inside me, I had been ready to agree to anything he wanted as long as he continued giving me access to unlimited orgasms.

After pulling ourselves out of bed yesterday afternoon, Theo and I rode out to check on the farm and met Margaret in the driveway. When we mentioned the swap to Margaret, she'd immediately asked to move into my apartment. At first, I had worried that she'd felt forced out of the farmhouse, but she explained that she was excited about the proximity to the bakery, and I hadn't argued with her after that.

The waitress walks by with my usual peach margarita, and I take a sip before grabbing a handful of chips to snack on until Margaret and Hannah arrive. After a few minutes of snacking and scrolling through Instagram, Margaret enters and makes her way towards our table.

"Hey, Caroline. How was your Monday?" she asks as she slides in across from me.

"It was good. I am exhausted though. How was yours?" I ask before stuffing another chip in my mouth.

"Ugh, it was fine. I cannot wait to get started with the

bakery. I am so nervous about getting everything going, but I'm excited at the same time you know?" Margaret asks.

"Well I totally get that, but you have nothing to worry about. I have never met anyone who bakes as well as you do. You are gonna kill it, and we will all be there to help you with the manual labor part," I tell her after she orders her own margarita.

"Yeah, you're right. I tried a few new recipes today that I need y'all's feedback on. I can't decide how many I should offer on the permanent menu," Margaret says looking stressed.

"Hey, you'll figure it out. And you know we're always here to help with the taste testing too," I say with a laugh as Hannah walks into the restaurant.

She throws herself into the booth and sighs. "I swear Leroy Scott is going to be the death of me."

Margaret and I giggle as Hannah orders her margarita, and we each take turns chatting about our day. After the last few weeks, I was grateful for a mostly uneventful Monday. There had been no fire drills, outbursts, or wild animals, so I was calling it a win.

After a while, the table gets quiet before Hannah and Margaret look at each other. "So, Caroline," they both say at the same time causing us to all burst into a fit of giggles.

"Yes, let's get this over with," I say with a laugh.

"We're totally gonna be sisters-in-law, huh?" Margaret asks and Hannah squeaks with amusement.

"I don't know. But I do know that I am completely in love with your brother. He makes me happy, and he's one of the strongest people I know. He's everything I want, and we are going to figure out the rest as we go," I say as Margaret's eyes fill with tears.

"Yep. Welcome to the family, sis."

CHAPTER FORTY-FIVE
THEO

I knock on the door of my foster parent's home Monday evening and try to act like my heart isn't about to beat out of my chest. I hear rustling on the other side of the door as Heather opens the door wide. Her smile is gentle, and there is no doubt in my mind that she's been waiting all day for me to arrive. I'd texted both her and Bobby this weekend to ask if it would be all right for me to stop by so it wasn't an unexpected visit.

"Theo, honey, come on in," she says, moving out of the way of the door.

"Hey, Heather. How are y'all tonight?" I ask as I take a seat on the sofa closest to the front door. "Where's Bobby?"

"He's coming. He had to help with something at the school this afternoon, but he should be back any moment. Do you want some cookies while you wait? Margaret sent me her secret recipe because I've become obsessed," Heather says with a laugh.

"Sure. Those things are addictive," I say as she walks into the kitchen and comes back with a tray of cookies and a bottle of water. She sits it on the sofa between us as Bobby comes in the door. "Hey, Bobby. We were just talking about you"

"Theo, bud, I am so glad to see you," he says, walking over, hugging me quickly before leaning over, grabbing a handful of the cookies sitting beside me, and collapsing into his favorite recliner on the other side of the room. "What brings you here this evening?"

"Well, I just wanted to talk. A lot has happened since I moved to Springside, and I want to let y'all know before anything else happens," I say before taking a breath and launching into an abridged version of the last two months. Bobby glares at me as I detail the rough start I had in Springside, and Heather interrupts to chastise me for cursing in the halls of the school.

I tell them about Caroline, and the incredible way she has made me believe in good again. I tell them about being 'voluntold' into coaching the Saints, and I see the hurt in their eyes that I had robbed them of the opportunity to be on the sidelines for the beginning half of the season. I tell them about Zach and his sister along with the accident from Friday as they just sit and listen.

Finally, after I feel like they have a big enough idea of my current situation, I stop and look at each of them. Heather leans over and takes my hand as she wipes the tears that have accumulated from her eyes while Bobby gets up from his chair and comes to sit with his wife.

"Well, Theo. You've had quite a few weeks it sounds like. I am so sorry you've been through all of that even though you might have deserved a bit of it. I can't believe you were so ugly to that woman in front of her students," Heather says, shaking her head at me. "As for the rest, I am so proud of you for working on getting some support. I think moving to Springside might have been one of the biggest blessings you could have received."

"I agree. That's actually why I'm here. I know you haven't met her, but I just wanted to come tell you both that I am going to propose next week. I snuck away tonight while she was with Margaret and Hannah at Maracas because as much as I wish things were different, Margaret and I wouldn't be here without you. Y'all took us in and never looked back. I know you would have loved to adopt us, but I wasn't ready to have new parents after I had just lost mine. But even then, you two have never given up on us, and I love you both so much for that."

I look up at Heather and Bobby, who are both failing at hiding their tear-filled eyes. I have never expressed any type of legitimate feelings towards them, and I have to admit I feel bad for waiting so long.

"Oh, Theo, of course. We love you too!" Heather says. "I have to go grab something okay? Promise not to run on me?"

"Yep," I reply simply as I pop another cookie into my mouth.

Heather stays gone for less than five minutes before she comes back with a large envelope. "I have something you need to see." As soon as she says it, I notice that the envelope is in my mother's handwriting. My heart stops.

"One night, your Mom and Dad went on a date, and as they came back home, they saw the worst car accident either of them had ever seen. They'd left you and your siblings at your grandparents and gone out to dinner on the beach, but as they came back from Crestview, they saw a car wrapped around a tree. They called 911 and sat there until the first responders could get there. Your Dad went and tried to help them, but they were both already gone. There was a car seat in the back, but the child wasn't with them. It really shook your Momma up. She kept asking what that baby was gonna do because in less than a minute, she had lost both her parents," Heather explains.

I swallow down a gulp because that situation is incredibly

similar to mine. Fire, car accident, or terminal illness—I'd come to learn it didn't matter because the outcome was the same.

"Anyway, she decided to write letters for each of her children for the moment that they knew they had met 'the one', and had them placed with their will. The instructions were for your guardian to keep them safe until the time came. And, it sounds to me like the time is here," Heather concludes before handing me the large envelope. "Here you go."

I feel like I am going to pass out if my heart beats any faster, but as my fingers tremble, I do my best to open the letter. I pull out a page that is once again full of my mother's loopy cursive and swallow the lump in my throat the best I can. Taking a deep breath, I begin to read.

Dear Theo,

My sweet, fearless, protective boy.

I pray this letter never finds its way into your hands. I pray that when you find the woman who turns your world upside down, your father and I are there to dote on her. I pray I am there to dance with you when you decide to say "I do," and that your father and I get to fight over which one of us gets to hold our grandchildren first. I pray there is a lifetime of family vacations, laughs, and memories between us all before your father and I are forced to leave this world. But I have learned that life can be full of moments that are out of our control. So, I decided, just in case, I wanted to make sure you and your siblings know just how much your father and I adore you.

Theo Johnson, you are worthy of that once in a lifetime kind of love. Your father and I have watched you grow into a young man who loves harder than anyone I know. There is nothing in this world that you won't do for your family, and watching you thrive has been one of the deepest joys of my life. I will never forget the morning your sixth grade teacher called because you had duct taped Johnny Stewart to the flagpole for calling your sister ugly. I knew then that anyone lucky enough to have your love would never wonder if you would protect them.

I have no doubt that the woman you have chosen to spend your life with will never know another day without your fierce devotion. The babies that will one day fill your home have no idea that they will never find someone as loyal as their daddy. But in protecting everyone else, remember that you will need a shelter too.

I hope you find the kind of love that makes you brave. The kind of love that makes you confident that you can face whatever life throws at you. The kind of love that makes you slow dance around the kitchen at two in the morning to the glow of the refrigerator lights because you can't imagine your

life without them. And once you find it, fight like
hell to keep it.
    All my love forever and always,
    Mom

My hands shake as I fold the letter back up and put it back in the envelope. I wipe the single tear that had accumulated in my eye and look up to Heather who is crying silently beside me.

"She and your Dad loved you so much. And I have no doubt they would have wanted you to have this too," she says, holding out a small jewelry box.

I take it from her hand and let out a choked sound of shock when I see my Mom's engagement ring and wedding band perfectly preserved in the box in my hand. "How? This was lost in the fire," I say, blinking to make sure that I am not dreaming.

"We thought so too. But a couple of months after the accident, I got a call from a jewelry store in Crestview. One of the small stones on the side of the engagement ring fell out, and your Dad dropped them both off the day of the accident so that they could check the prongs and clean them. The store obviously didn't know about the fire, so it took them a while to piece together what had happened. The jeweler had a friend here in town that he called when no one came to pick them up, and that's how they got my number," Heather explains.

"Go find your forever, Theo," Bobby says with a smile, and I stand on my shaky legs to do just that.

I take my time driving home from Bobby and Heather's, thinking about the emotional roller coaster that today has become. I had gone to tell Bobby and Heather about Caroline, never once considering it would turn into what it did. The letter that was sitting like a dead weight in my pocket had somehow helped me feel more free than I had in years. I pull up to Maracas and put the truck in park, knowing it will probably be over an hour until Caroline is ready to go.

Grabbing the letter, I read back through it a few times and realize that my mom is right. Before I had moved to Springside, I had been so consumed with grief, I had stopped living.

After sitting for a while, I see Caroline, Margaret, and Hannah walk out of the small restaurant. Caroline hugs them both as they walk toward her old apartment and her face lights up when she sees me sitting in the parking lot. She darts through the dark lot before jumping in the truck and leaning over to give me a long kiss. "Let's go home, Cowboy."

CHAPTER FORTY-SIX
CAROLINE

The following Monday, the girls and I sip our margaritas and I can't help feeling like there's something I'm missing. We've been here less than an hour, but Margaret and Hannah have already scarfed down their quesadillas and are sitting across from me twiddling their car keys in expectation.

"Y'all are acting so weird. What aren't you telling me?" I ask them suspiciously.

Margaret's eyes widen slightly, just enough to assure me that they're up to something.

The day started with Theo claiming something was wrong with my car, even though I haven't noticed so much as a check engine light since the last time it was serviced. He insisted he needed to dropped me off at work this morning, and Margaret was waiting to pick me up from practice because he said he was caught up at work. Thankfully, I still had clothes at Margaret's that we hadn't gotten around to moving yet, so at least I'd been able to freshen up by throwing on an old pair of jeans and one of my favorite pink tops.

Hannah just rolls her eyes at me and shrugs. "I told you we

have to get some of Margaret's stuff from the farm. I don't want to be moving shit at midnight tonight. Plus I drew the straw to DD tonight, and I miss tequila."

"Alright, fine," I say, finishing my margarita. "Let's go then."

We stand and make our way out to Hannah's car where we jump in and she throws the car in drive. She cranks nineties country music the whole way to my new home so loud it's impossible to have a conversation, and we laugh as we sing "Heads Carolina, Tails California" at the top of our lungs.

The lyrics die on my lips as we pull up at the farmhouse. The entire driveway and porch is covered in hanging lights, and I see Theo standing in the middle of the drive with a bouquet of flowers along Will and Seth on the porch waving at us.

"What–" I stutter, and I turn to the backseat where Margaret is wiping tears from her eyes. I look back in bewilderment at my best friend, and Hannah leans over to squeeze my hand.

"Well Caroline, I think you might have found your brighter days. Let's go," she says with a watery smile.

I get out of the car and slowly walk to Theo as Margaret and Hannah join the boys on the porch.

"Theo, what is all of this?" I ask when I am close enough to wrap my arms around him.

"Caroline, I never imagined I could love someone as much as I love you. You helped me realize that I don't have to live in the dark anymore, and I don't want to know another day on this earth without your light. I've already told you I'm yours for as long as you want me. And I was just wondering if forever felt like too long?" Theo asks as he drops to one knee and holds out the most beautiful vintage engagement ring I've ever seen. "This was my momma's ring, and I know you never got to meet her, but I have no doubt she'd be proud to see you wearing her ring. Will you marry me?"

I wipe the tears from my eyes and stare down at the man

who has completely transformed my life. "Of course, Cowboy. Forever sounds pretty damn good to me."

With that, Hannah, Will, Seth, and Margaret cheer, and Theo kisses me hard. He slides the ring on my finger, and I choke back a sob when his mother's ring fits my finger perfectly.

Margaret screams from the porch, "I told you we were gonna be sisters-in-law!"

All of us laugh at her outburst, and I walk over to take her hand. "Margaret, you know I love your brother. But are you okay with me wearing this ring?"

She wipes a stray tear from her eye before she leans over and hugs me hard, "Caroline, I hate that my Momma never got to meet you, but there's not a doubt in my mind that your finger is where that ring is supposed to be. She would have loved you as much as Theo and I do."

Walking back to Theo, I take a moment to look at the friends surrounding us. If you had told me this summer that I would fall in love with a grumpy fire chief and be living on a farm with a mischievous jackass, I would have asked how much Mrs. Sally'd had to drink before starting that rumor. But now, I can't imagine my life any other way. Our group was proof that we didn't get to choose our family or our circumstances, but we do get to choose to chase the sunlight and believe in brighter days. And I was pretty damn excited about mine.

EPILOGUE- ONE MONTH LATER

THEO

Monday afternoon, I make my way into the farmhouse with a shout, "Sunshine, I'm home!"

Caroline peeks her head up from the sofa where she's sprawled out with Bear lying on top of her and resting his head on her shoulder. "Hey, baby! I missed you today. I'd get up to kiss you, but you can see this big guy has other ideas."

"The little bastard," I mutter under my breath as Bear looks at me and lets out a loud sigh.

I walk over and glare at him before leaning down to kiss my girl.

"How was your day, Chief Johnson?" Caroline asks with a big smile on her face.

"Pretty good, Miss Tyler. It's so nice to have Zach back at the station. It was a slow day so we filmed some content. Margaret has given us some recipes to use, and I cleared it with Brian for part of the proceeds of this year's cookbook to go towards a college fund for Bethany. I told Zach and the rest of the guys today, and I don't think there was a dry eye in the station. How was your day?" I ask while lifting her feet and placing them on top of my lap.

"It was a really good day. We played a game that went along with the Salem Witch Trials since we're studying *The Crucible*, and my students enjoyed it. Michael also came by after class to tell me his adoption is going to be finalized next week. He told me to tell you he wants us to come to the courthouse with him when it's made official."

I smile at my fiancée and tease, "Did you cry?"

She rolls her eyes at me and pokes me with her foot, "You know I did. That kid's been through so damn much, but I am proud of him."

"Me too. Are you meeting the girls tonight?" I ask, rubbing the bottom of her bare foot.

"Cowboy, you know the answer to that. We never miss a Monday," she says while stroking Bear's head.

"Yeah, yeah. Well, text the girls that you're gonna be late tonight," I growl, and Caroline's eyes widen as she looks at me.

"Why am I gonna be late?" she asks as a mischievous smirk takes over her face.

"Because you're not leaving this house until after you've moaned my name and you're full of my cum," I say, running my hand up the inside of her leg toward her tiny pajama shorts.

"Theo," she groans, as Bear gives me a murderous look and jumps down onto the floor. I continue tracing my fingers higher and higher up her leg until I graze the fabric of her lacy thong. Her breath catches, and I lean forward and push her shorts to the side so that I can tease her clit through the rough material.

"Oh, my God," she cries out as she withers under me. I look down to smirk at her and firmly wrap my hand around her throat the way I know she likes as I slide my other hand inside her soaked panties. I flex my hand around her throat and groan as I feel her inner walls contracting along with my hand.

"So damn perfect."

I tease her with my hands until I can tell that she's on the edge of an orgasm before withdrawing my fingers. She whimpers at the loss of contact until I free my cock and push into her. I keep the pressure in my hand around her neck steady, making sure she's able to breathe freely as I fuck her hard. It doesn't take long before I feel her walls tightening around my cock, pulling a low groan from my throat. "God, Caroline. Come for me, pretty girl."

With that, I feel her walls spasm and grip my cock, and we both finish with a moan.

"Damn. Is that all you got?" she asks with a wink, swaying her hips as she runs to the bedroom and locks me out to get ready for dinner.

"When are you gonna learn I'm never gonna be through with you," I mutter as I step into the bathroom to take a shower. "When you get home tonight, you're mine."

Caroline

"Caroline, the farm is going to be so perfect. Are y'all still planning to have the ceremony in front of the barn?" Margaret asks as we sit in our usual booth at Maracas and sip on our final margarita of the evening.

"Yeah, we are. And you're okay with taking care of the cakes?" I respond as I check my phone and see a text from Theo letting me know he's outside.

"Of course! I have so many ideas I can't wait to show you!" Margaret says excitedly. "Let's do a tasting one day next month"

"Sounds good to me, but you know we love everything you make," I tell her honestly as Margaret smiles.

"Have you decided on a color for the bridesmaid's dresses?" Hannah asks, and I can hear the curiosity in her voice

"I am still leaning toward pink since it will be late spring.

But you two are the only ones in the bridal party, so do y'all have any strong opinions?" I ask while I break a chip in half and dip it in the queso sitting in front of me.

"It's your day! Whatever you want is fine with us! I am just so damn happy for you!" Margaret exclaims with a squeal.

"Me too. Whatever you want, Caro. But just don't make me walk down the aisle with Will," Hannah says with an eye roll.

I laugh loudly before saying, "Trust me, none of us want to hear y'all fuss all day, Hannah."

"I promise I'll be good," Hannah interjects with a scoff. "I'd never ruin your special day. He's just such an ass."

Margaret and I share a look, and I fight to contain my laughter. "I'll bet you the next round of Scooter shots they hook up before Christmas," I whisper as Hannah goes on about how much she dislikes the football coach, oblivious to the fact that neither of us are listening.

"You're on," Margaret shoots back as the waiter drops off our checks.

"Y'all ready?" I ask, and my friends nod at me as we make our way to the old-fashioned cash register and pay for our dinner. After that, we step into the cool October air and say our goodbyes before splitting off towards home.

I make it to the dark parking lot and run to Theo's waiting truck before throwing open the door and peppering his face with kisses. He lets out a low laugh before kissing me back. I swear I can never get enough of this man.

When we finally pull back, he grins at me. "Did you have fun?"

"I did. We talked about wedding stuff. I missed you though," I say as I reach for his hand while he backs out of the parking spot and starts driving home.

"Fun. I missed you too. You know, I can't wait to marry you, Miss Tyler," Theo says, leaning over to squeeze my thigh.

"I can't wait to be your wife. Speaking of which, I was thinking..." I say hesitantly.

"Yeah?" he asks expectantly.

"I don't mean right away, but all of this with Michael has me thinking. Have you ever thought about becoming foster parents eventually?" I ask, nervous to see what his reaction will be.

Theo looks over at me as we sit at a stoplight on the way out of town. I see emotion taking over his features as he brushes a piece of hair out of my face once again.

"Sunshine, there's nothing I wouldn't do for you. But I can't think of a better way to honor my family. You found a way to heal the brokenness inside of me, and I have no doubt that you can do that for some of the kids like Michael," he says, bringing my hand to his lips and kissing it gently.

"Theo, you saved yourself. You just had to believe you were worth saving. And I'm so damn proud of you," I say with a smile.

"Thanks, Miss Tyler. So, remind me, what was it you asked me earlier?" Theo asks with a mischievous glint in his eyes.

"Uhh... Is that all you got?" I say sheepishly.

"Well, Caroline, why don't we go find out?" he asks as we pull up at home.

I laugh before jumping out of the truck just as he puts it in park. "You'll have to catch me first, Cowboy."

READY FOR MORE FROM SPRINGSIDE? HANNAH AND WILL ARE COMING MARCH 2025

ACKNOWLEDGMENTS

Wow! I cannot believe that you are actually holding this book in your hands right now! I have joked that this book has been to hell and back with me, and I really do believe that. However, for every low in this journey, there's been a hundred highs. I have felt incredible support from so many people, and I am SO grateful!

First and foremost, Theo and Caroline's story would still be floating around inside my brain without the love and support of my sweet husband. C, you have always believed in me more than I believe in myself. Thank you for taking care of the house, talking through the farm scenes, and forcing me out of the writing cave every once in a while. I love you always, babe.

To my Mom and Dad, you have always told me there's nothing in the world I can't do. I'm not sure a spicy romance novel was what you had in mind, but thank you for always encouraging me to chase my dreams. Nonnie and Dah- thank you for your unwavering support. I'm sorry for all the missed visits, but I am so grateful for the way you've encouraged me. The four of you have made me into the person that I am, and I never could have done this without you. I love you all bunches! Also, this is still the only page you're allowed to read.

Brittni, you were the first person to hear this story, and there is no way I could have gotten started or figured out this process without you! Thank you for answering my million questions and always encouraging me to keep writing.

Ali, oh my goodness! Who would have thought in June that

we would end up here? From my sweet logo to the most perfect cover in the whole world and a million graphics in between I literally couldn't do the whole author thing without you! Thank you for always reading my mind when I have no clue what I'm talking about.

Erica, thank you so much for taking my chaos and helping me turn it in to an actual book. You are a rockstar!

Emma, you were absolutely incredible! Thank you for all your comma help!

Emily and Christa, y'all deserve an award. The number of times I slid in your DMs with another idea or chapter... Thank you for beta reading and talking through every word of this book with me. Y'all are the best cheerleaders and I'm so grateful.

To my betas, Caroline, Lauren Brooke, Madison, and Tabitha, y'all are literal angels. I am so appreciative of every comment and suggestion! Thank you for your help making this story what it is!

To my ARC readers and the rest of the bookstagram community, you will never know how much I appreciate you. It brings me to tears to think about how quickly y'all jumped to support me with this endeavor, and I love every single one of you. Thank you for every share, post, and tag!

And finally, sweet reader, thank you for taking a chance on me and my debut! I hope you always remember there's brighter days ahead!

BE THE FIRST TO KNOW

Want to stay up to date on all the things? Join my newsletter, sign up for alerts on upcoming signings, and follow my reader group here!

LIST OF CONTENT WARNINGS

Explicit Sexual Content
Tragic Loss of Family
Parental and Sibling Death
PTSD and Panic Attacks
Parental Abandonment
Nightmares
Discussions of Foster Care

ABOUT THE AUTHOR

Hollie Luckie is a small town girl that wholeheartedly believes in happily ever afters. Between teaching English and writing romance, she is always getting lost in a fictional world. She resides in south Alabama with her high school sweetheart, her dog Memphis, and her own farm of quirky farm animals. You can find Hollie on Instagram at @authorhollieluckie or on Goodreads.